EVEN IF THE SKY IS FALLING

edited by TAJ McCOY

EVEN IF THE SKY IS FALLING

LANE CLARKE   TAJ McCOY   SARAH SMITH
FARAH HERON   CHARISH REID   DENISE WILLIAMS

CANARY STREET PRESS

CANARY
STREET
PRESS™

Recycling programs
for this product may
not exist in your area.

ISBN-13: 978-1-335-45255-9

Even If the Sky is Falling

Copyright © 2023 by Taj McCoy

All the Stars
Copyright © 2023 by Taj McCoy

Keep Calm and Curry On
Copyright © 2023 by Farah Heron

My Lucky Stars
Copyright © 2023 by Lane Clarke

Bunker Buddies
Copyright © 2023 by Charish Reid

Interlude
Copyright © 2023 by Sarah Smith

Anything You Can Do I Can Do Better
Copyright © 2023 by Denise Williams

Epilogue
Copyright © 2023 by Taj McCoy

For questions and comments about the quality of this book, please contact us at CustomerService@Harlequin.com.

Canary Street Press
22 Adelaide St. West, 41st Floor
Toronto, Ontario M5H 4E3, Canada
CanaryStPress.com

Printed in U.S.A.

For the ones who hold up the stars for us even when the sky is falling. You know who you are.

CONTENTS

Introduction

Dear Reader,

Picture this: the sky is falling. Literally. And the world as we know it is about to end. (Or so everyone thinks.) What would happen next? Would you reveal your long-standing crush on your grumpy boss? Would you reach out to the one who got away? Or the one you ran away from? Luckily for us, some of the romance genre's most exciting voices—Taj McCoy, Farah Heron, Lane Clarke, Charish Reid, Sarah Smith and Denise Williams—have come together to answer that very question. Now, I don't want to be too spoilery, but one of the stories features the ultimate hero trifecta: (1) he's wearing a Henley (2) that shows off his strong forearms (3) as he reads a feminist romance. Perfection, right?

I'll let you in on a little secret: "If The World Was Ending," a song performed by JP Saxe and Julia Michaels, is one of my favorite songs ever. In it, two former lovers declare that if the world were ending, there's nowhere they would rather be than with each other. To say that the premise of this anthology is the stuff of my tender heart's dreams would be an understatement. Reader, I know you're going to love these stories filled with tension, hope, all the swoons and, yes, plenty of sexy moments. So grab your favorite beverage and settle in for a good time—you're guaranteed to have one.

Hugs,

Mia

ALL THE STARS

TAJ McCOY

"Willy Song, we are leaving this base and heading to the station in eight minutes, with or without you," Halley growled through gritted teeth into her phone. She hung up before he could respond. *This is the last time I allow this joker off base before a mission.*

The dry air kicked up dust in the breeze, but the September heat radiated off the tarmac outside a small hangar. Halley Oakes was one mission away from being promoted from a NASA senior communications specialist to project manager, and it all depended on the success of this team. Based on those she'd been assigned, Halley had her doubts that her promotion was any closer than it had been a year before. More than once, Song had put her in a bind that left her with egg on her face in front of her superiors. He could complete most of his job, but not before making matters worse. She was sure someone had been joking when she read the team roster days before.

"I'm here, I'm here!" Willy jumped out of an SUV that hadn't come to a full stop with a cloth grocery bag, clanging its contents in one hand and a mission binder in the other. "Man, I hope we have time for a pit stop, because I think I had some bad shellfish last night, and a three-hour ride with me could be unpleasant." He scrunched up his nose, waving a hand in front of his face comically until he caught the arctic glare of his superior. His wiry hunched form straightened, and he pushed his floppy dark hair back so it wouldn't fall into his eyes.

Ew. "What the hell is that you're carrying, Song?" Willy Song was the tech specialist that no one chose for essential missions. Between his inappropriate jokes, his constant need to overshare and his record for accidents, there was no way he should be assigned to this detail. Of course, tell that to the chief—Song happened to be his only nephew.

Song hesitated briefly before a sly grin spread across his face. "Have you ever tried a peanut butter stout, boss?" He held open the bag by its handles to show off its contents—a six-pack of beer and a bag of pretzels. He practically danced with excitement, his feet tapping the tarmac to the beat of a rhythmless drum. "It's locally made at a brewery here in Boulder. It's supposed to be amazing, with subtle hints of chocolate and peanut butter." He chef-kissed his fingers as his eyes rolled back.

"Ew, no, and don't call me that. I like Oakes just fine." Halley wrinkled her nose. Beer was never really appealing to her, and adding peanut butter wasn't likely to make it better. She smoothed her hands over a self-imposed uniform of black cargo pants, work boots and a thin V-neck sweater with a small NASA emblem embroidered high on the left breast. Her curves felt understated in this uniform, and her thick halo of curls was pulled back into her standard "work attire" bun. She pushed the sleeves up her forearms, wishing she'd opted for something short-sleeved in this heat and running through the inventory of other clothes in her go bag.

"Everyone else here, boss?" Song eyed the black Escalade loaded with equipment for the installation.

"Glenn is already in the truck. We're just waiting on Simmons." Halley checked her watch for what felt like the millionth time. Jake Glenn, their systems engineer, always arrived like clockwork. Lynn Simmons, a part of the protective detail, usually beat everyone there and would nap until it was time to move. *Where is she?*

"Simmons? I thought she got reassigned for that detail in Florida?" He shifted his binder under the arm holding his prized beer so he could scratch his head before unsuccessfully trying to smooth his wrinkled clothes.

Halley's head snapped in Song's direction. "What?" she barked. A twisting sensation pierced her gut, and she blinked hard before staring at him with laser focus. "She was reassigned? Who is her replacement?"

Song's eyes widened as if he knew more. "Umm…"

Halley snatched her phone out of her pocket to go through her emails from the chief. Surely someone would have told her that her team assignments changed. Sure enough, Chief Henry had emailed her while they were in the air on their Colorado-bound flight from Andrews Air Force Base, outside DC. She scanned the email, inhaling a sharp breath when her eyes fell on the last name she wanted to see. *Griffin Harper.*

Seeing the murderous glint in her dark eyes, Song retreated to the SUV as Halley's cell rang. *Shit, it's the boss.* "Sir," she answered on the first ring, her tone devoid of emotion.

"Oakes, I sent you an updated roster while you were in

the air." The chief's no-nonsense tone was enough for Halley to understand that there would be no talking her way out of these last-minute reassignments. She assumed he came out of the womb scowling.

"Yes, sir, I saw the update." Her mouth formed a straight line. Protesting would just piss off the chief, and Halley was trying her hardest to advance in her career at NASA— something she'd been focused on since she started out as a summer intern in grad school. It had taken a decade to rise through the ranks and gain the trust of her superiors, first by becoming a specialist, and finally having "senior" attached to her title. Halley had built a reputation of reliability and strong leadership, and she could feel that she was right on the brink of advancement yet again. She could taste it. Complaining about assignments wasn't something that many comms specialists could get away with while still being assigned to lead missions.

Over the years, Halley had become the chief's go-to specialist on the team; he relied on her efficiency and quick thinking. He especially liked that she didn't bombard him with questions on how to get things done. Her initiative was a constant topic whenever he had to dress down a slacker in their unit. There were colleagues who teased her for being a favorite, but no one could deny Halley's work ethic.

"This won't be a problem, will it, Oakes?" Usually, Halley's commanding officer wouldn't have any knowledge of her personal relationships, but she and Griff had had a huge blowout argument in the mess hall the last time they saw each other—right after he'd sent the text that ended their relationship. She'd gone after him to give him a piece of her mind, and when he had nothing to say in response, she blew up. The chief and several other senior officials were present. Over a year had passed, but Halley had never shaken her frustration at being led on by a man who promised the world when he ultimately wasn't ready for an actual commitment or even to communicate his feelings like an adult. Because of her outburst in front of the senior team, her advancement had slowed, as if the higher-ups were waiting to see if she would rally or unravel altogether.

"Not at all, sir. We will conduct ourselves professionally and make sure that the system is installed flawlessly." Halley stood at attention, her voice firm, even though her insides were swirling.

"Good. Has Song arrived?" *Of course, he has to check up on his nephew.*

Sweat began to gather across Halley's smooth brown forehead as she cleared her throat. She whisked it away with the back of her hand. "He has. He's already in the transport vehicle. We're just waiting for Harper to arrive, and then we'll head for the base."

"Good." His voice softened slightly, as if he'd stepped away from the earshot of others. He was constantly surrounded by a team of people monitoring any number of projects and emergencies. "Now listen. Song looks up to you, and he could benefit from your guidance, Oakes. Make sure that this mission goes off without a hitch, yes?" The firmness of his tone indicated there was only one right answer. Being on the chief's bad side could mean a six-month detail in a place no one wanted to go.

"Yes, sir. We won't let you down, sir." The phone disconnected, and Halley bit her lip, wondering whether she would be able to keep her promise. Her shoulders rounded slightly as she fell deep into thought. The chief's nephew had already shared that he planned to sneak contraband into the station, and Halley's emotionally unavailable ex was on his way to distract her and bring back all of the feelings that she never processed. She sucked her teeth, brooding over the inevitable. Sensing movement behind her, Halley's back snapped straight, and she waited for the figure to identify itself. His smell-good cologne gave him away first.

"Hi, Halley," the voice behind her rumbled with a gravelly bass tone that reverberated at her very core. "Been a long time." That voice used to be enough to curl her toes, but Halley had built up a wall that turned her eyes hard and her face to stone. She no longer lit up when he spoke to her; instead, her senses dulled and she carried a constant air of cynicism.

Halley turned, rolling her shoulder blades down her back—narrowing her gaze to lock eyes with the one who decided he wasn't ready to be with her. He'd pulled his aviators down enough for her to get a glimpse of his thick, curly lashes and arresting stare. His dark hooded eyes trailed from hers to survey her from head to toe, eliciting a scowl from the recipient of his assessment. She took in his black tactical garb that stretched tight against his muscular chest, the dark brown skin of his arms crossing in front of him brandishing black ink tattoos, and that goofy look he made when he found her amusing. "Griff."

His lips twitched at the corners, threatening to curve, and she prayed that he wouldn't smile as he slid his sunglasses back up his nose to shield his eyes from her scrutiny. Beads of sweat gathered on his forehead and temples, his close-cut beard framed that strong, flexing jaw that Halley tried to forget. He looked good—better than the last time she saw him. He must have filled out some while on assignment abroad. A former marine, Griffin was a part of NASA's protective services team, and he traveled with several of the communications specialists as they assisted different countries with the implementation of the ADGWS—the Aerial Debris Global Warning System.

A couple of years ago, this program wasn't even on anyone's radar—it wasn't until a strange series of meteor showers slammed into a bunch of space junk in the Earth's atmosphere that anyone thought about creating a notification system that would alert people on the ground to take cover. Most of the meteor showers hit old decommissioned satellites or other junk that burned up in the atmosphere—the visuals looked like comets and shooting stars but were far too close for comfort. People began to believe some form of apocalypse was coming—that burning projectiles in the sky signified the end of times—but scientists continued to present data that explained the phenomenon, assuring people that they could track potential dangers and signal when true danger was imminent. However, back then they didn't have a universal means of transmitting a warning.

Even then, the idea wasn't adopted as policy by global leaders until a fiery chunk of an almost disintegrated old space station crossed the flight path of a transatlantic plane just seconds before a catastrophic impact would have landed hundreds of passengers in the middle of the ocean. Citizens of the world began to protest, demanding that they be warned to seek shelter if something invading the airspace threatened to reach the ground—or worse—could collide with something else that threatened harm upon impact with one hundred percent certainty. Governments began to hold summits to come up with a worldwide plan that would be recognizable by all inhabitants—no matter their country of origin.

Eventually, world leaders agreed that they would each

install an alert system, and NASA teamed with other space agencies around the globe to lead the charge in implementing the siren systems. Deaf and hard of hearing citizens were provided with all-hazard radios, which could emit visual and vibrating alerts. News agencies worked with local governments to come up with approved language to transmit should the sirens be employed. The space center teams strategized hundreds of scenarios so that countries could assemble local guidance. Halley had been all over Asia and the Middle East. She'd heard that Griff was assigned to details with teams in Central and South America. She never expected to see him at the home installation—especially not even more burly and chiseled than before. Yet there he was, staring her down with a boyish half smirk on his face like he hadn't broken her heart just last year.

He removed his mirrored aviator sunglasses, those dark brown eyes crinkling at the corners. "Don't you think it's ironic that we came up with the idea for a universal alert system and we're the last ones to install it?"

"No, I think that we created some goodwill in prioritizing other countries that needed help with implementation. We could have used other forms of PSAs to get the job done if something was on course over the US." Her tone held a twinge of annoyance. He knew all of this, so why was he asking this question? *He probably just wants me to talk to him.* She had zero intention of falling for any of his antics on this trip.

He shrugged, observing her openly. His gaze made a slow descent over her body once more—the curves he used to ache for—before traveling back up to meet her lash-lined glare. His playful, boyish smile made her stomach do backflips, but she narrowed her gaze, aware of two sets of eyes watching through the blacked-out windows of their transport vehicle.

"Listen, Griffin Harper, I don't know what's running through your mind right now, but I am going to remind you just once that I have point on this mission. I don't want to hear a peep out of you unless it has to do with your protection detail for this team. Do anything to piss me off, Griff, and I swear I'll make good on the promise I made the last time you saw me."

His smile simmered to an amused curl of his lips. "The one where you promised you'd shove your foot up my ass?"

She batted her lashes sweetly. "Good. You remembered." She tossed the keys in his direction and moved toward the passenger door of the SUV. "Now load up. I want to be there and set up well before sundown. Jake Glenn, Willy Song— eyes front if you know what's good for you," she snapped, climbing into the truck.

"Yes, ma'am," Griff whispered, his thick lips curving into a tight-lipped smile. He grabbed his bag from the ground and proceeded to load it into the trunk.

Two hours and thirty-six minutes. Halley squinted at her phone, hoping the estimated time of arrival on her GPS would change to a shorter length of time. When it didn't, she sighed, leaning back against her seat, her eyes squeezed shut. The air conditioning pushed curly wisps of her hair out of her face and made her shiver—the only reprieve from the dry heat rising outside the barrier of her window. Halley hummed to herself, welcoming the cool air, trying to drown out the sounds around her.

"Not a bad idea to recharge while you have the time," Griff observed, keeping his eyes on the road ahead of them.

Halley opened one eye and turned to focus it on the driver,

his eyes shielded by his sunglasses. "You really think I can sleep with Song making all of that noise?"

Griffin cracked a smile. "I would think that with all the travel we do on these details, you'd get used to sleeping with a little noise in the background."

"A little noise" was an understatement. They didn't bother playing the radio because none of the team would be able to hear the music. In the back row, Song sat with his back against the arm rest and his feet propped up on the seat. His head leaned against the darkened window, his mouth agape as he snored loudly. Every inhale rumbled like a grating motor struggling to start. In the middle row, Jake sat with noise-canceling headphones and his head against the headrest, but his fidgeting and cutting scowls toward the back indicated he still heard Song's throaty grumbling clearly.

Song sucked in a breath loudly, his soft palate rumbling as the air pulled inward, his exhales soft and unencumbered. Jake squeezed his blue-green eyes closed and then reached back and flicked Song in the middle of his forehead, jolting him awake. "Huh, what? Dude, what's your problem?" Song repositioned his head so that his cheek pressed against the window.

"Man, you sound like a broken air vent," Jake muttered. He moved his headphones off one ear to wait for a response, the bronzed skin of his forehead wrinkled from his raised brows.

Song was already sound asleep again, his snoring muffled only by his closed mouth. *He probably won't even remember that Glenn flicked him.*

Halley cracked a smile in Jake's direction as he shook his head with annoyance. "Permission to strap him to the back of the SUV, boss?"

Her grin widened. "We have a rack up top if it gets to be too much."

Jake nodded, satisfied. He returned the ear cup of his headphones back to the side of his face and shut his eyes. Glenn was never the kind to exert any kind of violence, but Song tried his patience. The most capable systems engineer Halley had ever worked with, they'd traveled the world together to implement warning systems and to provide guidance to other countries considering alternative ways of reaching rural areas with warning communications. His gruff, steely glare caused many to assume that he carried a cold demeanor, but Glenn was a gentle giant and extremely quiet until he got a little *añejo* tequila into his system—then you couldn't keep him from a dance floor or karaoke stage. Halley crushed on him early in her career, but after her failings with Griff, she vowed never to date another colleague. Jake's honey-brown curls wound around the band of his headphones as his fingers tapped along with the beat of his favorite playlist.

Halley faced forward, her shoulders relaxing a little more. She tried to remember the last time this team had been assembled, thinking back to her first detail several years prior. Her ambition motivated her to be proactive and earn quick points with their superiors. Some thought she was a brownnoser, but Griffin had backed her up, praising her quick thinking and ability to anticipate obstacles. She'd barely looked in his direction before that day, but his words stuck with her, and soon after that, they'd started dating secretly.

They fell hard, even though they shouldn't have—relationships were strongly discouraged among unit members. Halley couldn't help how she felt, and Griff seemed so sure that she was made for him, so they'd agreed to keep their relationship quiet. A few colleagues had figured out that the two were an item, but Halley didn't want their superiors to reassign one of them away from headquarters in DC. The chief never seemed to let on, and, with all of their travel for work, they agreed that it didn't make sense to have two apartments, so they consolidated into Griffin's place since it was bigger.

Halley picked at her nails, wishing she'd gotten that mani-pedi before the trip as she'd planned. "Do you remember that first detail?"

"That training workshop in Egypt?"

"Yeah. Song couldn't handle all of the dust from the sand. His snoring was ten times worse on that trip."

"Remember Jake panicked and thought he was waking up to a bear?"

Halley almost smiled, but she remembered who was sitting next to her. How his strong hands made her feel so safe and also seemed to hold her heart in a vise. Even now, she wasn't sure she was completely released from his grip. The one she almost risked it all for—her reputation and career. "A bear, that's right," she mumbled, staring up into the mountains.

Griff smirked as he glanced in the rearview mirror. "That guy has notoriously bad allergies. I'm sure the elevation here doesn't help him any. It's dusty here too."

Halley sucked her teeth, keeping her gaze straight ahead. "I'll be sure to buy him some eucalyptus oil. He sounds like a clogged drain."

The highway was packed with Friday traffic, but most cars were headed east toward downtown Boulder or south toward Denver. The team's westerly direction remained relatively clear, the bright sun shining onto the dried grass and dark shrubs that peppered the sides of the lower foothills. The Rocky Mountains loomed behind the foothills—the highest peaks still capped with snow even after the heat of the summer months.

Griffin glanced at her quickly before returning his eyes to the road. "Do you want to put on some music or something?"

"Uh, sure, if you think we'll hear it." Halley reached for the radio controls and a familiar song burst through the speakers—one that she and Griff danced to before. The impassioned lyrics hit Halley in the gut and Griffin stiffened at the sound, gripping the steering wheel more tightly. The heady voice of H.E.R. crooned melodically over a slow beat and the strum of an electric guitar. Flinching, Halley fumbled to quickly change the station, turning the music to a smooth jazz station with instrumental piano playing.

Griff mumbled thanks, and Halley turned to stare out the passenger window, but she was too deep in thought to take in the scenery. The last time they heard that song, "Every Kind of Way," they'd slow danced in their apartment, celebrating an anniversary. Halley squeezed her eyes shut, remembering their bodies pressed together as they moved along with the sensual song. She'd hummed the lyrics with her face pressed against his neck as Griff held one of Halley's hands to his heart as he ran the fingertips of his other hand along the small of her back.

Halley remembered his muscular body felt so hard against the softness of her curves, and when he dipped his head to kiss her, she tasted the remnants of the lemon torte cake they'd shared at the anniversary dinner. That night, she was sure that, whatever their trajectory, they were meant to be together. Two months later, she learned via text that she was moving out, and they'd avoided each other anytime they were both at headquarters ever since. In the past year, Halley never got further than a couple of dates; her walls were raised to barricade heights to protect her from ever falling so deeply again. Instead, she threw herself into her work, taking each promotion as assurance that there was nothing wrong with her while closing herself off to new possibilities of love.

She opened her eyes and stared out at the terrain. They'd left the city behind and houses were more sparse with large plots of land. The highway was paved at the foot of two large mountains, splitting the space between the two like a dividing wall. Halley pictured Griff on one side of an invisible barrier with her on the other.

"Just sit tight for a couple of minutes, I have to clear the station." They'd pulled up to the gate of the station, which looked dark inside. The back of the building abutted the base of a mountain, with satellite dishes and safety sirens affixed to the roof along with solar paneling. Griffin put the SUV into Park, surveying the property in front of them.

Not far from the Rocky Mountain National Park, the team had turned off the highway onto a dirt road that wound around foothills and brush to a secluded area unlikely to be visited by random hikers or passersby needing a rest stop.

Halley rolled her eyes from the passenger seat. "Come on, Griff. No one is here. The team assigned to this station is a skeleton crew, and they don't have anyone working here on Fridays." She looked at the empty parking lot and the dark windows as indication that no one was present, even though she knew from experience that there could be unexpected visitors within the station.

"People do stupid things all the time, Halley. Let me do my job," Griff muttered. He side-eyed Song, whose bag of stout bottles clanked as he jumped out of the SUV. "Song, I just said to sit tight. What are you doing, man?" His six-foot-three frame towered above Song's five-foot-six.

Song opened his mouth to protest and then climbed back into the truck.

Halley leaned over the center console to look at Griffin through the driver's-side window. "Fine, just hurry up. If we get everything implemented, we can get back to the airport in time to go home tonight," she replied gruffly.

"What's the rush?" Griffin's eyebrow raised slowly. "You got a hot date or somethin' waiting for you back home?"

Song shifted uncomfortably in the back seat, his bottles clinking together as a reminder that this conversation was in a public forum.

Halley clicked her tongue and shook her head as she turned to stare out the window while he moved to open the gate and secure the station—his service weapon on his hip. *Home.* When Halley and Griffin broke up, she moved out of their spacious two-bedroom town house in Alexandria, Virginia, and found a small studio with enough space for her cat to roam and a closet big enough for her shoe collection. These days, poor Luna spent more time being watched by Halley's sister, Nova, than she did with Halley. Just before this last trip, Luna left an unpleasant surprise in Halley's suitcase, forcing Halley to use a duffel bag and buy some fresh clothes.

"Guys, I'm gonna make a couple of calls. I'll be outside," Halley said over her shoulder, exiting the vehicle before she received a response. Holding up her phone, she dialed the first person listed on her Favorites list.

"Hey, sis, did you make it okay?"

"Hi, Nova. We made it to the station. Griffin is here." She lowered her head and her voice, assuming the two in the truck were actively attempting to ear hustle.

Halley was met with a moment of silence. The last time Nova heard anything about Griffin, she said she would choose violence on sight if she ran into him around town. "Ugh. So he hasn't crawled up his own ass and died," Nova observed. "Is that weird for you?"

"Weird doesn't begin to cut it." She sighed. "How's my Luna?"

"Chile, your cat is fine. How's my couch is more like it," Nova snapped. "Just know that if this cat ends up missing, it's because she's scratching up all my damn furniture and peeing in my shoes."

"I'm so sorry, sis. I should have warned you," Halley groaned.

"Is this some sort of cat phase or is she punishing me because I'm not you? Or is this some sort of comedy that I don't appreciate? Like, what kind of animal mastermind is at work here for this level of foolery?"

Halley pictured Nova's tilted head and pursed lips complementing her tone. She coughed to stifle a laugh. "Honestly, it could be either."

"This is why I like dogs. You can tell that they're happy to see you, there are very clear boundaries as far as excrement and I don't have to worry that they might decide to overthrow humanity and smother me in my sleep."

Halley could hear Nova moving around her apartment—she worked remotely as a strategic consultant. Drawers and cabinets were opening and closing in the background, which meant she was probably getting ready to make dinner. Complain as she might, Nova secretly loved when Halley left town and Luna came to stay. Halley grinned. "Luna had better be in perfect condition when I get back or I'm telling Dad that you have his missing wine Coravin."

"Now that's just dirty, Hal. Jesus. Let me live one wineglass at a time!" Nova cackled into the phone, and Halley pictured her full head of honeyed curls bouncing along.

Halley chuckled. "Try me."

"But seriously, how is the installation going?" Nova knew Halley's role in implementing the US system and often joked around about the sky falling, but that was before the piece of the old space station fell into the Atlantic and freaked out residents all along the East Coast. "We don't have anything to worry about, right?"

Halley exhaled slowly, shaking her head. "Nothing to worry about, Nov. We haven't received any reports of activity that would be cause for alarm, and if there was a cause for concern, you know better than most what to do if there is any issue. Right?"

"Yes, Hal. You've practically drilled it into me—if I hear the siren go off, I'm to immediately go to the basement and stay away from the windows until we get three siren blasts or the text alert that we're all clear," Nova exasperatedly repeated to Halley the instructions she'd heard over and over again.

Halley opened her mouth to add a piece that Nova had forgotten, but Nova continued before she could say anything.

"And yes, I would take Luna with me. She already has a care package in the basement, just in case." Nova clicked her tongue at her older sister. "You're lucky I love you, you know."

Halley rolled her eyes lovingly. "I love you too. Fingers crossed that I'm on my way home tonight."

"Just be safe, Hal. We'll be here."

Halley disconnected the call to find Griff standing right behind her. She jumped at the sight of him. "Jesus."

"Sorry, did I scare you?"

She glared in response.

"Right. Was that Nova? How's my Luna-Toons?" His voice light, Griffin offered that easy smile that often made Halley want to punch him.

"*Your* Luna?" she scoffed. While she got Luna two years before Griffin even came into the picture, Luna took an immediate liking to him, often acting like she preferred Griffin over Halley. Of course, Griff never let her forget it.

"Luna would have stayed with me if given the chance, you know."

Halley scowled. "Right. The only way your exit would have been a bigger dick move would have been if you broke my heart *and* stole my cat. Fuck outta here, Griff."

He grimaced. "Come on, Halley. I thought we were past that now. Aren't we friends?"

She grabbed her go bag from the trunk. "No, Griff. You decided you were past this and you left. I still have screen shots of that lovely text you sent me to let me know."

"Okay, I admit, I didn't handle it the best," he ventured, his hands spread wide in front of him as if to surrender.

"No, you didn't handle it at all, Griff, but now really isn't the time to get into this." She stared hard into his eyes, jerking a thumb toward the station. "Are we clear or what?"

He blew out a sharp breath as his shoulders dropped and his back hunched a little. The image made Halley picture a deflating balloon. "Clear."

Halley patted the doors of the SUV with the palm of her hand twice, keeping her eye on Griff. She projected her tone from her chest, intent on giving orders only once. "Alright, team. Let's get set up. I would prefer not to have to overnight out here, so make moves."

Song and Glenn climbed out of the truck, wary of the

other two staring each other down. Song's bag of beer clanking at his hip as he grabbed a duffel of equipment.

Halley's head snapped in his direction. "Willy, the beer can wait, man. Get set up."

Song nodded. "I got it, boss. Just trying to be efficient and make as few trips as possible." He didn't put down the beer, but he did grab a second piece of equipment and struggled to carry it all into the station behind Jake, who handled twice the amount of gear. Jake would bite his tongue, but Halley sensed his annoyance. His clenched jaw was his tell—the more it flexed, the closer he was to going off the rails.

Halley threw up her hands in frustration, making quick eye contact with Griffin as he scowled after Song. "He never listens," she whispered, "but he is the one that is *always* guaranteed to fuck up. Peanut-butter-fucking-stout."

"Just calm down, Hal—" He scratched at the back of his neck.

"No, Griff. Literally, anyone else would be out on their ass by now. It's just because his uncle is who he is that we deal with all of his bullshit."

Griffin waited for a beat. "You're right, but stressing about this isn't going to make you feel any better. Keep him in line, let's get the job done and we can get the hell out of here. Mission first, right?"

Halley sucked in a breath, hating that he was right. Hands on her hips, she dropped her head, closed her eyes and nodded, taking in a couple of deep breaths.

"Come on, let's get to work." He nudged her arm with his elbow before picking up the remaining equipment.

She trudged in behind him, the station a long hallway of rooms with digital locks. Halley pulled her NASA credentials from a retractable lanyard and held the badge against the electronic pad, unlocking the largest room of the station. The long wall had thick glass windows looking into the control room from the hallway; the room was set up with stadium-style seating facing a huge multiscreen-in-screen monitor. Glenn stepped inside, followed by Song, and they immediately began to unpack laptops, cords, hard drives and other materials that would help them hardwire the warning system for the entire country to headquarters and their local satellites.

Halley continued down the hall, familiarizing herself with the layout of the station. Lavatories, a lunch room and several single-occupancy bunks were farther down the hall. There was also a communications room directly next to the control room along with several supply cabinets with emergency equipment. "There are enough MREs to feed a team for a year," she murmured.

Griffin grinned. "I'm partial to the chili."

Halley turned green just thinking about it. Hearing a large thud and a yelp, she and Griff exchanged a look and doubled back to the control room. "Everybody okay in here? Song? What the—"

Jake was on the far side of the room connecting cables to the servers, his jaw flexing actively as he cut his eyes in Song's direction. Willy had a bucket of ice in his hand and was limping on one foot, but he signaled with his free hand that there was nothing to worry about. "Okay in here, boss. I just dropped some equipment on my foot while I was making room for—"

"In what world do you think it's okay to have ice buckets of beer in the control room, Song? What. Is. WRONG. With. You?" Halley bellowed. "You really think this is that much of a priority?"

"Well, if you'd just try it, boss—"

"Do you even understand why we are here right now? We are implementing a national warning system—our *entire country* is depending on this system, and I'm sure they'll take comfort that this fucking beer takes priority over their safety."

Song's gaze shifted nervously from Halley to Griffin. "I just thought that maybe we could celebrate the final installation with something special."

"He didn't mean any harm, Hal," Griffin coaxed gently.

Halley's neck swiveled sharply as she gestured in Song's direction. "He also didn't mean to get his job done efficiently. Now he's hobbling around, and we could have damaged equipment. But at least the beer is safe." She threw up her hands and rolled her eyes. Song hung his head a little.

"Come on, Halley, don't you think you're being a little too harsh?" Griffin asked quietly, reaching for her arm.

Halley yanked her arm out of reach. "Is it really necessary for me to remind everyone that it's *my* ass on the line if anything goes wrong?" Just as she finished her sentence, her phone rang. Halley swore under her breath, answering her phone on speaker so that everyone could get a taste of reality. "Yes, Chief. We're here and getting set up now."

"I want a report as soon as you're ready to go live with the system, Oakes. This one is for the home team, so I don't need to tell you what is at stake, do I?"

At the sound of his uncle's voice, Willy's back snapped straight, jostling the ice in his bucket. He winced at the noise and mouthed "sorry" to Halley. Griffin pinched the bridge of his nose between his thumb and forefinger. Why he was taking up for Song right now confused Halley, but she figured any sense of siding with her could no longer be expected either.

She chewed her lip, ignoring Song. "No, sir. We are making every effort to have a smooth and efficient install. Our goal is to get this done, get the tests scheduled and be on our way home tonight."

"Your ass is on the line here, Oakes. If the team has to stay the weekend to get it done right, you do that. I don't want any mistakes, and I want a full report ASAP."

"Will do, sir. We will be set up in no time and will check in as soon as everything is up and running." She tried to keep her voice positive and confident to assure the chief that they were on task.

"Tell your team to get it done, or this could be your last detail for NASA. There are plenty of competent comms specialists who would kill for your job, Oakes."

The call disconnected before she could respond, and Halley pocketed her phone, staring straight ahead but focusing on nothing in particular. The team stood in silence for a moment before Halley turned on her heel and headed toward the hallway. Griff tried to follow her, but she held her hand to stop him, her tone faintly above a whisper as she said, "Just gimme a minute."

Halley stared at herself in the mirror for a long moment before turning a handle on the sink and splashing cold water on her cheeks. She blotted her face with a dry paper towel and then wiped the perimeter of the sink before throwing the paper away. Placing her hands on the counter, she leaned forward, looking herself in the eye. "Pull it together, Oakes," she whispered.

It had been Halley's dream since childhood to someday work for NASA. She wasn't the great scientist and astronomer that her dad was, but she knew her job and took every detail seriously. Sometimes, it felt like the chief was setting her up to fail when he attached his nephew to her teams, but as she stared at herself, she considered the possibility that the chief was trying to help his nephew as best he could by attaching Song to Halley's details. *Maybe I should listen to Griff and cut him a little more slack.*

Cutting him slack was an almost impossible task, given the number of times he'd been assigned to Halley's detail and created problems for her. Problems she kept from Song's uncle out of fear that she'd be held responsible for his mistakes. Song once almost electrocuted himself because he was downing a Big Gulp while rewiring servers at HQ. He broke one of Jake's toes by accidentally dropping a case of equipment when he thought he saw a bug. Of course, it was actually just a dried leaf. The more Halley considered Song's blunders, the heavier the weight on her shoulders.

The lights flickered as if the power threatened to go out, and Halley rushed back to the control room. Jake rushed in from the galley with a wad of paper towels, and Song was on the floor, frantically mopping up a puddle of beer. Griffin stood in the doorway, his mouth slack. Apparently he was all out of defenses for Willy.

A cloud of fury built between Halley's brows. "Song, you had better start talking. What the hell just happened?"

"Boss, I—" He looked back and forth between the stout on the floor and Halley's death glare, a panicked expression in his eyes.

"Oh my god. Oh my god. Oh my god." Halley stared at the static flickering across the big screen monitor in their control room. "Does that mean what I think it means?" She pointed at the screen. "Why are we not picking up satellite feeds, Song?"

"I—uh... Um, well..." Willy stammered, his cheeks flushed red as sweat poured from his temples.

"None of those sound like cogent explanations, Song. Get me a sitrep and don't make me ask you again!" she yelled.

Song nodded, seemingly near tears. "Yes, boss. Right away."

Everyone stilled as the sirens began to blare. The same chilling sound that had been broadcast around the world on the news and in virtual town halls so that citizens everywhere knew what to listen for. Local authorities had been provided with the instructions and funding to have sirens and alert transmissions work anywhere that people were likely to be, and with so many hikers and rock climbers in Colorado, Halley was still surprised at the clarity of the sound within the station. She glared at Song, the intensity of her words flamed through gritted teeth. "What the fuck, Song? Turn. That. Off." Her voice boomed as wasps of warning swarmed in her belly. *I'm so getting fired for this.*

Song grimaced, his eyebrows knitting together as he frantically flipped switches and attempted to type commands into his portal. "Boss, I can't. I think that the system shorted out. It's not responding."

Halley stared at him, unblinking. All of the breath from her lungs carried one word. "How?"

"I—I spilled some of the stout. It was an accident. I was trying to put the bottles on ice..." He stopped as Halley held up a hand.

"You thought it would be a good idea to have open beers on ice in the control room? What did we *just* talk about? There is an entire break room with tables, a refrigerator and snacks, where it would make so much more sense to chill down your beer."

"I tried to tell him that he should just put that in the break room until we were ready to celebrate, but he just doesn't *listen*." Jake chewed on the side of his lip as he tried to swap out some of the damp wiring, but a spark zapped his fingertips, and he drew his hand away, shaking it out. "Song, go get more paper towels," he barked.

Willy turned to go to the break room, muttering, "I just thought that, since I had already brought the ice in here, I might as well put the beer on ice and let it chill while we worked."

Jake squeezed his eyes shut, and Halley pictured a tiny person inside his brain screaming at the top of their lungs. The sirens continued, and Halley rushed outside to make sure she wasn't dreaming. The blaring echoed from the mountains as flocks of birds scattered, undoubtedly confused by the commotion. Her mind raced, as she pictured accidents on the highways, people panicking and running through the streets and Nova running to the basement with Luna in tow. She ran back inside, praying the guys had found a resolution.

Jake was removing wires from another server as one sparked close to his hands. "Shit!" he shoved a finger in his mouth. "We are so fucked," he muttered.

"Please tell me that's not true," Halley begged. "Song, where is my situation report? Move!"

Song looked like he could both cry and puke at the same time. "I—I don't have answers right now, boss. I need more time to assess what's happening."

An emergency alert sounded on Halley's cell phone, then Song's, then Griffin's and then Jake's. Halley looked down at her phone. "We're fucked alright," she whispered.

Griffin stepped to her side, not bothering to look at his own. "What is it?"

Halley's hand shook as she read the alert on her phone. "'This is an official announcement—aerial debris detected. This is not a drill. Please find immediate shelter in an underground bunker or interior parts of a building away from windows. Remain sheltered and wait for an all-clear.'" She set her phone down and then snatched it up again. "The chief."

Song's eyes widened.

Halley pressed Chief Henry's contact information, but the phone wouldn't connect. "I'm not getting a signal. We didn't do that, did we?"

"No," Jake responded matter-of-factly. "It's more likely that the panic of over three hundred million people trying to use their phones at the same time is jamming cell towers. Calls aren't going to go through via radio frequency right now." He continued to reroute different cables on the servers. "Honestly, I could really use a line to HQ right now, because I don't have time to read through eighteen system binders to figure out what all these servers control, but half of them are pretty fried."

Song's shoulders slumped so far down that he bowed over his desk. "Boss, I don't know what to report. I don't have answers for how long it'll blare, or how long it'll take to get to an all-clear signal. I—I'm sorry. I should have listened to you."

"Song, we don't have time for apologies now. We need answers and we need them fast, or we're all getting pink slips right at the start of the weekend." Halley pressed her hands against a control panel, leaning her weight on it.

Jake interrupted, "Boss, I'm losing telemetry on our local satellites. I think a hard reset may have been triggered by the shorted servers. The entire system is going to reboot starting in five minutes."

"Jesus Christ. Turn on the TVs."

Jake and Song flipped on several television networks on their big monitor, and all had digital monikers—all stations had posted an immediate emergency warning for everyone to get underground. News agencies were warned not to try to capture panic—that everyone needed to move safely to bunkers, including their people. Halley stared at the lifeless screens. Everyone across the country was waiting to hear the three blasts to alert them that they were safe.

"Okay," Halley breathed. "So we have a full system reset that's about to happen, and then what?"

Jake shrugged. "We've likely got hours for the reset to complete before we can have everything fixed, but we won't know for sure until we can get back online and Song can see all of the systems that were tripped." He jutted a finger in Song's direction. "Honestly, we could have messed with other systems or station communications outside of what we've currently identified and simply have no idea."

"Do you think cell phones will be down the entire time?"

Jake turned his palms face up by his sides. "It could be a number of things. The siren system might be interrupting radio frequencies, or just the sheer number of people trying to use their phones at the same time is doing the job, which could overwhelm the bandwidth of cell towers. Given the sirens, the latter makes a lot of sense. The amount of network traffic across the entire country is certainly enough to knock out signals. People will probably receive random texts, but likely after long delays. They could probably reach each other if they had a landline phone in their bunker, but I think most people wouldn't have had the forethought."

"Hmm…that's something we didn't think of." Halley's eyes swept the control room for a hard-line. "I know we have one in the control room at headquarters, but is there a landline phone in the HQ bunker?"

"I honestly don't know, boss. I didn't get to visit the bunker at base."

Shit, I should have worked a bunker visition into our implementation plan. Perspiration beaded on Halley's forehead, and knots turned in her stomach. The more she looked around the control room at the sizzling servers and a six-pack of beer on ice, the more she wanted to scream into oblivion.

"You don't look too good, boss," Jake whispered, eyeing her closely, his blue-green eyes observing her. He leaned closer for privacy. "Maybe you should go lay down for a little while. We'll update you once we have anything determinative."

It didn't feel right to leave, but Halley felt the walls closing in her, as if she was suffocating. She turned to Song. "Willy, if you don't get this figured out and we somehow manage to get out of this with our jobs still intact, I will make sure you are never assigned such a big detail again. I don't care who your uncle is—I will make it my life's purpose to end your career. Understood?"

Song blinked slowly and nodded.

Lights began blinking across the control center, and their control screen went completely black. The sirens finally stopped sounding. Halley looked around the room feeling completely out of her depth, unable to contribute any working knowledge to the technology issues they were facing.

"The reset just started, boss. It's going to be at least a few hours, so best hit the barracks for some shut-eye. We'll come get you when we have something." The corners of Jake's mouth turned upward slightly—the closest he got to a reassuring smile. "We've got this, Hal. Don't worry."

Halley patted away the sweat on her forehead with the palm of her hand and nodded. "Okay, but don't worry about waking me—I want to know the second you know anything."

"You got it."

Halley stepped out of the door and headed down the hall, Griff right behind her.

Halley stormed down the hall and thrust open the door to a small private sleeping quarters. Against one wall, a couple of scratchy surplus blankets and a white sheet dressed a drab mattress on a twin cot, which was topped with a thin white pillow. A red-and-black-plaid throw blanket was folded neatly at the foot of the bed. Across from the cot was a work desk and open shelving filled with emergency supplies. The wall connecting the space was bare other than an old pedestal sink and a small wastebasket.

Griffin squeezed into the room before Halley could slam the door shut.

"What the fuck am I supposed to do, Griff? We've incited nationwide panic!" She tore a couple of paper towels from a roll on the work desk, then blotted the sweat from her forehead and the bridge of her nose. Her heart pounded in her chest, and her breath was short. She stood with her hands on her hips, willing herself to calm down.

"You don't know that, Halley. We don't have any reports to indicate that anyone is hurt."

"Oh, you really think that people just went into these bunkers and aren't freaking out right now, worried that the world is going to end? Like people hear those sirens and are like, bet—let me just proceed in an orderly fashion??" She thunked down onto a corner of the cot harder than she intended—the cot's springs creaking sharply in response.

His full lips curved into a lazy half smile as his dark brown eyes bore into hers playfully, his head tilted slightly. "What would you want to do if you thought the world was possibly coming to an end?"

She scoffed, rolling her eyes. "But it's not!"

"You and I know that, sure, but no one out there does. Come on, Hal. You don't even want to think about it?" He stretched his arms above his head, wrapping his fingers around the top shelf of supplies, his arms threatening to burst through the sleeves of his shirt. "I know what I'd do."

Halley felt the tug, as if he had become the center of gravity. She licked her lips with the tip of her tongue, willing herself to maintain her distance. "What's that? You know what? Never mind, I don't want to know."

"Oh, I think you do. Come on, the sky is falling, you wouldn't want to sit outside with me and watch for shooting stars? We could count them, one by one." He grinned at her, pulling his bottom lip between his teeth as his brow curved upward. He used to make that look at her from across the room whenever they were at some event that he wanted to leave—his signal that he was ready to take her home and take off her clothes.

She rolled her eyes. "Is that really where your mind is right now?" Of course, now that he mentioned it, that was all she could think of—how annoyingly romantic of him. *Here is Griffin, king of bad timing, first of his name. Why is he still so sexy?* Halley watched the way Griff's chest expanded with each breath below those sculpted shoulders. She hated how she could remember the tickle of his stubble against her sensitive skin. She glared at him, angry that he took her mind to this place so easily.

Griff leaned back against the supply shelves. "My mind is always there a little bit, but honestly, right now I'm just hoping to distract you enough to calm you down. You're so focused on Song, and while he deserves to be within your crosshairs right now, is this really about what he did, or are you just projecting your anger with me onto him?"

"Are you kidding me? Millions of people are sheltering right now because of that fool! What the hell does that have to do with you? But you know what? Yes, let's talk about you, because apparently I have time today." She blinked at him, resting her elbows on her knees.

He shrugged. "What do you want to know?"

Halley felt her intuition split into two—the pros and the cons resting on either of her shoulders. The pros wanted closure, while the cons believed nothing good could come from reopening the same can of worms. Closure won. "Why did you do it, Griff? We were great together."

"It's like we're right back to the same argument. I thought we were both past this." Griffin rubbed the back of his neck, a pinch between his brows.

"How am I supposed to be past something when I don't understand why it ended? You broke things off without any explanation—you sent a text, you refused to talk about it and you completely shut down. I'm just supposed to magically know what happened? I couldn't fix it, I couldn't move on, because I didn't even know what went wrong. I mean, what the fuck did I do to you?" She gulped in a breath, tears threatening to spill. "Can you just give me that so that I can finally move on?"

Griffin rolled his eyes, staring at something on the ceiling.

His chest heaved, as his thick arms crossed in front of him. He bit his lip, shaking his head as if he was holding back.

Clearly he's not interested in having this conversation. "You know what, Griff? Never mind." Halley narrowed her eyes as she pointed at him, standing up as if to leave the room.

"You know what, Hal, maybe I didn't want you to move on." His tone resigned, he fixed his gaze on her.

"What? I don't understand." Halley shook her head. *None of this makes sense.* "Why wouldn't you want that? You moved on first, so why wouldn't you want that for me?"

Griffin's face twisted as he snapped at her. "Don't you know that was the biggest mistake of my life? Walking away from you was the worst thing I've ever done—I didn't know what 'being ready' meant. I just knew I was supposed to be ready first—that's what Pop always said. I thought that I was supposed to have all my shit together, but I didn't have any sort of plan, and I was afraid of my feelings for you."

Confused, she stared at him, as if he'd grown another head. "What was it that you were supposed to do though? We already lived together. I wasn't pressing you for anything—we both had work goals that we wanted to achieve before we took any next steps." She felt like she was missing some of the figures in an extremely complicated equation.

"That's true, but I *felt* like I was supposed to be ready to propose or make some other big gesture. The second that I knew I loved you, it's like this ticking clock hung around my neck. Everyone was waiting for me to make a move, and I couldn't handle the pressure. You didn't ask me to do anything, but friends would joke, and you know my mom has been asking me since the day we moved in together when I was going to 'make an honest woman out of you.'" He rolled his eyes as he made air quotes with his fingers. "By the time

I figured things out for myself, you had already moved out, and you wanted nothing to do with me. We got assigned to different teams and that was it. But I never stopped loving you, Halley."

"How am I supposed to believe you now? I didn't just opt to move out. You told me that you couldn't do this anymore." She gestured between them. "You ended this and let me think for a year that you stopped loving me—that I wasn't enough or had done something wrong."

Griffin turned to face her, a pleading look in his eyes. "The sky could come falling down tomorrow, Hal. I don't want to be anywhere that isn't with you. If that means we're engaged, or married, or you're barefoot and pregnant, I'll be the happiest man alive because I'm living my dream with you. I'm sorry that I didn't realize it right away—honestly, it took me losing you to really get it. And I'll do whatever I have to convince you. For starters, there's this." He pressed his lips against hers, cradling her face with his hand.

Their lips touched softly at first. Halley pulled back briefly to press her lips together and frown at him, but something inside compelled her to lean forward and kiss him again. Her cheeks flushed, and he stroked his fingers against the nape of her neck. Her lips parted, and he kissed her hungrily, gliding his tongue against hers before sucking on her lower lip. His fervor ignited her appetite, and she let down her walls, throwing herself into his kiss.

Neither wanted to stop for air. Frantically, Halley pulled her sweater over her head as Griffin removed his tactical belt. He took off his polo shirt over his head and lifted Halley to her feet, pressing her against the wall. "The cot is going to make a lot of noise," he whispered, returning his mouth to hers before trailing his tongue down the side of her neck.

She whimpered, his hands deftly unhooking her bra and cupping her breasts. Her back against the wall, Halley panted as Griffin's kisses inched downward, over her nipples, lapping at them before moving lower to the waistband of her slacks. She kicked off her shoes, and Griffin unbuttoned her pants, kneeling before her as his fingers dug under the waistband of her lacy black panties. He looked up at her and she nodded, looking to her sides for something sturdy to hold on to. As he guided her panties to the floor for her to step out of them, he kissed the inside of one of her thighs, pulling it over his shoulder as he buried his face between her folds.

Halley covered her mouth with one of her hands as she gasped, gripping the pedestal sink with the other. Her knees could give at any moment, but Griff kept her pinned in place. He licked and suckled her clit, holding her against his mouth by gripping her ass tightly. She was so wet—she could feel moisture dripping down the thigh of her standing leg—the pleasure emanating from her core made her wrap her other leg around Griffin's back more firmly.

"Mmm," he responded to the added pressure, using his fingers to spread her folds apart, exposing her core. "I missed this." He ran his tongue over her slowly, again and again, feeling Halley's thigh tighten around his neck and shake as she got closer to the brink of orgasm. His tongue painted slow, intense circles that coaxed muffled moans from deep in Halley's throat. She rotated her hips, grinding against his mouth, gripping the sink with her other hand, as his tongue speed increased—the painted circles spinning at a dizzying pace until lights danced behind Halley's closed eyelids.

"Fuck, I'm about to—" Halley's mouth dropped open as she gasped for breath.

Griffin held her steady as she rode his face through wave

after wave of orgasm, her body tightening and convulsing as her back arched and curled forward. He didn't stop until her last wave of spasms jolted through her body and she expelled a deep breath, her eyelids heavy with lust. He kissed her one last time before standing, a sheen over his mouth and his closely cut beard.

Halley beckoned him to her with two fingers, eyes low with want, her breath ragged. She wiped the moisture from his face with the palm of her hand, pulling him close. As they kissed, she could still taste herself on him, his thick lips warmed by her center. Halley ran her tongue over his mouth until he captured hers with his own. "I can't believe we're doing this right now."

"If the sky was falling, there's no place I'd rather be than right here with you," he murmured.

Halley wrapped her arms around Griff's neck, giving him a slow, searing kiss that made him groan against her lips. "Oh yeah? Show me," she breathed. "I want to see all the stars."

He grunted in response. Griffin's strong hands squeezed her ass before grasping the backs of her thighs, hoisting her up and setting her ass on the pedestal sink. His muscular arms bulged as he unzipped his pants, and Halley yelped from the cold ceramic. Grinning at her, Griff's pants dropped to the floor as Halley's eyes homed in on the bulge below the waistband of his boxer briefs.

She chuckled haughtily, shaking her head in reverence. "Old friend."

Griffin's lips curved into a sinister smile. "He missed you too." He pulled Halley closer so that her ass balanced on the lip of the sink before leaning her head back to expose her neck. His lips and tongue traveled a winding path down her throat, across her collarbone and between her breasts before taking detours across the tightened buds of her nipples. He carefully rolled them between his lips and teeth, as Halley writhed against him, arching her back to bring herself closer to his mouth.

As Griffin savored Halley, he rubbed himself against the slickness between her thighs, eliciting a soft moan from her as she leaned her head back against the wall. Griffin waited for her to open her eyes, mouthing the word *okay* as his firm tip undulated against her. His brown eyes imploring her for an answer.

She nodded, sucking in a breath through clenched teeth as his thick length slid inside her. "Fuck," she whispered, tilting her head forward to watch him ease in and out with delicious deliberateness. Halley wrapped her legs around Griff's waist, coaxing him deeper inside, his hands resting on either side of the sink. The skin between his brows pinched as he focused, his breath warm and uneven.

He dipped his head forward to kiss Halley, pulling one of her legs over his broad shoulder. His forehead pressed against hers, he tilted his hips slightly above hers and drove into her faster, jostling the sink—the back of Halley's head tapping against the wall. Griff cupped the back of her head in his hand, kissing her tenderly before returning her leg around his waist. "Hold on to me, babe."

As Halley wrapped her arms around his neck, Griffin lifted her, pinning her back against the wall where she stood before. She gasped as her skin pressed against the cool surface, Griffin pummeling into her, their bodies clapping together. Each thrust grazed her G-spot, building pressure that pushed Halley toward the edge of orgasm. Halley sank her teeth into his shoulder to keep from screaming. Gasping for breath, her eyes widened as she cried, "I'm about to—"

Griffin's mouth crashed against hers, muffling the high notes escaping from her throat. His thrusts slowed as he neared his own climax—Halley riding the waves of her own. He grunted, his brows furrowing and then rising as he came. Breathing hard, Griff buried his face in Halley's neck, his solid body pressed against hers in a full embrace, her legs tightening around him. His beard caught her hair as he pulled away to search her face, touching his fingertips to her jaw and tracing them to her bottom lip. "I missed you," he whispered, beads of sweat pooling at his temples.

"I missed you." She took in those deep brown eyes with their curling lashes, the orbs laser-focused on her in a way that felt different this time.

Griffin pressed his lips against hers gently, his eyes closing as he pulled back and touched his forehead to hers. After a long moment, he stepped back, cupping her ass and lifting her off him as she uncrossed her ankles and loosened her grip around his waist. Griffin grinned. "You've still got that vise grip, you know."

Halley smiled mischievously. "Thick thighs save lives, Griff."

As he pulled on his boxers, he threw back his head and laughed, eventually nodding in agreement. "I believe that to be true." He eyed her. "They sure saved mine." He closed the distance between them as Halley wrapped herself in a flannel blanket from the foot of the cot, pulling corners of it over her shoulders and crossing her arms.

Halley stretched her neck back to look at him, jutting her chin in his direction. "How do you figure?"

Griffin gripped her waist before extending his arms around her to rest his hands on top of her ass. He shrugged, smiling a little to himself. "You've never noticed how much energy I have after we have some quality time? You got that sauce, babe."

Halley giggled. "Shut up."

He stooped down to brush his lips against hers. "You do. It's addictive. I could be out with the fellas getting into all kinds of foolery, but I'd rather be right here." His hands spanned the curves of her hips. "I could never get enough of this."

She shook her head, pressing her lips together before craning her neck to stare into his deep brown eyes—his magnetic focus was so intent on her that her stomach contracted and heat flooded her entire body. Her cheeks burned crimson as her stomach gurgled loudly. "Uh, sorry about that," she laughed.

Griffin's wickedly sensual mouth curved into a grin. "Hungry?" He pointed to the shelving filled with supplies. "I'm sure there are some MREs with the supplies. They're not super appetizing, but they get the job done."

Halley shook her head. The last time she sampled a pouch filled with an emergency meal, she couldn't keep it down. "I've got some snacks in my bag, but I'm not hungry for food right now."

"No?" He looked at her curiously.

She met his gaze and shook her head suggestively as she pulled her bottom lip between her teeth. "No."

"Well, what is it that you have in mind, Oakes?" His voice dropped deeper, a sexy, teasing tone that could make her toes curl if she were off her feet.

She scanned the supply shelves and stepped out of Griffin's arms briefly, retrieving a couple of rolled sleeping bags from the bottom shelf. After unrolling and unzipping them, she spread them out on the floor, one on top of the other.

She grabbed the pillows and blankets from the cot, dropping them onto her makeshift bed before sitting down in the middle of it, the blanket still wrapped tightly around her body.

Griff raised an eyebrow, amused. "Are we camping? It's been a long time since I've made a fort."

She grabbed his hand and pulled him down next to her. "Call it what you want. You said the cot would be too noisy."

With his smoldering orbs locked onto hers, he sat on his knees, rubbing the top of her hand with his thumb. "But I thought you were hungry."

She nodded, her lips against his as she opened the cocoon of her blanket wide enough to pull him inside, his hands immediately finding their way to her warmth. "I am. For this."

A quick rap at the door woke Halley. "Yeah?" she yelled through the door as she sat up with a start, the cot squeaking from the shift of weight. At some point, they'd moved off the floor to save their backs from the polished concrete.

"Uh, sorry to interrupt, boss, but I think I've got everything all set. We should be coming online in five," Song called from the other side.

"I'll be right out," she responded, carefully swinging her legs over the edge of the cot in an effort to make as little noise as possible.

The cot still shrieked as she moved, and Griff smiled, though his eyes were still closed and his face was partly buried in the pillow. "That was a nice try."

Halley pulled on her pants. "Well, you're going to need to get up too. I can't leave a smiling naked man in the sleeping quarters—the others will have questions."

Griffin sat up slowly, surveying the room before locking his gaze onto Halley as she slipped on her bra. "What time is it? How long has it been?" The windowless room gave no indication of how much time had elapsed or how long they'd been asleep. He stepped out from under the blankets, naked and solid, his deep brown skin chiseled and glowing.

Halley's cell phone was almost out of battery, but it flickered to life when she touched the screen. "Oh god. It's been almost twelve hours, Griff."

He pulled on his boxers and closed the space between them, gripping her shoulders. "Listen, Halley, if anyone can handle the chief, it's you. Just get all of the information that you can from the guys, and prepare your report accordingly. He's going to be on edge, as he should be—he's been unable to give answers to people like the president for half a day."

"There's no reasonable explanation for this, Griff." She sighed. "My whole career is flashing before my eyes."

"You have the most reasonable explanation possible." He dipped his head to kiss her cheek, nudging her with his jaw when she looked up at him questioningly. "Song."

She expelled a deep breath and nodded. "Song." She pulled on her sweater and smoothed her hair into a fresh bun, a couple of curly tendrils loose near her temples. "Fuck yeah, let's do this."

Griffin finished dressing in record time, and Halley threw the door open, rolling her shoulders down her back and walking down the hall. She donned her best scowl as she returned to the control room. Griffin was a few steps behind her. "Song, where's my sitrep?" she barked.

"Boss, it took a full eleven hours for the system to reset. Once that was complete, Jake and I were able to rewire the servers both for the warning system and to get the local satellites reconnected. The ADGWS is fully installed, with a test date scheduled for one month from today. Once we flip this switch, the all-clear blasts should sound, and we can get out of here." Sweat poured from Song's brow, and Halley was sure he'd need a hydro pack on the flight home. He looked tired but more afraid than anything, his thin frame practically buzzing with nervous energy.

"What about cell phone service?"

"We still anticipate substantial network traffic, but if we can't get you connected to the chief from here, we should go back to town and call HQ from a landline," Jake suggested. Light brown stubble pushed through his light brown skin, but his alertness energized Halley.

Halley paced slowly, taking it all in. Song stepped into her path, an anxious look on his face. "Please, Halley, I know that I put the entire mission in jeopardy. I know you guys don't like when I get assigned to your details, because you think I'm going to screw it up somehow, and you're probably right. I do care about this job though, so if you can find it in your heart to forgive me and maybe to think of something so that I'm not fired for my mistakes, I promise I'll be better."

Halley's face softened. "I can't make any promises, Song. Hell, I don't even know if I've got a job after all of this."

"I may not be the best, and sometimes I make things difficult, but I respect you and I always learn from you. I will *never* make that mistake again."

Halley tsked. "You're damn right."

"What are you going to tell the chief?" Song's eyes pleaded with her.

She motioned for him to flip the switch, and three sharp blasts immediately sounded outside the station. A second later, her cell phone rang. "The truth."

"Oakes—" Chief Henry shouted into the phone.

Halley took a deep breath. "Sir, I can explain." The three

blasts complete, she walked outside for quiet, to be away from prying eyes and ears as she gathered her thoughts.

"You'd better have a good explanation, because I am about five seconds away from telling you to turn in your credentials. What is happening over there?" Chief Henry didn't have to yell to sound intimidating—his voice was a deep growl.

Halley turned toward the front wall of the station, covering her eyes with her hand. "Your nephew happened, sir."

For a moment, there was no sound, and then the speaker on the chief's phone was muffled as if a hand was covering the receiver. When he began speaking, his voice was hushed, as if he had relocated himself somewhere more quiet or with less of an audience. "What exactly happened, Oakes?"

Griffin stepped out the front door and looked to Halley for answers. She shrugged, holding up her hand to ask him to wait.

"Sir, permission to speak frankly?"

"Granted."

"Song is reckless, and he's always picked last for missions because there is a ninety-nine point nine percent chance that he's going to screw something up—"

"Now you listen here—"

"Sir, he usually fixes the issue, but he does have missteps. Most of these missteps could be prevented if he didn't take liberties like sneaking contraband into the station. He takes these liberties because he thinks people won't question him, being your nephew and all." Halley bit her lip, waiting for Chief Henry to process what she'd said.

"What kind of liberties are we talking about here, Oakes? And why haven't I been informed?"

"You know how it goes, sir. Remember when Major Heim's daughter was assigned to lead that project to decommission the satellite and almost ended up ramming it into the space station?"

He sucked in a breath. "How can I forget? That cost us millions."

Halley nodded. "She had no business being in that position without passing all of the required protocols, but she was advanced because of who she was. No one was going to ride her to complete her protocols because she acted like she didn't have to. Song does the same thing. It's not malicious, but he is well aware that he's breaking protocol. He practically dares us to report him, and honestly, I should have. So this is my responsibility. I am to blame for what happened here."

"Uh-huh. What did he sneak into the station, Oakes?" Chief Henry articulated through gritted teeth.

"I believe it was a six-pack of peanut butter stout, sir. From a local brewery in Boulder. A bottle was spilled in the control room, which shorted the servers and set off the warning system prematurely while also disconnecting several of our local satellites."

"Christ almighty..." The Chief swore under his breath.

"Listen, sir. No one knows but you and the team. At the end of the day, we had a successful emergency trial, with no injuries from what I understand from initial news reports. We had a real-time look at what one of these warnings can look or feel like, and there's no way that we would have had people take a scheduled test as seriously as they'd take the threat of the real thing. As far as anyone else is concerned, this was a secret test that allowed private citizens, businesses, first responders and government officials to get a sense of what a true, unscheduled warning will look and feel like.

"We acknowledge that it was a surprise warning test in advance of the scheduled test we were going to do next week, so we apologize and offer that it was meant to help people and businesses think through their sheltering plans from an informed perspective. We've rescheduled next week's test to next month, to give folks time to make more realistic plans and prepare their bunkers." Halley gave a wide-eyed shrug to Griff as she bit her lip and waited. Griff kept his eyes on Halley.

"Huh."

He might actually buy it. "They don't have to know that we didn't plan it, sir," she pressed, crossing her fingers as she made eye contact with Griff.

"You're going to need to complete reports alluding to this plan. You'll also need an explanation as to why you believed twelve hours was the right amount of time for a test." His breathing was measured, as if he'd calmed.

"I'll have drafts for you first thing on Monday, sir."

"Good. And, Oakes?" His voice sounded like he held the receiver closer to his mouth to make himself more clear.

"Sir?"

"Don't cut Song any slack. You ride him like you would any tech specialist who wasn't carrying their weight. The next time he's on your team—and there will be a next time—you better snatch the goodies out of his hand or you *will* be held responsible for any mishaps as the mission leader. Do I make myself understood?"

"Yes, sir. Thank you, sir." She swallowed hard, praying that Song wasn't assigned to another of her teams anytime soon.

The line disconnected, and Halley squealed as Griff whooped and swept her up into his arms, swinging her around in a circle. Willy and Jake joined them outside, Willy looking pitiful with his arms behind his back.

Griff released Halley, and she turned to Song and Jake, a relieved smile on her face. "The truth saved us this time, gentlemen. We've all got jobs to return to on Monday. We've got flights home from base this evening, so let's tie up any loose ends we have here so we can get back on the road. Maybe we can grab something to eat."

Willy looked close to collapsing. Jake clapped him on the back before reaching out to shake Halley's hand.

She held Jake's hand in both of hers before reaching over and squeezing Song's arm. Song bowed his head. "Thank you, boss."

"Don't thank me yet. Your uncle basically gave me a green light to ride you like Seabiscuit anytime you're assigned to my detail."

Song's eyes widened. "You'd let me back onto your detail again?"

"Count on it."

"While you were resting—" Song coughed, averting his eyes from Griffin "—Jake and I had a couple of beers while we waited for the system to reset. We saved the last one for you—it's nice and cold." Song brandished a bottle from behind his back.

"It's actually really good, boss," Jake added, the corner of his mouth angled upward slightly.

Griff took the bottle from Song to twist off the cap for Halley. She took a long swig, the smooth liquid cool against her dry throat. At the very finish, the taste of peanut butter crossed her tongue. She offered the bottle to Griff to sample. "That's not bad at all."

Griff nodded in agreement. "I'm not a stout guy, but that's damn good right now."

"Alright, well let's tie up everything here nice and neat, then we can go to the brewery for lunch. On the way, let's strategize the report that we need to have complete for the chief by Monday. I'm going to need each of you to provide me with details for this *planned test*." Her eyes shined as she emphasized those last two words.

"Really, you're down to go to the brewery, boss?" Song grinned.

"You and Jake already had a couple. Griff and I need to catch up," she smiled coyly.

Griffin wrapped an arm around her waist, pulling her close. "Yes, we do."

KEEP CALM AND CURRY ON

FARAH HERON

1

Maya Jafari had lived her entire life as if the sky would fall on her head at any given moment, so it was a huge surprise to her, and to everyone who knew her, that when the sky actually fell a few years ago (as opposed to figuratively falling), she drained her savings and started a small business. Seeing fiery streaks of lord only knows what fill the sky that day solidified to Maya that if she didn't open Masala Girls now, the South Asian sauce and spice empire she and her father had dreamed of launching for years would never be a reality. She'd be selling mortgages in a call center, and Dad would be driving that Atlanta Airport taxi for the rest of their lives.

But opening a booth in the Verona County Flea Market in the Blue Ridge Mountains didn't mean Maya had left her *glass half empty* tendencies behind her.

She leaned against the counter one Friday, scanning the

sales for the day. "We've sold thirty percent fewer sandwiches than we did by this time last Saturday."

Maya's only employee, Radha, who wasn't quite as pessimistic as Maya, shrugged. "We'll sell more at lunch. We always do."

Maya frowned. In the last few weeks, her paneer tikka sandwich had become the booth's main money-maker, thanks to a well-timed mention in the *Verona Market Bulletin* email newsletter, but it seemed the buzz was already wearing off.

"Masala Girls," a man at the counter said. Maya stood straight and smoothed her turmeric-yellow apron.

"*Masala* means spice in many South Asian languages," she said. "The name is a take on the Spice Girls."

"I know what *Masala* means," he snapped. He looked like he'd just walked off the set of *Sons of Anarchy*. "I'm surprised *you* know who the Spice Girls are," he said.

Why, because she was brown? Or because her youthful Pakistani genes made her look closer to nineteen than twenty-nine? "All our spices are sourced from ethical growers from around the world and roasted and ground in small batches. Are you looking for something specific?"

He picked up one of the sealed bags of spice mixes—this one Mughlai biryani. "I'm looking for the tikka sauce. The one from the sandwich. Best damn sandwich I've ever had."

Maya beamed, handing him a bottle of her famous (or hopefully soon-to be-famous) Masala Girls Tikka sauce, the one she used to marinate paneer every Friday for the weekend's sandwiches. The man studied the bottle's simple yellow label. Maya was used to this—she may have chosen this flea market because it was more likely to sell Stacey Abrams T-shirts than Trump paraphernalia, but this was *still* rural

Georgia, and Maya wasn't selling grits in flour sacs or south-
ern barbecue rubs. Even here, people were used to their food
colonized.

A white woman appeared, shaking her head. "No, Marcus.
That ain't it. The sandwich came from a food truck. What
was it called… Curry Junction. They sell their sauce there."

With barely a glance back at Masala Girls, the couple left
the booth, no doubt heading toward Food Truck Alley at
the end of the market, where there was apparently a truck
crushing Maya's dreams like elchi in a mortar and pestle. But
somehow, she doubted she'd get a warming cup of masala
chai after the destruction.

After selling barely any tikka sandwiches at lunch, Maya
asked some neighboring vendors about this Curry Junction
truck. She learned the following: they were based out of
Chattanooga and apparently had a real tandoor oven in the
truck, which sounded like a massive fire hazard to Maya.
Also? Everyone who had tasted their chicken tikka on naan
sandwich had proclaimed it to be the best in the county.
Considering Maya's was the only other tikka sandwich in
Verona County, this was troubling. Maya told Radha to
watch the booth—it was time to see Curry Junction with
her own eyes.

The Verona County Flea Market was made up of three
halls. Masala Girls was in Hall A, which mostly sold hand-
made things like artisan jewelry, prepared foods and wood
signs painted with inspirational quotes. In the middle was
Hall B, also called the Antique Hall. It was the biggest, and
was crammed full of antique furniture, creepy art, old toys
and dishes. Maya had never understood the appeal of buying
things that once belonged to people who were now dead, but

the antiques were the main draw of this flea market. Hall C was at the end of the antique hall, and was like Hall A, except it had Food Truck Alley—a row of seven food trucks. There was a taco truck, a smash burger truck, a barbecue truck, a bao and dumpling truck, a macaroni and cheese truck and two fried chicken trucks. Only now Maya could see that one of the chicken trucks had been replaced by Curry Junction, her new nemesis.

And of course, the truck was painted the same turmeric yellow as her Masala Girls apron. The name Curry Junction was splashed on the side in black Sanskrit-inspired font, along with a logo of a cartoon turban-wearing man holding out a platter of food. Maya frowned as she stepped closer. She was normally a *rising tides lifts all boats* kind of person, and she *wanted* to be delighted there was another South Asian food business in the market. But this truck was literally stealing her and her father's dream right out from under them.

On the counter at the window of the truck, she could see a neat line of sauce bottles. Bottles in the same shape and size as her Masala Girls sauces, but these said Curry Junction Tikka Sauce.

Furious, Maya stepped up to the window, intending to tell whoever was in that truck to cease and desist selling their copycat sauce at once.

"Can I help you?" the man at the counter said. And Maya forgot why she was even there…because *his face.*

Smooth brown skin. Wide smile. Large, expressive brown eyes. Square jaw.

It was delicate and strong at the same time. And the worst part, it was *familiar.*

Tarek Mizra. She hadn't seen him in years, but she'd never forget that face.

Without saying a word, Maya turned on her heels and rushed away, hoping he hadn't recognized her.

"Maya? Maya Jafari? Is that you?"

Ugh.

Maya speed walked past the other food trucks, through the antique hall and straight back to Masala Girls.

Radha was behind the counter. "Did that creepy clown doll in the antique hall look at you weird?"

Maya's eyes widened. "There is a creepy clown doll in the antique hall?" She shuddered. Why did she open her spice store *here*? There were hazards everywhere she turned. Possibly racist and ageist Southerners. Creepy clowns. First crushes looking as tasty as they had back when they were sixteen.

"What happened? Don't tell me the truck is an offshoot of one of those big restaurant conglomerates? Because you cannot compete with the Walmarts and Targets of food service."

"No. Worse."

"McTikkas?"

Maya exhaled, imagining the horror of desi food by American McDonald's. "Radha, I don't know who the fuck owns that food truck, but I *do* know the person working it."

"Who?"

Maya still couldn't believe it. She spat out the name, surprised that her mouth was still capable of making the sounds. "Tarek Mizra."

"Who's that?" Radha asked.

Maya blinked at her friend. Maya and Radha had been friends since college, and Radha had joined the family for Dad's chicken charga every Christmas. Radha was fully aware of the impact the Mizra family had on the Jafari family, even if she didn't know details.

"You know how my dad almost opened a restaurant years ago with a friend?"

"Yeah—he talks about it all the time. His friend betrayed him and deserted the partnership. OMG, that's who was in the truck? Your dad's old best friend?"

Maya shook her head. "No. His son, Tarek."

Radha leaned down and whispered in Maya's ears, "If the guy's a hot brown dude in a yellow chef's jacket, he's right behind you."

"So, you *did* recognize me," a voice behind her said.

Maya closed her eyes. He'd followed her here. Because of course he had. Because Maya was not just gifted in her ability to imagine worst-case scenarios, but apparently also in attracting them.

Maya took a deep, cleansing breath and remembered her therapist's advice of finding three positives in any situation. One—at least it was Tarek, and not his father, Arif Uncle, here. Two—Tarek now knew that the Jafari family *did* open their spice business, despite the Mizras' sabotage, and even if it wasn't anything impressive yet, it existed. True, the best revenge was living well, but living *adequately* after sabotage had to mean something, too, right? And three—Tarek was just as sexy as he'd been back when they were teenagers. Maybe more. Which might not be a positive for Maya specifically, but she was fully in favor of increasing brown joy in the world, and a face like that would bring a lot of joy to a lot of people.

"Excuse me," a female voice behind Maya said. "Is biryani masala the same thing as garam masala?"

Radha gave Maya a little pat on the arm before squeezing

out from behind the counter to help the customer. Maya had no choice but to turn and face Tarek.

And there he was. Tarek was a couple years older than Maya. Their fathers had been best friends when they first moved to Atlanta from Pakistan in the eighties, so she didn't remember a time when she hadn't known him. She still remembered the moment when she'd realized the weird hollow flutters in her stomach whenever Tarek said her name meant Maya had her very first crush. That crush only got stronger each year until the Mizra family moved out of Atlanta when Maya was fifteen and Tarek was seventeen.

"I can't believe it's you!" he beamed. "Little Maya! How long has it been? And look," he pulled on his yellow chef's jacket. "We match!"

It looked like the fabric for his jacket came from the same bolt as her apron. And also, why was he being so cheerful? Did he forget that their families were in a decade-long feud?

But that was another thing she remembered about Tarek. He was very…good-natured. Easygoing. The opposite of Maya in every way. As a teen, Maya had no interest in dark and brooding boys, since she was broody enough all by herself, thank you very much. Bright and sunny boys were more her catnip, although that preference could be because Tarek's sunniness combined with that jawline had imprinted in her brain in her formative years.

But unlike Tarek, Maya wasn't going to pretend everything was sunshine and roses in their past. Or, hell, in their present, either. Because the cherry on top of the *his father betraying her father* sundae was that Tarek was selling the damn sandwich that had unseated Masala Girls' tikka throne, and effectively taken money straight out of her till.

"Tarek Mizra," Maya hissed.

He smiled, apparently not picking up on the *I put a hex on you* tone in her voice. Glancing around the booth, he whistled with appreciation. "Masala Girls... This yours? I kept hearing about this awesome spice shop. Who'd have thought we'd have businesses in the same flea market!"

So, *he* owned that truck? "Curry Junction is yours?"

He rocked back on his heels. "Yup. You ran off before I could show you around."

Maya had no intention of faking any niceties. "You have to stop selling your tikka sauce."

"What? Why?" He looked confused.

"Because you are a *restaurant*. You sell prepared food for immediate consumption." She waved her hand to show the spices and sauces on the Masala Girls shelves. "I sell spices and sauces. You are *stealing* my customers, and I was here first."

Tarek finally lost his cheerfulness but unfortunately, his incredulous snort was as attractive as his grin. "Excuse me? I had no idea the flea market could only support one Pakistani food business. Also, aren't you selling a paneer sandwich? I've had at least three customers rave about it in the last hour alone."

People were raving about her sandwich? She filed that tidbit to celebrate later. "I need to sell my sandwich so people know how good my sauces and spices are!"

"And I need to sell my sauce because everyone wants it after trying my sandwich!"

Maya's lips pursed as she stared at him. "Why am I not surprised that a Mizra is a self-serving ass?"

He shook his head, disappointed. "Maya Jafari, you may look the same, but you're not the sweet girl I remember. I would say it was nice to see you again, but it wasn't." He turned and left her booth.

Maya hoped that creepy clown doll attacked that stupid-hot face on his way back to his truck.

2

The Verona County Flea Market was in the Blue Ridge Mountains in Georgia, about a two-and-a-half-hour drive from Atlanta. And since it opened at 7:30 a.m. on Saturdays, it didn't make sense for Maya to drive all the way to Atlanta Fridays after closing, only to come back so early the next morning. The market was near a quaint little village with an antique train as well as hotels and motels, but Maya didn't want to eat into her profits by renting a room. The van was comfortable enough to sleep in.

After closing at five, Maya tidied up and said goodbye to Radha, who was heading back to Atlanta for a date with her girlfriend before returning at ten the next day. Maya then headed to her van. She settled in the passenger seat to read before eating the dinner her mother had packed. After about twenty minutes, Maya's e-reader went blank. Damn, she'd forgotten to charge it in the booth earlier. She'd been looking forward to reading the new paranormal romance by her favorite author all week. The old van's battery wasn't great, so she never used it to charge electronics. She grabbed her e-reader and her bag, locked the van and headed back inside. It was six fifteen, so security should still be in the market.

She didn't see the security guard, Angela, as she headed straight to Masala Girls and plugged in the e-reader. The flea market seemed deserted, but Maya knew Angela did a final sweep before locking up around seven. Maya figured she'd charge until security kicked her out. She sat behind her counter and read.

But as usual when engrossed in a book, Maya lost track of the time. She'd just read a supersteamy sex scene when a loud piercing wail echoed through the building. "Fuck!" Maya stood and grabbed her phone.

It sounded like the disaster warning system...but that was supposed to be tested *next* week. Living in a world constantly primed for disaster was a challenge for a pessimist, and Maya coped with therapy, and by keeping on top of information, so the date of the test was burned in her brain. It was supposed to happen next week. The alarm had been created to warn people that something was hurling at the planet again to kill them all. Or kill enough of them to make earth into actual hell for those who survived. Maya was one hundred percent in favor of the government creating this alarm, but she didn't like that it was blaring now, outside of the scheduled test.

This was a real, actual disaster. Heart beating heavily in her ears, Maya checked Twitter to confirm.

But Twitter wouldn't load. Neither would Instagram, Facebook or even TikTok. Maya's phone *was* working, but she couldn't connect to any Wi-Fi or cellular service.

OMG. This was bad. Worst-case scenarios flashed through

her mind. Everyone was going to die, including her, her parents, her sister and her cat. Heart racing, Maya had to sit back down because her knees didn't seem capable of holding her up.

It *could* be a false alarm. The market management had handed out letters about what to do if the alarm sounded a few months ago. Maya, of course, remembered the instructions, but she still grabbed them from the paperwork under the counter to confirm.

Apparently, anytime the alarm went off outside of the scheduled tests, everyone should assume that it was an *active disaster*. And in an active disaster, everyone was required to take cover immediately. Underground was best, but failing that, far from windows and doors. Management suggested that the antique hall was the safest place to be since it was in the center of the building. Three loud blasts from the alarm system would indicate when it was safe.

Fuck. Fuck. Fuck. Maya could not...*would* not be stuck alone in a giant flea market for the end of the world. No, thank you.

Wait—not alone. The security guard was out there somewhere. Maybe she had a working phone. Maya grabbed her bag and useless phone and headed out of her booth to find Angela.

The antique hall was dim—since the overhead lights were now off. It was past seven, and the sun was already setting in the late-September sky. Turning on her phone flashlight, she searched the aisles for anyone. Thankfully, so far no creepy clowns. This was fine. As she passed a booth that sold only sixties TV show paraphernalia, Maya heard a noise behind her. She turned but didn't see anyone. She was about to start walking again when she saw some movement out of the corner of her eye. It was from a booth that sold old theater props. There was someone in there. Security hopefully? Or maybe the owner of the booth? Maya stepped inside. There was a dress form wearing a very ornate Victorian or Edwardian dress…and it was *moving*.

Great. A haunted, headless dress form come to life during the end of the world. Even Maya's most disaster-imagining self couldn't have dreamed this one up.

There is no such thing as ghosts, she repeated to herself. *Nothing can hurt me more than my own imagination.*

That last mantra was one her therapist came up with, but Maya was skeptical it did anything. Her own imagination was vicious. She leaned down and gingerly lifted the skirts and petticoats of the black velvet dress.

"Meow."

A cat. There was a cat in there. A big fluffy orange and white cat.

"Hello, beautiful," Maya said, putting her hand out. The cat cowered in the skirts, clearly frightened. "I'm not going to hurt you. Aren't you a pretty baby?"

The cat leaned forward to smell her hand. Maya had never seen a cat at the flea market before—whose was this? It was wearing a collar, so clearly not a stray. It nuzzled Maya's hand. She smiled as she scratched the top of its soft head. Maya was a total cat lady. Alone in a flea market for the end of the world was a nightmare, alone in a flea market for the end of the world with a fluffy cat was significantly less harrowing.

"Whoever you are, *thank God* you found Percy," a voice behind Maya said. A male voice. A male voice that startled Maya so hard she fell from her crouching position flat onto her butt, taking the dress form with her, and understandably causing the cat to bolt out into the darkness.

"Oh crap, I'm sorry, are you okay?" the voice said again, reaching for the dress form.

It was dark, but Maya closed her eyes and took a cleansing breath. She knew that voice. Apparently, she would be spending the end of the world with a fluffy cat named Percy, and Tarek Mizra.

3

"Fuck!" Maya grabbed her phone and faced Tarek.

"Maya? What are you doing here?" He had a flashlight—a real one, not his phone. His voice sounded concerned.

Maya stood, brushing off her black leggings. "I was looking for security."

Tarek looked amused. Not at all panicked about the whole *space debris falling from the sky* situation. And he looked hot. Him looking both calm and hot was incredibly irritating. He wasn't wearing that yellow chef's jacket anymore, but a gray long-sleeved Henley and jeans. "I was looking for Percy," he said. "Did you see where he went?" He pointed his flashlight down the aisle.

Maya looked, but did not see a cat. "Why is there even a cat here? Where's security?"

"I've been in the antique hall looking for Percy instead of

at my truck, so Angela probably left without realizing I was still here. Or you. She did this to someone last week, too."

"But the alarm! Didn't you hear it? Where did Angela go? She's going to get *fired* for leaving during the alarm…and you…why are you even here? What the hell is going on?"

He laughed, leaning on the back of an ornate velvet chaise. Maya couldn't believe it. The world was ending, and this man was *lounging*. "I told you, I don't know where Angela is. And yes, I think she *should* get fired, but the door locks from the inside, so she's not normally locking anyone in when she does a half-ass final sweep."

None of this explained why he wasn't panicked about the world ending.

"You *did* hear the alarm, didn't you?" Maybe she'd imagined it?

He shrugged. "Yeah, it's why Percy's freaking out. Don't sweat it. The three blasts should happen any minute now."

"So, we're *alone*? Is your phone working?"

That dumb grin never left his face when he shook his head. "Nope. Service cut out when the alarm went off."

"Fuck."

He raised a curious eyebrow at her. "You swear a lot more than you used to."

Nah, only difference was now she said it aloud instead of under her breath. "Sorry I'm offending your delicate sensibilities."

He snort-laughed. "No, I like the new swearing, sarcastic Maya."

She scowled. "Whose cat is that, anyway?"

"How do you not know Percy? He lives in the antique hall. Vendors take turns feeding him."

Maya had spent so little time in this hall because of the gloomy vibe, but if she'd known there was a cat here, she might have been willing to deal with dead people's dusty stuff.

"Hey, how's your family? I still can't get over seeing you again. Still living in Atlanta?"

Didn't he know that their fathers weren't speaking to each other? "Is this an interrogation?"

He snorted. "I mean, we're stuck here together. We may as well catch up."

Maya closed her eyes. *Focus on the positives.* One—there was a cat somewhere here. If she could find the cat this whole experience would be bearable. Two—she was alive. Three—she was not alone.

This last point, as much as she hated to admit it, was a positive. At least she wasn't alone. She'd prefer pretty much anyone else was here instead of Tarek, but Maya's own thoughts had never comforted her in her life, so she wouldn't enjoy being alone with them for the end of the world.

She sighed. "Look, I don't want to be here. I am assuming you don't, either. We have no idea what's going on… The world outside could be…" Her breath hitched. She paused to collect herself. "There could be a serious disaster out there, so excuse me if I'm not in the best mood on what could be our last night on earth."

He blinked, looking at her. She remembered those lashes well. Even as a child they were thick, dark and full. Luscious. "Isn't that an even *better* reason to get reacquainted with each other?"

Her eyes narrowed.

He chuckled, rubbing his chin. "Okay, fine. Let's *not* get

reacquainted. If it's easier, we can pretend we're strangers and that you don't hate me because of tikka sauce."

She didn't say anything. She had a lot more to hate him for than just the sauce. But they were stuck together. No matter how irritating he was, Tarek was the only one here.

He pushed himself off the lounge chair he was leaning on. "C'mon. I want to show you something." He started walking down the aisle of the antique market, and she had no choice but to follow him in case another mannequin started walking, or a clown smiled at her.

He took her deeper into the antique hall. It was a part of the market Maya had never been in before, where no natural light could reach them, and sounds were swallowed by the old furniture and textiles. As they walked, a familiar scent hit Maya's nose. She turned on her phone light and pointed it to the right—and yep—it was a booth filled to the brim with old paperback books. *Lovely.* She made a mental note to come back here and explore at some point in the future.

If there was a future.

Swallowing the lump in her throat, she hurried to catch up with Tarek. He finally stopped between a glassware booth and furniture booth.

"Here," he said. "Listen to that."

She frowned. "What am I listening to?"

He turned off the flashlight. "Just listen."

It was dark. All Maya could hear was the pounding of her heart in her ears. She squeezed her eyes shut.

She hoped her family was together. Dad wasn't working tonight, but her sister, Aisha, might be out with friends. Were they worrying about Maya? Maybe they thought she was alone in her car—with nothing but the thin metal roof to protect her.

Maybe they thought she was already dead. Maya choked back a sob.

"Are you okay, Maya?" Tarek's voice was closer. Close enough that she could feel his body warmth. She wanted to reach out and touch him…to feel another human here with her.

"I don't hear anything," she whispered.

"Exactly." He flicked his flashlight back on. "Nothing at all." The smile on his face was enormous…and almost incandescent. He'd always had that huge smile. She'd always been mesmerized by it. "The roof on this part of the market is metal. If something was hitting it, we'd hear it here. I think everything is fine out there. We'll hear the three tones soon, I'm sure of it."

They were in the middle of the mountains, though. There could be something falling from the sky in Atlanta, or Chattanooga, or any other highly populated area. It would be worse for humanity than if something was falling here.

"We have warmth, food and shelter," Tarek continued. "We can ride this out together. You, me and Percy."

At that, Maya felt a solid weight rub up against her leg. Percy was back, and he seemed to love Maya's leg a lot right now. She smiled. This cat was her first positive.

"Speak of the devil," Tarek said. He looked at Maya. "You used to have a cat. Do you know how to feed one? I've been assigned the task, but I've never done it before."

Maya snorted. Cats, books and spices were her three favorite things in the world. "Of course, I do."

Percy's food and his litter box were in a security office at one end of the antique hall, and he was thrilled with the trout pâté Maya selected for him. Her cat, Tatcha, liked fish best, too.

She was never going to see her sweet Tatcha again. Maya squeezed her eyes shut.

Positives: Cat. Alive. Not Alone.

"Hey," Tarek asked. "You okay, Maya?"

"No." She checked her phone… Maybe if it was working, she could get Mom to send a picture of Tatcha.

"Still no service?" Tarek asked.

She shook her head, putting her phone back in her bag. "It's probably a mixed blessing. I'd be hearing from my parents every ten minutes. You know what it's like."

Tarek shook his head. "You live with them?"

Maya nodded. "Just moved home a few months ago after…a breakup."

"Ah," he said. "I can't imagine living with my parents now. We don't really have much of a relationship anymore."

"You're not close?" Maya asked. The Mizras had been so much like her own family. Tight. He shook his head. Tarek's expression was closed off. He didn't want to talk about his family.

But if Tarek was estranged from his parents, then that made being stuck with him so much easier. She couldn't exactly hate him for his father's actions if he wasn't even speaking to his father anymore. Really, the only thing to dislike the man for was his refusal to stop selling his tikka sauce.

And…they were literally in the middle of a disaster right now, and Maya needed to get through however long it took until the three tones went off. What if she just…ignored the fact that they were rivals? Didn't think or talk about the sandwich or sauce?

The cat rubbed up against her leg. "Percy's done," she said. And at that moment, maybe because she was used to having her own dinner after feeding her cat, Tatcha, Maya's stomach growled loudly.

Tarek chuckled. "Hungry?"

Maya nodded. "My mom packed me a dinner, but it's in my van."

He grinned. "Any chance I could finally try the famous Masala Girls sandwich?"

Maya frowned, not loving the idea of eating the sandwich that was stressing her out so much.

"I have an idea," Tarek said. "Let's feed each other. I'll make you dinner from my truck, and you make me your sandwich."

Maya was hungry, and she was curious about Curry Junction, so she agreed. Maybe if he tasted how great her sandwich was, it would encourage him to stop selling his.

"This is such an adorable little shop," he said, while Maya grilled the marinated paneer on her little countertop grill. "I love your logo."

"Thanks. My sister made it. She's a graphic designer."

He nodded, impressed. "So, she's one of the Masala Girls?"

Maya shook her head. "No, right now it's just me. My friend Radha helps."

Tarek frowned. "Why is your name plural then?"

Maya narrowed her eyes. "Um, it's a play on the Spice Girls?"

"Do people call you Baby Spice?"

"Yes. Creepy old men."

He laughed. While she split a Portuguese roll, he explored the booth, investigating bags of spices and gleaming stainless masala dabbas.

"These are your dad's blends, right?"

"Most of them. Some are mine."

Tarek smiled. "I remember back when our dads used to cook together, your father used to roast and grind spices fresh."

Maya nodded. She remembered, too. Dad and Tarek's dad used to make the same dish over and over again until they got it just right. It was weird that the same memory lived in Tarek's brain. Maybe it was impossible to ignore their connection.

The paneer was perfectly blackened by now, so she slathered the bun with green chutney and her creamy raita sauce, then put two pieces of the cheese on it. She finished with a few pickled onions, fresh cilantro and a little extra tikka sauce. She put the sandwich on a plate in front of Tarek. "Voila. The *best* tikka sandwich in Verona County."

He laughed. "This looks delicious."

"Try it," she said, even though she was weirdly nervous about him tasting it.

He took a bite, licking the chutney when it slid onto his fingers. He had no expression as he chewed, and Maya honestly had no idea what he was thinking.

"So?" she asked.

"You really *are* the Masala Girl. Don't share that crown with anyone. This is amazing, Maya."

"Really?"

"Totally. Your marinade...fresh spices and actual heat! Great choice of bun. And your toppings are perfect." He looked at her. "I'm impressed. Actually, I'm a little nervous about cooking for you now."

Maya grinned. "As you should be. Let's see if you can top that, curry boy."

He cringed, then laughed at the moniker. After he finished the sandwich, making moans of happy pleasure as he ate, he took Maya to Curry Junction.

4

Maya's first thought after climbing into Curry Junction was that it was incredibly hard to breathe while locked in a tiny space with her first crush. It was *tight* in here. Really tight. In such a small space it was hard not to think about how Tarek Mizra still had an amazing laugh. About how his jeans were so perfectly worn and fit him so well. About how Henley shirts were without a doubt the sexiest shirts in existence. And then he slipped on that yellow chef's jacket, which made his warm brown skin glow in the dim light and gave the Henley serious competition. Tarek wasn't the most classically handsome Mizra—his brother, Salman, was Bollywood-level stunning. But Tarek had always had a certain something more to Maya. A sense of humor. A sparkle in his eyes. He was full of life.

Finding him attractive again wasn't making this situation easier. "So…what are you feeding me?" she asked.

He leaned on the prep counter as he fastened the buttons on his jacket. "Sorry, Maya, I can't make you my famous tikka—the tandoor takes too long to heat up. I could do almost anything else on the menu, though."

She picked up a menu from the windowsill. She'd figured a trendy hipster Pakistani food truck would be all fusion food, but that was not what was on the menu. This was real Pakistani food. There was chicken boti, biryani, kebobs, plus a whole section called the Curry Corner that listed many of Maya's favorites like chicken karahi, chana masala and even lamb korma. Maya frowned at the menu.

"You don't approve?" he asked.

"No. It's a good menu. I just thought your stuff would be all fusion-y or something. I'm surprised it's called *Curry* Junction?"

He smiled. "Why, Maya, because the menu clearly leans more into food cooked in a tandoor rather than *curries*?" He made air quotes around the word *curries*. "Or because the word *curry* is a loaded word based on a colonial misinterpretation, which really has no actual meaning in our culture, and which has diluted the vast diversity of the food of our family's homeland into a shallow one-dimensional item on a pub menu?" His eyes were twinkling with mischief.

Maya blinked...then laughed. "Yeah. That. The second one."

He shrugged. "I would argue that riffing off the name of a mostly white British pop group is also caving to colonial pressures."

"Touché," she said smiling.

He shrugged. "I used a branding company to help with the concept, and this name performed well in market testing."

"Is that what this business is for you? Market research and appealing to the masses?"

He shook his head. "Hell no. This business is a way for me to share food I love. And make some money doing it. To make money, I need to appeal to the people in my city. This name does that." He grinned. "But you know what I think we need tonight? Comfort food. Not restaurant food. Why don't you leave it to me? Go out there and sit—I'll be about five minutes with dinner."

Maya tensed. Sit alone *out there*? What if she started to actually *hear* the asteroids outside? Plus, they weren't far from a window here...and without the food truck as an extra layer of protection, something hurling through the window could...

"Or we could eat here in the truck," Tarek suggested.

How had he known what she was thinking? "You think I'm ridiculous, don't you? I mean we haven't died yet so..."

He shook his head. "I don't think you're ridiculous. If you're not comfortable, you're not comfortable. We are literally in lockdown because of an unknown issue out there—I think you're entitled to be a bit nervous, Maya." He handed her a bottle of water. "Here. Have a seat there, and I'll have something for you in about five minutes."

He said her name a lot. Maya couldn't think why he wasn't as nervous as she was. She sat at one of the tall stools that had been tucked under the window on the side of the truck and watched him cook.

He was mesmerizing. She honestly didn't remember if she'd ever seen Tarek cooking back when they were young. His father had been measured and methodical when he cooked. Tarek was a bit...chaotic. He flipped parathas on the tawa with his bare hands. And he chopped cilantro haphazardly on his board instead of gathering it to a neat pile.

The food smelled good, though. It smelled like her mother's cooking—like home. That should have made her sad since she didn't know if she'd ever see home again, but it didn't. The aroma loosened something in her.

Before long Tarek presented her with a plate containing flaky paratha, a mound of dry urad dal, and another of aloo gobi. Bright cilantro leaves and slivered ginger were scattered on top. It smelled heavenly.

"Dig in," he said, putting a plate with a little less food next to her plate. "The parathas were frozen, hope you don't mind. And the dal's not something I serve—just some I made for my lunches this weekend."

She ripped off a piece of paratha and scooped up some of the dal. The flavor burst in her mouth immediately—fresh spices, tomato, ginger, garlic and just the right amount of chili. Plus a hint of lemon acidity that was unexpected and delicious. "This is amazing."

"You seem surprised I can cook. I run a restaurant, remember?"

She didn't really know why, but she *was* surprised he'd made *this*. This was a home-style dish. Maya wasn't sure she'd ever had a dry dal in a restaurant—and definitely not in a trendy millennial food truck. She'd assumed Tarek was like his father, and Maya's own. The men cooked the fancy party food, or barbecue, but the homey food was left to the women.

"Why don't you serve dal on the truck?"

"No one would buy it." He slid another stool out from under the window and sat next to her. "Remember, I'm all about actually making money."

Maya took another mouthful of food. She didn't want conversation to stray closer to their families or their competing sandwiches, and she definitely didn't want to talk about the end of the world, so she asked him his favorite movie genre. Seemed a safe question. But his answer surprised her again.

She laughed. "You're kidding. Your favorite movies are *romances*?"

He shook his head. *"Rom-coms."*

"The rom part is right there, buddy. Adding a bit of comedy doesn't make it less of a romance."

He smiled. "Okay, fine. I love romances."

Maya shook her head, laughing. "You're a unicorn, you know that? You used to like adventure movies." She remembered watching *The Mummy* several times together with their siblings as kids. Although now that she thought about it, *The Mummy* was totally a romance.

"I like those, too, but a good rom-com is so stress relieving. Why am I a unicorn?"

"Because most men in my life don't like rom-coms. My ex-boyfriend used to take them out of my Netflix queue because he said they were rotting my brain. And he hated me reading romance novels."

Tarek cringed. "Ugh. Bad boyfriend."

Maya snorted. "*Horrible* boyfriend. I'm embarrassed it took me so long to figure that out." She took a long sip of her ice water. She was completely over Ben, but still incredibly angry at herself for staying so long.

Tarek was looking at her curiously when she put her water down. "Seems like a rough breakup," he said.

She huffed a laugh. "Yeah. I had to upend everything and move back home. I love not living with an asshole anymore, though." She took another bite of her food. She didn't want to talk about Ben right now.

But something about what she'd said caught Tarek's interest. "You lived with the guy? Your parents didn't care?"

Maya raised her eyebrow. "I'm twenty-nine—I don't need my parents' permission anymore." Maya's parents weren't the stereotyped strict Pakistani parents. So long as Maya was happy, they didn't question her lifestyle. They were fine when she'd moved out, but they were happier when she moved back. But that was because Ben was bad for her, not because she'd been living in sin. They accepted Maya as she was.

"Lucky."

Clearly, this was a sore spot for him. Maya was curious, but she also didn't want to pry. They weren't supposed to talk about family. After a few moments of awkward silence in the small truck, Maya asked another question so she wasn't obsessing about every sound she heard. "You ever read romance *books*?"

He shook his head.

"You should."

"Why?"

"Because romance novels are amazing. That is if you're a reader."

"I do read, but I wouldn't know where to start with romance. Hey, when we get out of this market, pick one for me and I'll read it," he said with a grin.

"*If*," she corrected.

"*When*," he said again.

He seemed so sure that they'd all be fine, but the longer they were here, the more Maya worried they'd never leave. She looked toward the front of the truck, hoping he didn't see the fear in her eyes. Suddenly there was a hand on hers on the stainless steel counter. He squeezed.

"I'm sorry," she said, blinking away a tear. "We just...we have no idea what's going on out there. I'm worried about my family." She shook her head. "My therapist would be telling me to focus on my three positives of this situation."

"What are they?" he asked, his hand still on hers.

Maya counted them off on the fingers of her other hand. "One, there is a cat here with us."

"*Seriously?* Percy?"

"Cats are always a positive. Two, I'm alive and well. And three," she wasn't sure she should say the last one. He might misunderstand. "And three, I'm not alone."

Tarek didn't say anything, just looked at her curiously for several moments. But they were so close together. His hand was on hers. He'd pushed up the sleeve of his yellow chef's jacket and she could see the corded muscle and smooth skin of his forearm. She swallowed.

He was close enough that he could kiss her right now while barely moving. They were the only ones in an enormous flea market but were squeezed together in this tiny truck.

She looked away, needing to break the spell. "Okay, so you like romance movies, what about music? Please don't tell me cheesy love ballads."

He laughed and took his hand back. They chatted aimlessly while they finished eating. About music, then the market and some of the wacky personalities there. They even talked a little about their recent past. Maya gave a brief background about the Ben disaster, and Tarek confessed he'd also had a big breakup in the last six months, but he didn't say much about it. Maya wondered if it had anything to do with his family, or his business, because they steered clear of those two topics.

But overall, Tarek was still so easy to talk to. He'd always been. Maya forgot about everything, including her business troubles and her father's dreams. Instead, she caught up with one of her oldest friends in a tiny stainless steel food truck during the end of the world.

It was lovely.

After he took the empty plates to the sink, he grinned. "What do we do next?"

Maya smiled. "I have an idea. Let me help you clean up, then come with me."

5

Maya took Tarek back to the antique hall. This was probably the first time she'd gone there by choice, but the
world was ending, and she wanted to surprise her friend.

On the way, they passed the theater prop booth and saw
Percy sleeping soundly on his back on the velvet chaise
lounge, his inviting white belly out for the world to see.
Maya laughed, giving it a rub. He looked like a romance
cover model against the purple velvet—fluffy cat style.

"Where are you taking me, anyway?" Tarek asked.

"It's a surprise," she said as they passed the music paraphernalia booth. "You don't mind surprises, do you?" Maya
herself hated surprises. They only led to her overthinking.
Well, honestly, everything led to her overthinking. But there
was one surefire way that Maya could turn off her brain. And
she was about to introduce it to Tarek.

"Ah! A bookstore!" Tarek said when they finally stopped. "What a good idea!"

"Sort of a bookstore." It was the used bookseller booth they'd passed earlier. Maya found a small shelf stuffed with mass-market paperback romances. Her e-reader had hundreds of books on it, but this was for Tarek.

He laughed. "You're going to pick me a romance book!"

"Yes. Unless…if you don't want to…" Maybe this was a bad idea. Just because this was her favorite way to pass time that didn't mean he was willing to spend this disaster reading.

"No, it's perfect. Pick one." He frowned, looking at the bright spines on the shelf. "There is no way you've read all these."

Maya laughed. "No. A lot of them, though."

"Okay, so which one am I reading?"

Maya ran her fingers over the spines. "Hmm…how about a paranormal?"

His nose wrinkled. "Like magic?"

"More like vampires and werewolves."

He shook his head.

"Cowboy romance?"

He cringed.

She grinned. This was fun. "A rom-com?" She found the brightest spines and looked for one she thought he'd like. "How do you feel about…" Maya bit her lip. How to ask about this? She turned, totally not realizing that Tarek was directly behind her. Like, very, very close. That did not make asking this particular question easy. She took a breath. "How do you feel about sex?"

He raised a brow. "Like as a general concept, or in specific situations?" He looked like he was trying hard not to laugh.

This was mortifying. She was sure she was pinker than

Percy's nose. "Like in books. Because romances have...sex in them. Well, not all, but a lot of them."

He shook his head, laughing. "I can't believe little Maya is reading smutty books now."

She'd been reading them back then, too. She slapped his arm. He was still wearing his chef's jacket since the market was a little chilly at night. "I'm not *little* Maya. Fully grown adult. Would you prefer something without on-the-page sex, or something more..."

He lowered his voice to a growl. "Spicy?" The way he said it...right behind her, with his voice lowered like that... Maya was amazed her legs were still holding her up. This was a terrible idea. What was she doing?

She turned back to the shelf. "I'm giving you an Amish romance."

He laughed loudly, and a shiver went down Maya's spine. This was worse than that sexy growl. "I really like this new smut-loving, grumpy Maya," he said. "And after trying my cooking, you should've known I'm always up for more heat. How about one of these sexy Victorian ones. I've always been curious about them. Seems like an oxymoron. Victorian sex." He picked up a historical romance with a heaving bosomed woman in a clinch with an open-shirted nobleman.

"That's a regency, not a Victorian."

He frowned because he clearly had no idea what she meant. She replaced the book in his hand with a different regency book. "This is the book I pick for you. It's got a feminist hero, a road trip and a search for dinosaur bones. And it's funny."

He laughed. "Dinosaur bones? Seriously?" He turned the book around and read the back. "This sounds hilarious. What are you reading?"

She pulled her e-reader out of her bag. "I started a book today."

"It's a romance, too, right?"

"Yep. A paranormal. I *like* werewolves."

They went to the nearby furniture booth to read, each sitting on either end of a big red couch—with a comfortable amount of distance between them.

After a while, Percy sauntered into the area and settled next to Maya. Tarek had snort-laughed at something in his book. Clearly, he was enjoying it, which thoroughly warmed Maya with pride. Maya lazily curled her legs under her and stroked Percy's soft fur. Her book was excellent. The cat was purring. And Maya was not alone.

"This is ridiculously good," Tarek said.

"Right? I don't get why people hate on the genre so much."

They continued to read silently. Maya forgot everything. Her father working too hard. Her uncertainty about whether dumping all her savings into a small business was a good idea. And most importantly, she didn't think about the world maybe ending out there. Mostly.

"Hey, Tarek," she said. "Your cell service working yet?"

He shook his head. "No."

She closed her eyes a moment to listen. She knew they were in the middle of the mountains, but there was still no sound of destruction. Maya would never have imagined that the apocalypse would be so peaceful. She checked her phone. It was past ten o'clock. It had been more than three hours since the alarm.

"What if we are stuck in here for days?" she asked.

He shrugged. "Could be worse. There's food, drinks and working bathrooms. Plenty of books. A cat. I bet we could survive here a month, no problem."

A month cut off from the rest of the world? Without her family and her friends and cat? Without her mother making her fresh rotis, and her father and her sitting at the kitchen table experimenting with new spice blends?

A month with no one who loved her?

Maya looked out into the dark distance. They'd turned a few of the lamps in this booth on, but everything outside their little sanctuary was dark. They'd found the main light switches in the security office earlier, but decided they weren't necessary.

It was so strange. She couldn't remember ever not seeing or hearing evidence of anyone else in the world. With four of them plus her cat in the family home, and her Monday to Thursday shifts in the busy call center, Maya was never alone. Even back in her and Ben's tiny apartment, she could always hear the families that lived above and below. Maya wasn't used to silence.

"Maya?" Tarek's voice was low.

"Yes?"

"I was thinking about your three positives, and I think they're mine, too." He slid closer to her and reached over her to rub Percy's back. "I like having the cat here. I'm also thankful we're alive. But my last one is different from yours. I'm not just grateful not to be alone, but happy to be *specifically* with you."

Maya didn't know what to say so she didn't say anything. But deep inside her, she agreed with him. She wasn't a fan of the end of the world. But was happy to be spending it with Tarek.

It started to get even chillier as the night went on. Thankfully, they had a whole flea market full of stuff at their disposal, so just past ten, they found a booth that sold cheap knock-off clothes, and grabbed sweatshirts, sweatpants and a thick furry blanket with wolves on it. They left an IOU on the counter for their purchases and went to the bathrooms to change.

It looked like they were going to be there all night. Maya still wasn't sure what was happening in the world outside the market since they hadn't so much as looked out a window, but she hoped people around the country were feeling as safe and secure as she was.

"I was up at six prepping food all day," Tarek said, yawning as they settled back on their sofa.

She was a little surprised that they'd wordlessly decided to continue to share the sofa. There were several other couches in this market—since there was more than one furniture vendor. But Maya didn't want to be the one to suggest going elsewhere. In a bizarre turn of events, Tarek Mizra was the only thing keeping her brain from falling into the spiral of despair right now.

And if at some point in the night the three tones went off, this moment...this *connection* she'd rediscovered would end. No more of Tarek's laughs. No more of him making her smile whenever he noticed darkness sweeping in to consume her. No more squeezing her hand before her tears fell.

And then life would go on. He'd be her professional rival and the son of her father's enemy again. This little protective bubble with their three positives would burst, and all the challenges that seemed almost insurmountable in Maya's normal life would be back.

And that was the best-case scenario. The worst-case scenario was that the asteroids that she couldn't see or hear but could be barreling toward earth right now would hit while they slept.

Maya's fists clenched and she squeezed her eyes shut. She

needed to be close to Tarek. To feel the comfort that only human contact could give her. Snuggling a cat was nice, but even a cat lady like Maya needed people.

"I probably won't sleep right away," she said. Or sleep at all. She was tired, but she was too anxious.

"Yeah, me neither. Plus...I kind of want to get back to this book."

Maya smiled. "So then should we just keep reading?"

He grinned, nodding. They got back into the same positions they were in before, except a little closer. They had to—they only had the one blanket between them. They read silently for a while until Tarek snorted.

"What?"

"Sorry, this is really funny. Are all these books like this?"

Maya shook her head. "That author is particularly funny. They're not all funny, though."

He turned to look at the cover again. "It's like...it's hiding something."

"What do you mean?"

"The book. You can't really judge it by its cover." He turned and looked at Maya. "I always thought that about you."

They weren't supposed to talk about when they were young, but she was curious. "Why?"

"You were kind of quiet, I mean. You still are, when you're not swearing or yelling at me about tikka sauce. But you were bookish."

She snorted. "I'm still bookish. I mean, I'm reading right now."

"Yeah, that's just it. You're quiet and read a lot, but it turns out you're reading very funny and *very* sexy books."

She laughed. "So, you're surprised I'm not a prude."

"I never thought you were a prude. That's my point. I never judged you by your cover. I always knew there was more than what others saw."

She believed him. Mostly because back when they were little and she'd had that massive crush on him, it was because he always…noticed her. She didn't think he could possibly return her feelings, but she wasn't *invisible* to Tarek. She had this memory of a big party at the Mizras. There were a lot of people there—and a lot of other teenagers. Her sister, his brother and sister, plus the kids of all the other aunties and uncles. They were all playing a board game in the basement and Maya had been eliminated early. Tarek played until the end, but Maya had the next book in her favorite series with her, so she sat in the corner and read. Really it was no wonder that she had a reputation for being dull and bookish. But anyway, the game must have ended because there was a commotion with all the kids heading up the basement stairs. Maya didn't know where they were all going, and it wasn't the first time she'd been left behind like that. She figured she'd stay in the quiet space and keep reading. But then Tarek was in front of her. *We're going out to the backyard, Maya. You're coming, right?* He had his hand out to help her get up.

It was such a small thing. But it was a memory that stayed with her—Tarek making sure she wasn't left behind.

She chuckled. "You haven't changed much."

He shifted a bit, settling into his seat. The movement brought them closer still, maybe unintentionally, but neither of them moved to correct it. They were touching now. Not quite leaning on each other or even pressed together, but there was no space at all between their legs.

"What did you think of me back when we were kids?" he asked.

She raised a brow. "Fishing for compliments?"

He laughed. "Yeah, maybe. Get back to me on that." He yawned, then rubbed his face. "I can't believe we're still here."

"We're never getting out of here." She'd said it lightheartedly, but still tensed the moment the words were out. They'd been alone for *hours*. Maya was used to assuming the worst was going to happen, but it was far past the time when even optimists should panic. Her breath hitched.

Suddenly, Tarek's hand was on her chin, gently turning her face so she could look at him. She'd love to say she found strength in his resolve. In his positivity. But the only thing in his eyes was the same fear she felt. His hand slid over her cheek. "I'm terrified, too, but keeping your three positives at the front of my mind is helping." His hand slid down her face, then he took her hand in his. She was pretty sure he was doing it because he needed to touch someone alive as much as she did. Maybe even more.

"Cat. Alive. Together," she said. She glanced at Percy curled up at the edge of the sofa.

"Yes," he smiled. "Cat. Alive. Together." He shifted again. "I should get some sleep."

Maya yawned. "Yeah, me, too."

Wordlessly, she shut off the lamp, and they arranged themselves side by side on the enormous couch, arms around each other, faces inches apart. He was warm, solid and smelled like garam masala and home. This was the only way she could imagine herself getting any sleep tonight. Alive, and together with Tarek Mizra.

"Good night, Maya," he said.

"Good night, Tarek." She smiled. He shifted a bit, coming even closer to her. She did the same. She could make out his eyes now. The fear was still in his warm eyes.

But there was comfort, too. And the space between them was gone. Maya wasn't even sure who started it, but it wasn't long before they were kissing. Maya was pretty sure it wasn't really happening though—it had to be a dream. Yesterday she'd been tense, and stressed and worried that her world was going to fall apart under her nose, and now it was the end of the world, and her first crush was gifting her easily the sweetest kiss of her life. She squeezed her eyes shut so she wouldn't wake up as Tarek gently explored her lips with his own. Tiny bites, a little bit of sucking. Soon his tongue reached out to taste, to explore. It was soft, sleepy and slow. Those full lips she'd fantasized about when she was fifteen felt even better than she could have imagined. She could feel his heartbeat against hers while they were cocooned together on an antique couch and wrapped in a furry blanket. They kissed like that, softly and lazily, for probably longer than they should have, until a long chime sound startled Maya. She sat up as Percy bolted off the couch into the darkness.

"It's over," she said. Their nightmare, or fever dream, or whatever it was, was over.

Tarek shook his head and took out his phone. "No. Sorry. That's my sleep app. Reminding me it's bedtime." He picked up his phone, but the sound had already stopped.

"What time is it," Maya asked. The spell of that moment was broken. Maya had no idea what was going to happen now.

"Midnight."

"Why do you have a sleep app?" Maya's therapist had once suggested she get one, but the sight of it on her home screen made her anxious.

Tarek shifted a bit, putting some distance between them,

then huffed an awkward chuckle. "My therapist recommended it. I have insomnia."

He didn't seem to want to say more, and Maya didn't want to pry. But clearly everything wasn't sunshine and rosewater in Tarek's world like she'd assumed. Estranged from his family and seeing a therapist? He looked at her with an awkward smile on his face, maybe worried he'd said too much.

"So...it's time to sleep then?" Maya said. She wasn't sure if she wanted to do that, or see where those kisses would have gone if his app didn't go off.

He seemed as torn up with indecision as she was. "Yeah. We should."

"It's just," Maya said, squeezing his thigh. "I don't want to do something even if it feels right, for the wrong reason, you know?"

He leaned forward and kissed the tip of Maya's nose. "Yes. I know exactly. Let's sleep."

Maya smiled, then turned her body so she could be the little spoon to his big spoon. She thought she wouldn't be able to sleep, but her last thought was that his breathing had slowed so his insomnia wasn't kicking in. Maya gave in to slumber, not knowing if the world was ending or not, and she'd never slept so peacefully.

6

Maya would have expected that waking up pressed tight against Tarek Mizra on a lumpy old couch with a furry wolf blanket thrown over her would cause a bit of confusion, but everything was crystal clear the moment she opened her eyes. She shifted a bit, squinting. It was still dark, but a bit brighter than earlier, as if a dim light was behind her. She could hear paper rustling. She turned to see Tarek reading by the light of his flashlight.

"You're up," Tarek said softly.

"What time is it?"

"Four. Can't sleep."

Maya smiled. "Book too good? Been there."

He chuckled. His sleepy face was...adorable. A tiny bit of stubble on that square jaw. Hair sticking up everywhere. And sleepy, hooded eyes.

"Any chance I slept through the *all-clear* sirens?" Maya asked.

He shook his head, putting his book down. "No. Still no cell service, either."

Maya sighed. She'd kind of hoped she'd slept through the rest of this disaster, but there was no way she was going to be able to get back to sleep now. She looked around—she couldn't see Percy anywhere, but she knew he was out there.

Three positives: Cat. Alive. Tarek.

Maya shifted up to a semi-sitting position and flicked on the table lamp. Should they talk now? Because they clearly had a lot to talk about. Like the *whole world possibly ending* part, but also? They'd kissed last night. A lot. Yeah, they were both exhausted and emotional and very scared, but exploring someone's lips wasn't usually how Maya dealt with fear.

She cleared her throat.

"Wait, Maya. Before you say anything, I have a whole speech planned. Can I go first?"

"Speech?" she asked.

"I woke up before you. I practiced."

She exhaled and nodded.

He cleared his throat. "Maya, I had a huge crush on you when we were teenagers."

Okay, that was *not* what she expected him to say. "No, you didn't."

"I did. The last year before we moved away."

So, nowhere near as long as she'd been crushing on him. Also, was this really happening? The world was ending, and Tarek Mizra had just admitted he was into her when he was sixteen? "Okaayyy…"

"And—" he ran his hand over his hair "—I had fun with you here last night."

"Except for the *we may all die a fiery death* part, right?"

He chuckled. "Yeah, of course. Without that, it would have been even better. But I was glad to be with *you* for the end of the world. If the world doesn't end, would you like to have dinner with me sometime?"

Tarek Mizra is asking me out. She'd pined for him for years, and all it took was one apocalypse and he was asking her on a date. Maya didn't want to just *go out* with Tarek. She wanted to wrap her arms around his neck and pull him in so they could finish what they'd started last night. Maya literally had to clasp her hands together in front of her to stop herself from grabbing him and mauling the man.

But mauling him, or dating him, or anything in between was a terrible idea. Even if he was estranged from his parents, he was still a *Mizra*. What would Dad say to this? Also, if the world didn't end, they still had their sandwich rivalry. And they didn't even live in the same city. "It would be very complicated."

"Yes, it would."

"We don't know if we'll walk out of here."

He took her hand. "You're right, we don't. But maybe enduring this would be easier if we had something to look forward to?"

She exhaled, squeezing his hand. "Look, Tarek, I'm… This is a lot for me right now. Can we put a pin in this conversation, and have it when we get out?"

He smiled widely. "Yes. Let's do that. We'll put a pin in it until we walk out of this place together."

It took Maya a second to realize that his enormous smile was because she'd said *when* we get out, not *if.* Apparently, the man's optimism was contagious.

To prevent herself from any more minefield conversations, Maya picked up her e-reader. "I think I'll read for a bit, okay?"

He grinned. He settled behind her, one arm loosely around her waist. "Yes. Me, too."

She did read, but not for very long. There was too much going through her head to focus. He didn't seem to be having a problem, though. He was so engrossed in his book; she almost didn't want to interrupt him. Almost, but she had to say something. The world was ending, and maybe the apocalypse was telling her it was time to be bold, just like when she opened Masala Girls.

"Tarek?"

"Yeah?"

"I had a crush on you before, too."

He chuckled and put his book down. "I know."

"You did?"

He laughed. "You were *very* easy to read back then." He batted his lashes suggestively at her.

Maya blinked. Well, this was embarrassing. She took a breath. "I think my teenage self would really, really hate that pin. She'd tell me the world was fucking ending and this could be my only chance with you."

He looked at her for a few moments, then smiled. And it was a different smile. Hungry. So fucking sexy Maya's toes were already curling. He put a hand behind her neck.

"Great thing about pins is you can take them out to try something on, then put the pin back in again." He pulled her close, so their lips were almost touching.

Maya swallowed. She *was* scared—her heart was pounding in her ears, but…if the world ended without her getting another chance to taste Tarek's lips she'd be both scared and pissed off. "What do you mean by *trying something on*?"

He pulled her even closer against his warm body. "Well," he said, smiling the playful smile that had been burned into her brain since forever. "I mean it *has* to be fate that you and I specifically are stuck here together. I am quite sure that we *will* walk out of this market—but getting through this ordeal would be easier if we had the possibility of more of this—" he kissed her briefly "—to look forward to. Committing to anything in a disaster is a bad idea. We're just trying it on. We can decide later if it fit." He kissed her a little longer this time, even briefly licking Maya's bottom lip. "And if nothing else, it will give us a way to pass this time that would actually be a longtime fantasy come true for me."

She was the one to lean in for a kiss this time. "For me, too," she whispered against his lips.

And his almost feral smile was back for a moment before their lips crashed into each other properly.

This wasn't sweet and slow like the last kiss. This was hot, urgent and insistent. They didn't need any preamble, any getting to know each other. They already did all that, and they had no idea how long they had together right now. Maya immediately climbed on his lap, straddling his strong thighs. His hands were all over her, and she couldn't believe how good he felt. Forget fireballs outside, the fire was right here between them. Maya arched her back, pressing herself into his hardness, aching to feel some release.

"Look at you," he whispered. "You're hungry, aren't you?"

She dipped her head to suck his earlobe, loving the moan he released. "So are you," she said, pressing his groin into her.

When his hands reached under her sweatshirt, then T-shirt, then bra, she pushed him away so she could remove them, tossing her clothes on the floor behind her. His hands immediately found her nipples and pinched, and she cried out with pleasure, then clamped her mouth shut.

He grinned at her. "You're a screamer. I *love* that, Maya." He leaned forward to lick her nipples. "We're all alone, *let go*."

He was right. This was the end of the world—why have inhibitions? She didn't hold in her cries of pleasure when he almost brought her to ecstasy with only teeth, tongue and fingers on her nipples. Eventually it was too much, so she gently eased off him and started taking off his shirt. And he let her.

He was amazing. He was Tarek, and that long and lean chest was bare and in front of her. He was her literal first crush, but really, he was so much more than that. He was the one who'd comforted her on what should have been the worst night of her life. He'd made her smile, laugh, read books with her and even made her a comfort food dinner. He wasn't some mythical teenage crush, or a family villain, or even a professional rival. He was the good man in front of her. The very *sexy*, good man. And even if nothing ever came from this, she knew with certainty that she was doing the right thing right now.

"I can't believe this is happening," she said, because she couldn't.

"You still want to?"

She grinned. "Yes. You?"

He took her jaw in his hands and kissed with such ferocity that Maya thought she'd explode. His bare skin felt amazing against her live-wire nerves. She needed more of it.

Maya hadn't been with that many guys. Ben, of course. And a few before him. But she didn't remember it ever feeling like this before. She felt wanted. He made her feel so powerful.

So she climbed off him and pulled him to the edge of the couch, then dropped to her knees on the floor between his legs. His eyes were wide with awe as she slowly started pulling down his sweatpants. He helped, lifting off the couch so she could inch his pants down, exposing more of him. His briefs came next, revealing an impressive, mouthwatering erection right in front of her face. Maya ran her hands up his hips, teasingly, ever so slowly, feeling him shudder under her touch. She leaned her head down and looked up at him.

"Holy fuck you're amazing, Maya. Do it," he whispered.

She smiled before opening her mouth and taking him inside. And oh god, he tasted *so* good. Maya loved this. Feeling a person quiver with unrestrained pleasure in her mouth. She worked him slowly, methodically, with one hand holding the base of his erection and the other gripping his solid thigh. His muscles were clenching as he held on to the back of her head, muttering words of encouragement. Words of affection. She was pretty sure he said, "Holy fuck, Maya, this is why I love you," at one point, but she was too far gone herself to process anything but the feeling of him in her mouth. His muscles tensed even tighter—he was close. She flicked her tongue against his tip before sucking deep, and he nudged her off him. She looked up at him, her lips still tingling.

"You are so fucking good at that," he said. "I'm close. I have a condom."

She nodded. "I want you in me when you come."

He hauled her back to the couch, then went searching for his wallet and his condom. Maya removed her pants and underwear, then watched as he rolled it on. When he finally climbed on top of her, she tossed the blanket to the floor. They didn't need it for warmth anymore. He was so beautiful balanced over her. Those eyes. That jaw. She wished she could have him like this all the time. She wrapped her legs around him and smiled.

"Are you ready, Maya?"

"Do it, Tarek."

He entered her slowly. "You are so beautiful," he said, going deeper while staring into her eyes. "Oh god, your *face*. You feel so good."

He felt amazing, too. Better than she could ever imagine. Despite their feverish beginning, now they moved slowly. She didn't want it to end, and it seemed neither did he. Their eyes stayed locked as he moved in her, and Maya actually teared up from the intensity. Before long, he leaned down to kiss her while increasing his pace. When she arched her back, he reached down and rubbed where they were joined, reading her body's reactions perfectly. That was all she needed. She screamed in ecstasy as the orgasm crashed through her, not holding back one bit. His climax came seconds later, and he shuddered as he clutched her tight and repeated her name like a promise.

They lay in each other's arms for a while after. He'd pulled the blanket over them, and neither said a word. Maya wasn't entirely sure she could say words anymore. But her mind was calm. Content. Not cataloging all the things that could go wrong. Not anticipating doom.

And she realized that she didn't want to put that pin back in. She was keeping Tarek, no matter what happened. He fit with her.

7

Eventually, Maya needed to get up and clean up. She retrieved her clothes strewn around the floor while Tarek pulled his pants back on. This was the awkward part.

"You okay?" he asked.

She nodded, locating her bra. "Yeah, I'm fine. I...I'm sorry. This is a little weird."

"You don't have regrets, do you?"

She looked at him. His jaw was set, but his eyes looked a little uncertain. She'd known that face pretty much her whole life, and although she'd never seen his after-sex glow before, it was still so familiar. She shook her head, then leaned down to kiss him.

"None at all," she said, then stood and pulled her T-shirt on. "I just need the bathroom."

He grinned. "Okay. Me too. After we're done, meet me at your booth?"

She frowned. "At Masala Girls?"

He nodded. "I want to show you something."

After cleaning up, Maya made her way to her booth in Hall A. She was feeling nervous—she still had no regrets about what they'd done, but maybe she'd let loose a little too much? Maya enjoyed sex, but she usually didn't show exactly how much she enjoyed it so soon with a man. But with Tarek...this didn't feel as new as it was. Even without the fact that she'd known him forever, the connection...the *intimacy* between then in the last ten hours wasn't like anything she'd felt before. But still. Had she gone too far?

He was already at Masala Girls when she reached it, dressed and waiting for her behind the counter.

"Okay, what's this about?" she asked.

"I have a proposition for you," he said, a huge bright grin on his face. "I thought of this before we...you know."

She raised a brow. "Did you sleep at all?"

He shook his head. "Not much. I'm an insomniac. Here," he said handing her a bottle of Curry Junction Tikka Sauce.

"What's this?"

"It's my sauce. I had an idea. This isn't because we slept together, which by the way, was amazing. You are so perfect, and I'm looking forward to talking later about how much I really, really like this new grown-up Maya and her...*skills*. But first...you don't want me selling my sauce because sauces are your thing. But prepared food is *my* thing. So why don't we compromise and stop selling each other's things?"

"What?" Maya was confused.

"You said earlier it's a pain in the butt to cook in this space. And bottling sauces is a pain in the butt for me. So, why don't we sell each other our tikka sauces wholesale? I'll use yours to make a paneer sandwich exactly like yours, with the Portuguese buns and pickled onions. I'll call it the Masala Girls Paneer Tikka Sandwich, and if people love it, I'll send them to your shop for your sauce. And you, you can stock the Curry Junction Tikka Sauce on your shelves. Tell people to come to the truck to have a chicken on naan sandwich that uses it, but not before you sell them some masala dabbas and biryani masala. We'll bring business for each other. There is no reason for us to compete when we can have a symbiotic relationship instead."

His face was so bright. His eyes twinkling. Tarek had the most expressive eyes. From confidence, to wonder, to arousal to fear, she'd seen it all in the last night. She'd been there with him for eleven hours and it felt like a lifetime. She certainly saw more of him than the fifteen years she'd known him as a kid.

His idea was a good one. Making the sandwiches *was* a pain in the butt. Without them, she could spend more time with customers or developing new sauces.

She smiled. "This is a pretty good idea. I think this is worth exploring. If we ever get out of here, that is."

He beamed and put out his hand. "*When.* Should we shake on it?"

She took him behind the neck and pulled his head down. "How about we kiss on it."

After a small kiss, he smiled. "Does that mean we're leaving the pin out of...*us*, too?"

She laughed. "For now. That pin was poking me."

"I'd rather be the one poking you." He waggled his brows suggestively.

She laughed, resting her head on his forehead.

"Look at you, Miss the glass is half-empty. You're making plans for the future."

"You're rubbing off on me."

He waggled his brows again, and Maya slapped his arm playfully. Honestly, Maya hadn't had this much fun with a man in a long time. No wonder she'd found a bit of optimism.

But really, this was a good plan. She wouldn't even mind stocking his bottle next to hers. She picked it up, studying it, and something printed below the ingredients made her freeze.

"Um, Tarek, why does this say that Curry Junction is part of the Mizra Restaurant Group?"

He raised a brow. "Um, because it is?"

She frowned. "What's the Mizra Restaurant Group?"

"That's all the family restaurants. Shahi Tandoor is the biggest one. We have two locations. Downtown Chattanooga and one right outside town. Upscale Indian and Pakistani dining. My brother opened Café Mizra a few years ago. It's in a more trendy part of town. Street food–inspired menu. And Curry Junction is my baby."

"I thought the truck was *yours*."

He frowned, confused. "Well, it is. But it's technically owned by the Mizra Group. I have full autonomy, though."

"You didn't tell me you worked for your father. I thought you were estranged."

He shook his head. "I didn't say that. I said we don't really have a good personal relationship—which we don't. But we do work together. He taught me everything I know about food service."

Maya blinked. *Shahi Tandoor*, the upscale restaurant, would have been the one that he opened after abandoning the partnership with her father. It would have been her father's dream.

Tarek wasn't *estranged* from his family. He fucking worked with them.

Maya's fists clenched. "I can't believe you didn't tell me this."

Tarek shook his head. "I didn't exactly hide it from you. And you said you didn't want to talk business. Why is this so bad?"

"Because I don't want a *symbiotic* relationship with the Mizra Restaurant Group! Don't you get it, Tarek? All this—" she waved her hands at the Masala Girls shelves. "Me working my ass off to make Masala Girls a success. Working full-time at the call center and in my spare time mixing spices, making sauces and marketing, this is all for my dad. His dream was always to have his own restaurant, and he was going to achieve that with your father years ago. But then your dad pulled out of their partnership. So now Dad drives an airport taxi and gets yelled at by racist tourists daily. Thanks to your family."

"Maya, look at me."

She did. His face...those eyes...right now they were a little surprised, and a lot sad. And so, so handsome. How could she have fallen right back into the all-consuming crush she'd had all those years ago? No, that wasn't entirely true. These were new feelings, and they were even stronger than the old ones. This was *real*.

"Maya," he said. He took her hand and held it to his chest. "This is me. Not the Mizra Group. *Tarek*. I had nothing to do with the past."

"I know," she said softly.

His eyes never left hers. "My father told me your father didn't want to move, and Dad saw more opportunities in Chattanooga than Atlanta."

Maya shrugged. She'd known Dad hadn't wanted to move, but Tarek's dad didn't have to abandon him. She shook her head, taking her other hand. "I'm sorry. I know it's not you, but I can't do this."

He blinked. "Can't do the symbiotic partnership, or the relationship?"

She shrugged. "Either. Both. What would your father say if he knew what we were doing an hour ago? What would mine say?"

He cringed. "Ew. We're not going to tell our fathers about that, are we?"

Maya hated doing this to him. "Tarek, I can't...won't...do anything to threaten my goals. I'm sorry." She understood how messy family was. She understood that he couldn't be blamed for his father's actions long ago. And his success, with his shiny food truck making so many people happy—Tarek deserved it.

But Maya and her father deserved success, too. What if Tarek's dad somehow took Masala Girls from them after they entered this partnership? Or what if Tarek's sauce outsold hers in her booth? Or what if Tarek stole her sauce recipe once she sold it to him?

Too much could go wrong. She couldn't rely on a Mizra to make Masala Girls' success happen. And she couldn't break her father's heart by being in a relationship with his rival's son.

Tarek shook his head. "I don't even know what to say. I know the last eleven hours have been a pressure cooker, but this was *real*. I didn't imagine that." He ran his hand through his hair and sighed. "And now you're walking away without even trying. But I'm not going to force something that you don't want. Goodbye, Maya."

He looked at her for a few long seconds, face washed with sadness, before he turned and walked away.

And Maya let him go. Fifteen-year-old Maya would have punched herself in the face for that. Hell, part of her was screaming to go tell him that he was right. The connection felt real to her, too. They could have been amazing.

But no. She couldn't risk everything for Tarek Mizra. Even during Armageddon. She squeezed her eyes shut and remembered her therapist. Cat. Alive. Not alone.

Well, she had no idea where Percy was right now. Yeah, she was alive, but the longer this disaster was going on, the less likely it was that she was ever getting out of this damn flea market.

And she *was* alone. So, so, alone.

She sighed as she picked up the bottle of Tarek's tikka sauce. Her bottle was nice, but his looked so much more professional. That's what happened when you had a whole restaurant empire that could afford branding experts instead of just a cab driver and a recent graphic arts graduate. Maya opened the bottle. Tarek's sauce was much redder than hers. Most tikka sauces had artificial color in them, but Maya didn't use any coloring in Masala Girls sauces.

She smelled Tarek's sauce and was hit with a burst of fresh spices and a hint of citrus. She smelled cumin, coriander and chili, but there was more there. Tamarind? She needed to taste it to be sure. She took one of the little cups she used for samples and poured some of the sauce in it. The bright color stained the cup, but the sauce had a similar consistency as her own. She dipped her finger and tasted. She could detect the other spices then…turmeric, ginger, definitely lemon and a lot of chili. Plus…mango powder? That's what the secret ingredient was. Maya pulled out another little plastic cup and poured some of her tikka sauce in it. She stuck her finger in it and put it in her mouth.

It tasted exactly the same. Not similar, not close, but *identical*. Other than the color, Maya would bet there was no difference between the Curry Junction sauce and the Masala Girls sauce. Which made sense. Maya got the recipe from her father, and Tarek's probably came from his father. And their fathers had created that recipe together in the old Jafari apartment back in Atlanta when both families were new to the country with dreams of a tandoori empire.

She put her finger back into Tarek's sauce and into her mouth. All those years he'd been cooking his chicken in the same sauce she'd been making her paneer in. Somehow, that made Maya profoundly sad.

In all honesty, Maya had no idea what her father would say about her joining forces, professionally or personally, with Tarek Mizra. But she did know that her father was as risk averse as Maya was. Years ago, when Arif Mizra tried to convince Dad that Chattanooga was the place to build their future, she could imagine exactly what Dad would have said. He would have listed all the things that could go wrong for them in a new and smaller city. He'd have said he couldn't possibly uproot the family and take a risk on an unknown.

And then Dad just stayed put while the Mizras went on to do amazing things. Maya had been the one who'd finally taken risks. She'd started therapy to help her with her chronic pessimism. She'd opened Masala Girls and worked her ass off to get it off the ground. She looked down at the little cups of Tikka sauce on the counter. Masala Girls was *hers*, not her father's. One day she hoped he would join her, but until then she had to make the decisions for its future.

This was yet another opportunity for Maya to take a risk

that could have a huge payoff. Just like the last time she thought the world was ending and the fiery streaks in the sky pushed her to finally start her business. This was fate. They might never get out of this flea market, but if they did, Maya wanted to walk out with Tarek.

She threw the little cups of sauce into the garbage—but not before taking another fingerful of Tarek's sauce. This whole nightmare could end, or not end, at any time. She didn't want to waste one more moment of it alone.

Tarek wasn't at Curry Junction, which made sense. An empty food truck wasn't exactly a comfy place to hang out. He was probably back at their sofa. She made her way through the antique hall toward their little bedroom, when something stopped her short.

It was Percy, sitting near the skirts of that Victorian dress on the dress form in the theater prop booth. Maya smiled and stepped into the booth to rub Percy's soft head, when she noticed that Percy wasn't alone.

Tarek was on the chaise lounge in the booth—the one with the purple velvet upholstery. He was lounging, on it, of course, because that's what one did on a lounge. He'd taken off his sweatshirt, and the sleeves of his worn gray Henley were rolled up showing his strong, naan dough–kneading forearms. And he was reading that historical romance she'd picked out for him.

Her mouth went dry. Why the hell had she sent this man away?

"For the love of God," Maya said, shaking her head. "Are you for real? Why are you doing that?"

He startled, then raised one confused eyebrow, which only made this tableau even more arousing. "You *told* me to read this book," he said.

She stepped closer. "Tarek Mizra, you are on a chaise lounge. In a gray Henley with the sleeves pushed up, and you're reading a sexy, feminist romance. You even have a fluffy cat nearby. All you need is a mug of masala chai. What right do you have to come back into my life *now* and be so utterly perfect that I can't think straight?"

He frowned, putting down his book. "I can't tell if you're being serious."

Maya shook her head and sat on the edge of the lounge, her legs touching his. "I'm being serious, Tarek."

He frowned. "You sent me away. Why are you here?"

"Two reasons. One, because I tasted your tikka sauce, and it tasted exactly like mine. Like...*identical*. There is no reason for us to sell each other our sauces for your plan."

He blinked, expression blank.

"Also—" she sighed and put her hand on top of his "—for the last year I've been trying to let more positivity in my life. And to take more risks when the payoff could be amazing. But I think I lost sight of *why* I'm doing it. It's not for my father or for anyone else but *me*." She squeezed his hand. "I was only willing to take risks my family would take, instead of doing what's best for me. Family is complicated. I'm not saying I'm choosing you over my father, but...I want to *try* to make this work."

He squeezed her hand. "Just the business relationship, or the personal one?"

She smiled. "Both. I think this whole positivity thing would be easier if I had an optimist in my life."

He grinned and sat up straight. "I'd be happy to put in an application for that role."

Maya laughed. "Done. You've got the job."

He put his arms around her, pulling her close. "Yay."

"I have a question, though. Why don't you get along with your family?"

He chuckled. "They think I should stop dating around and settle down with a nice Pakistani girl. I'm starting to see their point."

Maya frowned. "Um…you think they'd approve of me?" She knew her parents didn't like the Mizras; didn't his family dislike hers, too?

He put his arms around her. "I have no idea. Maybe this is what will make our parents finally talk again? Or not." He shrugged. "This is between you and me, though. Not them. We have time to figure it all out."

Maya smiled. And at that moment, she believed him. They had time.

Tarek gathered Maya in his arms and with one more incandescent smile, he lowered his mouth onto hers.

And they were kissing again. Maya had never had an apocalypse as amazing as this one. And when they got out of this flea market, she knew they were going to make this work. Because it was so worth any risk.

A loud noise startled them apart. Specifically, three loud noises.

A voice blared from the alarm system. *"This is an official announcement. Your area is now confirmed 'ALL-CLEAR' from aerial debris. Please exit your shelter safely."*

Half a second later, both Maya's and Tarek's phones started buzzing with texts. Maya checked hers and saw messages pretty much from everyone in her family asking her if she was well and saying they were all okay. She sent a text to her family chat saying she was absolutely fine.

"It's over," he said.

Maya's whole body relaxed. She laughed, then looked into Tarek's beautiful eyes. "It's not over," she said.

He smiled, putting his phone down. "No. it's not even a little bit over." And he pulled her down for another long kiss.

They could get on with their lives later. Maya and Tarek were busy right now.

★ ★ ★ ★ ★

MY LUCKY STARS

LANE CLARKE

Each photo passed by in a blur as Jones Miller scrolled through *his* Instagram feed. Him. Warren Cox. The man she was certain she was going to marry just three months ago. A certainty built more on inertia than romance, but a certainty, nonetheless. She had been wiped from his page like she had never existed. Five years' worth of anniversary posts gone in what felt like an overnight erasure. Quickly replaced by a blond-haired, blue-eyed debutante who had a toothy smile and a pronounced mole above the left corner of her stained red lips.

Jones zoomed in on the diamond ring taking over his most recent photo. Smiling faces and a balloon arch announcing their engagement. An acidic taste crowded the back of Jones's tongue as she read through the comments of ex-friends who had chosen Warren in the split. Even the friends who had been hers first, their solo to shared custody breaking apart in the wrong direction.

The door to the small room snapped open. Jones ducked her head on instinct. She was usually the only person in the Reserves Room, the small collection of textbooks set aside for law students like her who couldn't afford books that cost as much as her rent to serve as a doorstop for nine months. This was one of the few times Jones wished she still had her locs instead of the buzz cut she now donned instead. Locs were much easier to hide behind, even if it was the kind of hairstyle that stole attention and curious eyes. Sometimes even the curious, and disrespectful, touch.

Dianna Ellis rounded the corner in a blur. Even after two years, Jones was unsettled by the frequency at which Dianna seemed to vibrate. They didn't have anything in common. Where Jones was rough around the edges, Dianna was spit shined to a squeaky-clean gleam. Everything about Dianna seemed inauthentic. Her straight teeth purchased with expensive dental procedures, her waist-length sew-in. Her always made-up face and designer everything. Jones couldn't help but roll her eyes. Everything about Dianna screamed plastic. But worse, she didn't share the inherent mistrust that Jones had learned to have toward her mostly white classmates. Dianna didn't approach them with the hesitancy Jones's parents had taught her. And she most certainly did not have Jones's back like Jones had expected their first day of 1L Orientation.

Jones had been excited to see another Black girl as they registered. But the levity of not feeling so alone, both invisible and unavoidable, quickly faded when Dianna paid her as much mind as a paper bag in the middle of the street. Her mother had always taught her that not all skinfolk were kinfolk, but she had never experienced it until Dianna, who preferred to be accepted rather than heard.

Jones took Dianna in now. Her legs were practically bare

in fifty-degree weather, her skirt ending in that middling space between her hip and knee that was just low enough to be school appropriate and just short enough to be risqué. If Jones's mom was around, she'd scold Dianna for having open pores out in Chicago fall, the precursor to an eternally long winter. But Jones kept her mouth shut. The pneumonia her mother had always warned about might do Dianna some good. Maybe it would teach her that sweatpants weren't the devil and it was totally fine to wear them on the two-hundredth freezing cold day in a row.

Her mouth settled into a disapproving grimace, her tongue settled against the back of her teeth.

It was a sound Dianna knew as well as her grandmother's voice—the sucking of Jones's teeth. But her usual response, a roll of the eyes as quick as a blink, was halted when she saw Jones slumped into her favorite side chair. She had shoved it to the farthest corner of the room, directly below the heater. No matter what the temperature was outside, Dianna liked to maintain a body temperature of at least eighty degrees at all times. If she wasn't sweating, it wasn't hot enough. Blame it on growing up in Savannah but being warm just felt like home. And right now, Jones was squatting in her territory.

But unlike Jones, who Dianna felt made a precious attempt to make all social interactions as unpleasant as possible, Dianna clucked her tongue softly and shifted to the thinnest aisle in the room, housing the textbooks for environmental science. It was a small specialty for their law school class, where nearly everyone focused on corporate work at big New York and Chicago law firms or criminal justice work in DC. She was one of only six students on the Environmental Law track, and she liked it that way. There was no need to pretend to be someone bigger than she was in a room full of people who cared more about oil spill restitution than who wore what at the Met Gala. Despite the empty-headed fashionista that served her so well as her public persona amongst her classmates.

Dianna dragged her finger along the textbooks, looking for the one she used for every starting point she needed in her Law Review article. But the space where it usually sat was empty.

"What?" she muttered aloud, the echo between the shelving elevating her voice much higher than expected. For the past two years, the book had never left the shelf unless by her hand.

"What?" Jones responded.

Suddenly she was there, at the end of the aisle, her hands pressed firmly into her hips in annoyance. Dianna couldn't help but notice the way her fingers sat comfortably in the dip of her one-piece dungaroos. Dianna was pretty sure they were designed to hide her body entirely, but they weren't doing a good job. Or Dianna had become sensitive to the curves of Jones's body. If only the words that came out of her mouth were as sweet as the rest of her.

"Oh," Dianna said, becoming defensive. She wasn't sure why Jones despised her so much, but Dianna tried not to step on her toes as much as possible. "Sorry. There's just a book missing that I need."

She would have to ask the circulation desk, though she couldn't help but wonder what other person in the school both needed the free textbooks and had a sudden interest in factory pollution in low-income rural areas.

Jones's eyebrows perked up in interest, and the smug grin that Dianna had come to see whenever she closed her eyes settled on her lips, a perfectly pink shade that most woman had to purchase in lipstick form.

"What book?" Jones asked, in the tone of someone who already knew the answer. "Not this book." She turned around and grabbed the book from the small desk Jones had also pushed to the corner to accompany her perfectly placed chair. When she faced Dianna again, she was holding up the very textbook Dianna needed and had until that point considered hers.

Heat rose up Dianna's face, and she knew that her cheeks were becoming an embarrassing shade of cherry red. Out of habit, she lowered her head, letting her hair fall forward in order to hide her visible anger. The last person who was interested in environmental law was "Make as much money as humanly possible for soulless corporations" Jones fucking Miller.

Dianna took a deep breath through flared nostrils. She channeled her grandmother and every pageant coach she had ever had. *You catch more flies with honey.* She straightened her shoulders and put on her stage smile, one that stretched at the corners and gave her a headache from her clenched jaw. But it photographed well, and, more importantly, won any and everyone over.

"Do you know how much longer you'll be using it?" She tilted her head to the left like a puppy hearing its favorite word. Big eyes, even brighter smile. If she could make her ears flutter, she would.

"I don't know." Jones shrugged. "I'm not sure what I'm looking for. I might have to read every single page." She spoke slowly and deliberately, letting each word sink in as far as possible before twisting. She had watched enough Steven

Segal thrillers to know that's how you really went in for the kill. "I might even have to check it out."

Dianna grimaced. For once, her champion smile wasn't working. Which was even further proof that Jones Miller was not human. But worse, if Jones checked that book out, Dianna would never see it again, and she couldn't afford to buy her own copy. Ideally, Jones would turn it in on time, in the prescribed two hours the reserved books were out of the library. But this wasn't an ideal world, and the circulation desk was worked by Ms. Mindy, the nicest woman alive who erased so many fines for late returns that no one was ever incentivized to return anything to the library they had checked out.

"I can wait," Dianna offered. She walked toward Jones, who flinched as Dianna passed her, as if physical contact would cause her actual pain. Dianna brushed so close by that the fibers of her sweater brushed Jones's forearm, making every hair on her body stand on end. Jones's body emitted a warmth that one could usually only find emanating from beach sand. Hot in a delicious kind of way.

Dianna settled into the only other chair in the room. She shuffled around in the seat. It was definitely in the wrong spot, and the leather had not yet been broken in. It pressed against Dianna's bare thighs uncomfortably. But she was going to sit in this chair for as long as it took.

Jones returned to her seat, setting the textbook on her lap. She took ten minutes to read the table of contents, deliberately slow, and then proceeded to flip through each page. Dianna bit down on her tongue, her acrylic nails tapping on the arm of the chair. Jones was going out of her way to drive Dianna wild, but instead she was the one going nuts. Each tap against the leather made Jones twitch, the sound interrupting any train of thought she could muster. Like a leaky faucet that dripped through the night or a fluorescent overhead light begging to be changed. Jones had always had trouble tuning out noise, so much so that she felt crazy whenever she couldn't stop hearing something that everyone else quickly discounted.

"Do you mind?" she said finally, nodding her head at Dianna's still dancing fingers.

Dianna tilted her head again. Jones wondered if she knew she looked like a damn dachshund every time she did that. She refused to admit to herself that it was cute in an impossibly annoying way, like sloths who were mostly useless but still made her stomach soft inside.

Without a word, Dianna removed her hand from the arm of the chair, reaching into the large tote on the floor in front of her instead. Jones felt her body lean forward, trying to see what Dianna was conjuring before it was out in the open. She decided that if Dianna pulled out a mascara wand, she would lift the seat cushion and stuff Dianna beneath it. Primping in the library was at the top of her list when it came to irritating Dianna habits. Who really needed to look that put together all the time? There wasn't anyone here on a Friday evening but the two of them. Actually, she was surprised Dianna was here at all. Unlike Jones, Dianna had a social life.

Dianna pulled out a can of seltzer water, Blackberry Bubly. She slid her nail under the top and flicked it open, the sound exploding in the quiet room. Jones lifted two inches out of her seat even though she knew the sound was coming. She watched as Dianna banged a wrapped straw against her thigh until the paper popped open, revealing a lime-green paper straw that Dianna slid into the can. For someone so dainty, there had to be a quieter way to drink than the obnoxious slurping she was currently doing. Every so often she would take a deep sigh, the carbonation building in her throat and exploding through her lips. Jones tried not to stare, just as distracted by the sound as she was with the way Dianna puckered her lips around the straw. Like a kiss.

Jones blinked away, smoothing a phantom loc behind her ear. She still wasn't used to them being gone, the weightless feeling of her head. She cleared her throat loudly and nudged her head toward the sign plastered over the door.

"No food. No drink."

Dianna shrugged. "Turn me in then."

It was a challenge. Jones knew that if she left this spot, she'd lose her stolen seat for good. It would be like leaving land undefended during a war, ripe for the taking. And she couldn't leave the room with the textbook without checking it out first, which meant she'd lose that too. She didn't actually have any intention of taking the book home, nor could she. She had maxed out her checkout limit on books she actually needed, and unfortunately, while Ms. Mindy was a wizard with overriding the system, that was the one thing she couldn't change. She had hoped Dianna would simply leave before figuring it out.

"Do you go around being as annoying as possible?" Jones chided.

"Do you go around being as insufferable as possible?" Dianna asked. She slapped her hand over her mouth too slow. Despite how low Jones could go, Dianna had never responded to her remarks with a rude comment in return. She was taking the higher road, being a bigger person. But some people really could just grind your gears, couldn't they. "I'm sorry," she muttered between her fingers.

"Yeah, you really got me here," Jones said with a roll of

her eyes, hitting her palm against her chest. Dianna focused on Jones's face so as not to be distracted by the way Jones hand sat on the rise of her breast.

"I try not to engage in childish back-and-forth," Dianna said, pulling her straw back into her mouth. It didn't matter how attractive Jones was. Nothing could surpass how mean she could be. And unnecessarily so. Dianna had never done anything to her. She had only ever tried to be Jones's friend, but received nothing but derision in exchange.

"Childish," Jones scoffed. "Funny coming from someone wearing jelly sandals who can't follow a rule to save her life."

"I follow rules," Dianna responded. "But I'm thirsty and unfortunately, thanks to you, I have to stay in here until you're done. What are you doing anyway?"

"Trying to mind my business. You should try it sometime."

Dianna slumped back in her chair with her drink. "Someone got up on the wrong side of the bed." She was pretty sure Jones had never gotten up on the *right* side of the bed a day in her life. Though she wouldn't mind finding out. If Jones wasn't such a bitch.

Jones began reading the textbook more aggressively. It wasn't nearly as bad as she thought, it was even kind of interesting. Which shocked her, because she didn't think Dianna was into anything interesting. But she could feel Dianna's eyes drilling holes into the top of her head as it hung low to take in the minuscule text. Apparently, eye strain was a requirement of graduating law school because nothing was ever bigger than eight-point font Helvetica.

"This is good," Jones said aloud. "Maybe I'll change my focus to Environmental."

She didn't even have to look up to know Dianna was rolling her eyes. It was so aggressive that Jones could practically feel the shift in the room as they rotated up and back and settled in place once more.

"Sorry, can't get rich doing it," Dianna said.

"And here I was thinking you only cared about materialism," Jones responded.

"Well, you don't know me very well then."

"No." Jones shrugged. "I guess you'll follow the age-old plan of simply marrying rich."

"Why do you insist on thinking I'm a shallow person?" Dianna asked, leaning forward in her seat. Her hands gripped her can with such a tight grip that the aluminum was buckling in the center. The Bubly practically had a waistline.

"You're kidding right?" Jones asked, her eyebrow spiking upward with her heartrate. Despite having a quick tongue, she didn't like confrontation. Her heart was practically beating out of her chest. Especially since she couldn't help but be a little light-headed around Dianna. She blamed the obnoxious toxic fumes of Dianna's perfume, which always made her smell like cupcake frosting. "What was it, Miss Teen Savannah? You're from Shallow City."

"You do know pageantry is about a lot more than just pretty girls smiling into cameras, right? Or do you insist on being obtuse."

"I know it's not *not* about pretty girls smiling into cameras."

Dianna smirked. "You think I'm pretty?" It was a joke geared to irritate Jones further into leaving the room, and leaving the textbook behind. So she was shocked when what felt like a rock sank to the bottom of her stomach. She cared about Jones's answer. She maybe even cared a lot.

"I was just repeating *your* phrasing," Jones sputtered. "And you're obviously not the ugliest person I've ever seen. I do have perfectly working eyeballs."

"I can tell," Dianna said, nodding her head at how close Jones's face was to the textbook in order to see.

Jones slammed the book shut. "You know you are just a know-it-all drama queen who thinks the sun shines out of your ass. Would it kill you to, for just a moment, consider…"

But before she could finish, a long blare sounded through the room. At the same time, both Dianna's and Jones's phones shook so violently that they fell off their tables. Jones slammed her hands over her ears, the sound making her teeth hurt. Dianna reached for the phone that had slid under her chair.

"Chicago doesn't get tornadoes, right?" Jones yelled over the sound as her phone repeated it's shrill wailing.

"It's not a tornado," Dianna said, her voice shaking.

"Flash flood?" Jones asked. She could barely hear herself think.

Instead of answering, Dianna flipped her phone around so that Jones could read the warning splashed across her lock screen. She had to squint, but the words fell into place. Big red exclamation marks bookended words that made bile rise her throat.

"This is an official announcement—aerial debris detected. This is not a drill. Please find immediate shelter in an underground bunker or interior parts of a building away from windows. Remain sheltered and wait for an all-clear."

Jones, with her head hunched in a pathetic attempt, scrambled for her phone on the floor. Maybe Dianna was playing a cruel joke on her. Though she couldn't ignore the pallid look that stretched over Dianna's face like a veil. Her phone, while it had ceased its screaming, had the same life-altering message as Dianna's. Meteoric debris was heading for Earth, and it was likely that sometime soon, she would be dead.

Jones threw her phone with a squeal, rushing toward the door. She yanked, but the door failed to give. She pushed, thinking that maybe her head was just as jumbled as her body. Everything she did was useless. The door stayed shut.

"What the fuck?" Jones shrieked.

"It's not going to open," Dianna said.

"What are you talking about?" It came out of Jones's mouth in a whine that Dianna didn't expect. Tough-as-nails Jones was afraid.

"Don't you remember our orientation packet 1L year? The Reserve Room in the library is one of the designated bunker rooms." She pointed to the walls. "No windows. Cement framing. Underground."

"No," Jones said, refusing to believe her.

"Yes." Dianna nodded, like she was talking to a toddler one second away from the temper tantrum of the century. "We're stuck in here."

"No," Jones repeated. "I am not dying in a library with you."

"We're probably not going to die," Dianna said, smoothing her skirt before she sat down. She ignored the shaking in her fingers as she picked up her can to continue drinking. She told herself that it was just the siren putting her on edge, which had been going nonstop for the last four minutes.

"Oh, are you also focusing on astronomy too, Galileo?" Jones asked through gritted teeth as she continued to manhandle the door.

"Wow, you're even a bitch when you think you're about to die. No last-minute repentance?"

"You think this is funny?" Jones said, her eyes narrowing

into slits. "Of course, you do. You've already gotten to see the world and travel and date and do all the things. While I'm just some lame girl who gets dumped and replaced in a matter of seconds. The universe is so unfair that I'm actually starting to believe in a higher power. Because there is no way that my life is this much of a shit show by accident."

She tilted her head up and screamed at the blinking lights. "Are you there, God? I hope you're getting a really good laugh."

And just as suddenly as it had started, the siren stopped. Jones stilled, looking around the room. Dianna ducked, just in case.

"Is it over?" Jones asked.

Dianna grabbed for her phone. The warning was gone. She pulled up Twitter. If there were updates, that was the best place to look. Contrary to what her grandma had believed about social media, it was way better during catastrophes than relying on local news sources, which were mostly behind paywalls anyway.

But her home page would not refresh. *"Tweets failing to load"* was the only new message she could see each time she swiped. "Oh," she said aloud.

"What's wrong now?" Jones rushed beside her. It was the closest they had ever been and Dianna felt like her skin was leaping off her body as pinpricks of heat reached from her fingers to her toes. She had never noticed that Jones smelled like oranges and eucalyptus. She had never been near enough to notice. It made her want to bury her head in Jones's neck and breathe in until her lungs exploded.

"Twitter's down," Dianna answered, trying to find her words again through the brain fog caused by Jones's aroma. "Check yours."

"I don't have one," Jones said. She sounded remorseful, like starting up a Twitter page in high school would have been the one thing that saved them now.

"Well, check something else," Dianna said, as she rushed to Instagram. Down. Snapchat. Down. TikTok. Down.

"I don't have anything."

The bars at the top of Dianna's phone were still showing three bars, but for the life of her she couldn't get a single page to load. "Well, see if you have service. I don't."

"Who do you have?" Jones asked, as she opened her email.

"Sprint," Dianna responded, impatient. The quicker they figured this out, the quicker she could calm down. She hated not having every piece of information available. She hated being left in the dark.

Just as the thought crossed her mind, the Reserve Room actually went dark. Dianna shrieked, dropping her phone and her Bubly.

"Shit," she said, as she felt the water soak through her skirt before the can made a now-empty echo on the floor. All she could see was the flash of Jones's face in her phone's light before the backup generators kicked in and the room was filled with the blue-gray light that was always present in industrial freezers in every zombie movie she'd ever seen.

"My email's down," Jones said in disbelief. "My email is never down. I have Verizon." She tried to send a message to Naima, her incredibly reckless younger sister, who since turning eighteen was responsible for at least half of her recent gray hairs. Dianna herself could claim the rest.

Jones tried not to worry as she received a *"failed to de-liver message."* Her sister wasn't reckless enough to ignore the alarm and stay hanging out at whatever friend's house had the most booze. Right?

"Sorry for your loss," Dianna said as she wiped at her skirt. She hadn't drunk nearly as much of that water as she had pretended to when trying to get on Jones's nerves, and she was paying for it now as every last drop soaked through the fabric and made her thighs sticky.

Jones fixed her mouth to retort before noticing the wet stain spreading across Dianna's skirt. "Oh," she yelped. She moved to the door again, forgetting for just a moment they were trapped there, as she barreled into it. "Oh!" she groaned before rushing back to her backpack to pull out paper towels. Being helpful would distract her from trying to send one hundred more texts to Naima that would do nothing but go straight to the ether.

"Why do you have so many of these?" Dianna asked as Jones helped her dab at her skirt with a handful of paper towels and napkins that looked like they came from every restaurant on 53rd Street.

"Ragweed," Jones muttered as she focused on pressing at the spot between Dianna's legs.

Dianna stilled. "What?"

Jones looked up finally. In the near dark, her brown eyes were nearly black. "I'm allergic to ragweed pollen. I keep tissues on hand so I'm not a snotty mess."

"Oh," Dianna said, distracted as Jones's hands continued to move. "Maybe I should..."

"What?" Jones asked before immediately dropping her hands to her sides. She was both thankful that it was so dark and that she was a deep brown that hid embarrassment from her face. "Sorry."

"That's okay," Dianna said. It was the most cordial conversation they'd ever had. She didn't want Jones to think she was upset with her and set off the attitude she was so used to receiving. Plus, it hadn't been that bad letting Jones's hands work over her thighs. Jones was surprisingly gentle, Dianna thought, for someone who approached every interaction with a sharp edge. "I just hope it's not ruined. It's vintage."

"So expensive?" Jones corrected, handing the rest of the dry paper towels to Dianna to finish drying off.

"Probably not." Dianna shrugged as she pressed the paper towels against herself. Dabbing was always more effective than scrubbing. "It was my grandmother's. She died six years ago and I inherited her closet. Well, I inherited everything, and her closet was all she really had." Dianna's voice broke at the end of her sentence. Jones pretended not to notice.

"Oh," Jones said, surprised. She inspected the skirt more closely now, at least what she could see in the shadows. "It's nice."

Dianna stared at her, the paper towels forgotten. "It's nice?"

"I like vintage clothes," Jones explained with a shrug. "Better than the stuff we've got now."

"Well, thank you. And agreed." Dianna smiled and the most surprising thing of the evening so far happened—Jones smiled back. You could have knocked Dianna over with a feather. Jones had a beautiful smile. Her lips pulled all the way back to show two even rows of teeth, and her eyes brightened. All of the frown lines settled in Jones's forehead and the corners of her eyes disappeared, making her look softer.

"I bet that caused quite the stir," Jones offered as she watched Dianna press into the fabric.

"What?"

"Your grandma shafting the rest of the family," Jones laughed. "In my family, there would have been a no-holds-barred, knockdown, drag-out fight between my mom and sister for clothes." Her fingers twitched at her side as she restrained herself from texting the family group chat. It wouldn't make it to them, and that would just further stress her out.

"It was just us," Dianna said, the words barely loud enough to reach Jones just a few feet away.

Jones realized Dianna hadn't reached for her phone even once after they received the warning. There wasn't anyone she needed to reach because there wasn't anyone. Her stomach twisted. Maybe needing to be accepted by everyone was how Dianna avoided feeling alone. Jones didn't know what she would do without her family.

Dianna dumped the used paper towels into a pile on her abandoned chair. She reached behind her back and unzipped her skirt. Jones leaped away like Dianna had pulled a boa constrictor out of her back pocket.

"What are you doing?" Jones asked in nearly a whisper.

"It's wet. And sticky," Dianna answered, sliding the skirt down her legs and stepping out of it. "And it'll dry better flat." Luckily it was just seltzer water so it hopefully wouldn't stain. She would just have to get it to the dry cleaners as soon as possible. She laid it flat on the carpeted floor. And then she shimmied out of her tights, rolling them into a ball before shoving them in the trash can. Hopefully it wouldn't be too cold when they got out of here. *If* they got out of here.

Jones's eyes burst open like tiny saucers. It was never quite warm enough in Chicago for Jones to see much of her classmate's skin during the school year, and she had never seen so much of Dianna. Her legs were stronger than they looked when covered by tights or jeans, because Dianna would never be caught dead in yoga pants like the rest of the student body. And despite how body-shaping Jones had considered Dianna's clothes to be before, she was realizing now how much they had left up to her imagination. In just her panties, Dianna was slender but muscular, sinewy tendons rippling beneath her skin even in the dark. The kind of body that Jones had only seen on professional athletes during her biennial watch of whatever Olympic event was on television. Her legs were slightly paler than her face, which was already gold medallion, but still sunlight soaked.

Dianna caught Jones's glance, which was concentrated on a small dimple settled into Dianna's skin. She anticipated the slick comment that was probably nestled at the tip of Jones's tongue and she rolled her eyes in anticipation. "I'm not going to walk around in a pair of tights. I would look ridiculous."

Jones cleared her throat and looked away. Dianna was surprised by her continued silence. She had usually emptied her clip by now. Dianna sat on the floor beside her skirt and continued to dab. The skirt was stiff but it didn't look stained from what she could tell in the shoddy lighting. It was one of the few things she had left of her grandmother, but she was trying not to get emotional about it now. Jones would surely use any weakness she learned about her in here for future commentary.

Jones sat down across from her, leaning her back against the shelving. "How long do you think we'll be in here?"

"I have no idea," Dianna answered. "How early do you think they send out the warning before the meteor actually hits something?"

Jones leaned her head back and knocked it repeatedly against a shelf, like she could wake herself up from this nightmare. "This is so stupid. We're just supposed to wait here with no cell service for God knows how long?"

"Looks like it." Dianna shrugged.

"Why are you so chill?" Jones asked, suspicion settling into her glance.

"Because freaking out isn't exactly helpful. I could panic, but it wouldn't open that door and it wouldn't save me if that meteor is headed in our direction. Might as well sit quietly with my existential crisis."

"Hmm," Jones muttered.

Dianna sighed, deep from her stomach. "Okay, let's hear it. What are you thinking?" Usually, Jones made her every thought vocal. Never in her life did Dianna think she would be urging Jones to speak her mind. But these were strange circumstances, and Jones was acting even stranger.

"I just figured pageant girls were all about the drama."

"Did you get all of your pageant knowledge from *Miss Congeniality* or something? I already told you, pageantry is more than just smiling and waving and learning how to walk gracefully in heels. Some of the most powerful women in the world were in the pageant circuit. And we always did a ton of community service."

"Are you trying to sell me a product or something?" Jones asked. But instead of her usual smirk of disdain, laughter was laced through her smile. "You sound like an infomercial for *Toddlers and Tiaras: All Grown Up*. I'm sorry, but don't you ever get sick of…performing."

"Well, it gets really old when everyone just assumes you don't care about anything but makeup and Kate Spade purses."

Jones worked her lip between her teeth, because she *did* think Dianna only cared about makeup and handbags, though she had no idea who or what a Kate Spade was.

"So what *do* they teach you in pageants? Because it looks like a lot of dressing up in pretty gowns and sound-biting world peace." She stayed silent before continuing. "And no, none of my pageant knowledge comes from *Miss Congeniality*. It comes from *Drop Dead Gorgeous*."

Dianna couldn't help it. A laugh spilled from her mouth and bubbled into her lap. "Oh, my goodness, that just about explains it, doesn't it? Sorry to disappoint, but I was never in a single pageant where girls died in asinine ways and not once did a float explode."

She couldn't hold in her giggling as her body rumbled with it. No wonder Jones judged her so much. That's what happened when satirical films took on the one hobby taken the least seriously. Her laugh got stuck in her throat, however, when Jones reached over with her foot and tapped the inside of her calf with it. Even through Jones's boots, it set Dianna's entire body on fire. She swallowed until her laugh settled back down into her stomach.

"What do they teach you?" Jones repeated. She was no longer tapping Dianna with her foot, but had settled her toe in the concave arc of Dianna's ankle.

"Um," Dianna started, trying to clear her head. She pulled her legs toward her and crossed them. She couldn't trust her body, it was acting way out of whack. "Well, they stress philanthropy and scholarship. That's why I started doing them, actually. To earn scholarship money for college."

"You needed scholarship money for college?" Jones asked in a tone of disbelief.

Dianna rolled her eyes. "Yes, Jones. Not everyone at this school was born with a silver spoon in their mouth."

"I guess I just figured," Jones said, but she shrugged instead of finishing her sentence.

"I know what you figured. Here comes Dianna Ellis, rich beauty queen with a stick up her ass. Trust me, you're not the first person to make assumptions about me that are totally wrong. I had to get scholarships for college and law school. What my grandma left me definitely couldn't send me to a place like this."

If Jones could sink into the floor she would. She had called Dianna every stuck-up name in the book, and had thought of several more that weren't appropriate in mixed company lest she give their white classmates reason to believe they could repeat them, but she hadn't for a second thought that Dianna did pageants for money and not because she wanted some validation that she was beautiful. Jones's mother had always said that making assumptions turned you into an ass, and here she was, proving her mother right.

"Well, since you are a smarty-pants, what do you know about this thing?" Jones pointed to the roof as a metaphorical stand-in for the meteor falling from the sky.

"Not much," Dianna said, shifting on her butt. She hated sitting on floors. They always put too much pressure on her lower back. A few downward dogs would probably help, but she was too self-conscious to splay herself out in front of Jones. "All I know is that we have to stay in here until they tell us we can leave. *If* they tell us we can leave. If it doesn't flatten us."

"Oh, it's definitely going to flatten us," Jones said.

"You think so?"

"I'm not exactly a religious zealot, but if I were a god, I would definitely take out the worst place on Earth, which, surprise, we are currently in. This law school is chaotic evil."

"Well, that's positive," Dianna laughed. She ignored the nagging in her head that these really might be her last moments. She had never thought much about death. She was surprised she had survived her grandmother's passing and felt like she counted down the minutes until she saw her again in some promised afterlife. She never expected it would come so soon. No matter where the meteor hit, it was bound to kill them all one way or another. She found it shockingly easy to find peace with that. It wasn't useful to stress about things beyond her control. Her therapy and Zoloft must be working, maybe a bit too well.

"Congratulations, I am the last person you're ever going to see. What did you do in your past life to deserve this?" Jones leaned forward, and Dianna could make out the shadows her irises cast up to her eyelashes like dandelion petals.

"It could be worse," Dianna said. "I could be trapped in here with someone who wasn't nice to look at with bad BO."

This time, despite the deep hue of her skin and the lack of lighting, Jones couldn't hide her blush. Even her lips were warm with it. Dianna wasn't the first woman who had ever made her entire body feel like it was in a toaster oven, but she was definitely the first to ever even slightly get Jones to put her guard down. Not even the man she had thought she was going to marry had successfully done that. Maybe it wasn't such a surprise he had so easily replaced her—she had never really been his. Or at least, he had never really been hers. It was easy to write over data not deeply embedded.

Jones watched as Dianna glanced at her phone and then crawled over to where she'd left it on the floor. Jones wasn't sure if Dianna had forgotten she wasn't wearing pants or simply didn't care. But for just a moment Jones let herself watch as Dianna's butt was cast straight into the air as she crawled.

"Do you want a snack?" Dianna's voice felt far away and Jones had to concentrate to put the syllables together into recognizable words.

Dianna dragged her bag back to where Jones was sitting.

Upturning its contents, snacks cascaded out onto the floor. Along with a first aid kit nearly exploding with bandages, a small pack of wet wipes, an eyeglass case, a pair of flats rolled into a ball and an AirPods case.

"Why do you have all of this?" Jones said, grabbing a tube of ChapStick that had rolled toward her. The girl was prepared for anything—zombie outbreak, contagion, lockdown in a meteor bunker.

Dianna tossed Jones a bag of Cheetos, taking a small bag of fruit snacks for herself. "If you stay ready, you don't have to get ready." There was more to it than that, but she wasn't comfortable sharing that part of herself with Jones just yet. Until an hour ago, Dianna was pretty sure Jones hated her. The best she could hope for now when, if, they finally left this room was indifference, or maybe Jones would forget everything that happened here. End-of-the-world chatter was fickle. She wasn't about to open up with an uncertainty like that.

Instead, she rose from the floor and snatched the textbook she had been waiting for from Jones's long-abandoned seat. She pulled a notebook from the pile that had once been a mess of crap at the bottom of her tote bag.

"You're not seriously about to do work are you?" Jones asked, incredulous. And she thought she was intense.

"Why not? We've got nothing but time." Dianna dug out a pen and dated the corner of the blank page.

"If that's how you want to spend your last moments."

"Well, I could come up with something better." Dianna tilted her head like she so often did. Except this time a flirty smirk lifted up one side of her mouth.

Jones looked away first, leaning back on her hands to create distance. It might be her last day on Earth, but she wasn't sure she was ready for whatever that smirk promised. Especially not with Dianna Ellis. She pulled her arms through her sweater and folded it into a square. Lying down, she pushed it beneath her head as a makeshift pillow.

Dianna smiled conspiratorially, bringing her books closer to her chest as she began to scan for the most important passages, making note to cite them in her article. Her eyes strained as she angled the book beneath the dim emergency backup lights, but it was worth the distraction. What was a few more ticks down on her next eyeglass prescription in the grand scheme of things?

She didn't know how many minutes passed when she finally looked up to find her once blank page now full of her handwriting, scribbled neatly until about halfway down, when her cursive became nearly illegible. She liked to call it "study blackouts," when she was so in the zone that anything could have been happening in the world and she would never know it.

A small snore from just in front of her pulled her attention away from her notes. She tilted her book to the side to see Jones, huddled against the bookshelf with one arm thrown over her face. Snores squeaked out with each rise of her chest.

As if she could feel Dianna's eyes on her, Jones jerked upward, awake and alert. Her head slammed into the corner of a bookend above her. She screamed and pressed her shirt against her mouth, trying to capture the drool falling from the corner of her lips. Only then did she realize she hadn't screamed at all.

Dianna was rushing toward her in a crawl, speaking too many words at once for Jones to assort into comprehensible sentences through her grogginess. Dianna grabbed at her face, and before she knew it, Dianna was so close that she could feel her breath on her face. The blackberry from her Bubly still clung to her lips, which were so close to her own that if she leaned forward she could capture them.

"Lips," Jones said aloud. Her brain was still moving far too slow. She felt drunk. With sleep, with something else she was still too afraid to name.

"What?" Dianna asked.

Jones puckered her lips and then laughed. Maybe she was drunk. Or concussed. Her legs had that buzzy feeling she only got after a few shots of tequila, when all of her synapses were racing to figure out which limbs needed them most. Even her face was tingling.

"Oh, you slept good," Dianna laughed, sitting back on her butt. "My nana called it being high on z's."

Jones's mind came back slowly until once again her brain was full of too many thoughts. Anxiety pressed against the back of her eyes. She had almost kissed Dianna. Dianna still wasn't wearing her skirt. These things felt related.

Dianna dug a small pouch out of the pile on the floor. She held it and if Jones could read minds, she was sure that she'd drown in whatever was going through Dianna's head right now. She tapped the pouch with her fingers and then sighed.

"Can you help me?" she asked finally. "I need some light." The generator lights were getting dimmer by the minute and the small device had barely enough battery power to illuminate the small numbers. That would teach her to stop forgetting to plug it in before bed.

"Sure," Jones agreed. She found her phone shoved beneath her thigh and pressed the small flashlight button. She got a ten percent notification and turned on low power mode. Hopefully they wouldn't be in here much longer. No way

out was one thing, but no way out with no phone felt like a
horror movie waiting to happen.

She held the phone over Dianna's hands and watched as
Dianna unzipped the pouch. A small device fell out. Dianna
took the device in one hand and held out her thumb on the
other. Jones watched silently, holding her phone as steady as
she could as Dianna pressed the device against her thumb.
A sharp and sudden sound popped—the needle pricking her
skin. She moved the device from her thumb, which now had
a small bead of blood at the tip.

Jones moved closer as Dianna tilted the device toward
her, trying to read the numbers in the light. Dianna nodded
as she read and then dropped slowly to the floor, shifting
through the rest of the pile until she found her first aid kit.
She pulled out a small antiseptic wipe, ripped it open with
her teeth and pressed it against her finger.

"Do you…need me to do anything?" Jones asked her, following her movements with the light so Dianna could see
what she was doing.

Dianna smiled up at her. "You're doing it."

Dianna checked her phone service again, though it was
futile. They were still totally disconnected from the world.
She grabbed her bag once more. Apparently, there were some
things that hadn't managed to tumble to the floor. She took
out a bottle of orange juice and drank half the bottle before
coming back up for air.

"Are you okay?" Jones asked.

Dianna nodded. "My blood sugar's low, but I don't know
how to tell my insulin pump that." She waved her useless
phone in the air. "You can turn that off by the way."

Jones flicked the flashlight off and then shoved her phone

in her back pocket. "How do you normally tell your insulin pump."

Dianna lifted her shirt, exposing a small patch at the side of her stomach that looked slightly squishy to the touch. Jones moved her hand to test it before stopping. She didn't know the etiquette, but it probably wasn't kosher to touch someone's medical devices without permission. It was a part of her body, and you couldn't just go around touching people's bodies just because you were curious.

"Go ahead," Dianna said.

Jones touched it like it was a rare gem, gently and with barely a press of her fingers. She didn't know if it hurt, but she didn't want to find out. Dianna shivered as Jones's cold fingers brushed against her too-warm skin. She blamed it on her blood sugar—she tended to break into a sweat when her levels were off. Especially if there was an impending event, like a crash. Her mouth was already starting to dry and her thoughts were getting fuzzy around the edges.

"How does it work?" Jones asked.

"I test my blood sugar levels with this." Dianna picked up the small device. "It's called a glucose meter. And it's connected to an app on my phone, so it inputs the numbers and then this—" she held her hand over the small patch, trapping Jones's hand in between. A small squeak escaped Jones's lips but she kept her hand in place. "Gives me however much insulin I need based on all of that data," Dianna finished explaining.

She moved her hand one finger at a time. Jones felt her face get warmer and warmer, thankful once again she had inherited her mother's deep chestnut skin instead of her dad's cool umber.

"It's supposed to be revolutionary and super high-tech, but

I guess relying on technology for everything is bound to bite you in the butt at times like this." Dianna sat heavily into the plush chair, bringing her orange juice bottle back to her lips. She was already starting to feel better. She would have to pay better attention now that she didn't have her phone to keep track. She manually inputted her numbers so she would have them for later. Twenty years managing her diabetes and she was about to die from either a meteor or lack of insulin from being locked in this room. Cool. She let her head drop back as a deep groan of frustration escaped her.

She should have paid more attention to the innumerable times her doctor tried to teach her how to manually override the connected system. You know, in case of a global blackout or world-threatening meteor, because it would be ridiculous for life-saving devices to require an iPhone. But she had put too much faith in the tech.

A part of her had never quite taken her diabetes as seriously as she should have. She was young, otherwise healthy, worked out five days a week. She had a skincare routine, drank a metric ton of water every day, and had even qualified for the Boston Marathon twice. She wasn't the type of person who should have diabetes. How could a body like hers be *disabled*. So she could be lax about it, she had thought.

She had played stupid games and now she was winning stupid prizes.

Jones sat on the floor in front of her. She plucked a bag of snacks that seemed the least necessary—a small packet of miniature Nutter Butter cookies. She figured the fruit snacks were the better option for blood sugar regulation, just like the orange juice. A shot of easily and quickly digestible sugar.

"You never told me," Jones whispered. She didn't mean it to sound like an accusation, but it was laced through her words.

Dianna snorted. "Would you have been nicer to me if you'd known?"

"Honestly," Jones said. "Probably. Is that fucked up?"

"Very," Dianna nodded. "I'd rather you be a bitch to me and treat me like an equal than be nice just because you think I'm broken or something. Yeah, I'm diabetic. But I'm also top of the class and still going to whoop your ass in our Con Law final."

"Okay, calm down," Jones laughed. "Not on your best day."

"There she is," Dianna laughed. "Seriously though. I'm not ashamed of it or anything. It's just a part of who I am. And yeah, I have to do things a little differently than other people. I have an invisible disability that makes me feel not sick enough to feel like I can ask for help sometimes. Which is messed up, because it's not like there's a hierarchy. And I shouldn't have to hide this because I want people to treat me like a *'normal'* person, whatever that means." She used air quotes around *normal* and released the word like it was acidic on her tongue.

"Don't worry, next time you go around demanding we all bow down, I will certainly remember that it's just because you're a little bit of a bitch and not because of anything else." Jones nudged Dianna's knee with her shoulder.

"When have I ever demanded anything from you? Or anyone?" Dianna asked.

"You don't have to," Jones said. "You just flash your pretty smile and swish your pretty hair and people just do whatever you want."

"That is so untrue."

"Oh, really?" Jones sat up now, swiveling on her butt so that she was facing Dianna, eye level with Dianna's thighs pressed into the leather. Her T-shirt under her dungaroos stuck to her back with sweat from being pressed into the chair. It was a flimsy cotton, a relic of her ex and his love of obscure bands. "Did you have to fight for your spot on Law Review?"

"What are you talking about?" Dianna threw her hands up in frustration. It was just like Jones to create false narratives in her head, even after everything they had been through today. Every day, it was a new victim card being pulled like Uno Draw Fours. It was exhausting. "Everyone earned their spot. We all did the same application, the same Bluebooking challenge, the same article edit."

"Yeah, and every year the existing editors find ways to exclude Black students from making it on. They go out of their way to find the smallest reasons to reject us. Even when we have the grades. They care more about maintaining status quo than being fair."

"Hello," Dianna said, flourishing her hand over herself. "I'm Black."

"But you're different. They accept you. You're the Black Poster Child to them. Light-skinned with fine hair and green eyes. Thin so that pencil skirts don't ride up your ass. Demure and docile. They look at me, tightly coiled hair and dark skin and dark eyes and a full body and all they can latch onto is how different I am, how aggressive they presume me to be because I don't smile in their faces. And you gobble up their acceptance like you've earned it, never once stopping to realize the privilege you carry. And it makes me so angry that I can't stand to look at you sometimes. The first day I saw you, I thought…"

"You thought what?" Dianna urged. She knew that she got along with her classmates more than the other students in the Black Law Student Association. She had never found it helpful to separate herself. But she had, of course, missed the community that the other BLSA members seemed to have with one another. Like they were more like family than friends. She had never looked at herself hard enough to determine if the opportunities she had been given were *because* she had latched onto power. The power. The rich classmates. The legacy students. But at what cost?

"I thought I had a built-in ally. A friend." Jones shrugged. Her mouth worked over her words like they were sour candy. "Someone who would look around the room with me and acknowledge the bullshit. But then you just fell in line with *them* and I felt betrayed."

"I—" Dianna began, but she didn't know what to say. She had always felt like she was the one who had been rejected. She had never considered that it was she who had done the rejecting. She had sought certainty in her success, but that had required her to forget the people who were already like her and understood her in exchange for people who never would, and probably would never care to.

"Just don't do it again." Dianna was surprised to see Jones smile at her. Before today, she could have counted on one hand the number of times Jones smiled at her, and she wouldn't even need all of her fingers to do it.

Dianna released the breath that was caught in her throat. She felt guilty, but mostly she felt sad. She might have had better friends in her life, friends she was comfortable opening up to about things like finances or diabetes or her grandmother's passing if she hadn't been, well, Jones had said it well. A bitch.

"Seriously," Jones said again, placing her palm on Dianna's knee with a squeeze. She was starting to touch Dianna more, with more ease and greater comfort. It was starting to feel like she couldn't stop herself from touching Dianna actually. "You know now."

"Well, I am sorry," Dianna responded, her eyes fixed on Jones's hand. She had always known she ran hot, and Jones was cold to the touch right now, but it felt right. Like when you flash froze molten lava and were left with something crystalline. Something uniquely beautiful.

Jones kept her hand in place, like she had completely forgotten where it was. It had happened quickly, but being near Dianna, touching her, breathing her in, had become comfortable. Natural, even. Jones had always wondered how lovers' hands always seemed to find one another. While walking Michigan Ave. Between the sheets in the middle of the night. But maybe she was starting to understand it. The magnetism of infatuation.

"Good thing you have the rest of your life to do things differently," Jones said.

"Too bad the rest of my life could be just a few minutes." Dianna tried to laugh, but dread sank through her body like lead.

The comment reminded them both of why they were stuck in this room in the first place. Doom. A meteor ricocheting toward Earth, God knew how close to them. Or when. They could be alive for minutes, or hours. They could leave this room and have years. Maybe together, maybe not. It felt necessary to do something, anything, that would make their possible last moments spectacular. Dianna refused to die having lived half a life.

Once again, Dianna placed her hand over Jones's. Jones looked up at her, long lashes heavy against her bottom lids. Dianna did not stop with just her hand. She moved her whole body. Jones felt the air quiver with static. Or maybe that was just her, shivering.

Dianna was close now, so close. Even in the lighting, Jones could make out the sparse beauty marks splashed haphazardly over Dianna's face. One above her left eyebrow. One below her right nostril. One near the corner of her mouth, which was parting.

"Did I ever tell you I liked your haircut?" Dianna asked, the finger of her free hand tracing Jones's hairline. She needed a new lineup, and all she could think about other than Dianna's orange scent getting stronger, was that she hoped Dianna didn't notice.

"What?" she responded, but before she could clarify, if she even could clarify, Dianna's lips were pressed against hers.

She had known it was coming, but her body still responded with surprise. She hiccupped into Dianna's mouth, earning a chuckle that grated across Jones's teeth. It was a soft kiss, but kinetic energy built beneath their lips. Jones pressed harder and Dianna scooted to the edge of her chair, making Jones's head tilt farther up in order to not break contact.

Dianna released Jones's hand on her knee, moving her own to cradle the back of Jones's neck. Her nails swirled through the curls at Jones's kitchen, a different curl pattern from the rest of her hair. Dianna noted that the back of Jones's neck was impossibly soft and instead of thinking about what it would feel like, she released Jones's lips and dropped her own to the space between Jones's chin and collarbone.

Jones sighed, the noise filled with more yearning than she thought existed within her. Jones's hand moved from Dianna's thigh to her waist, pulling her even closer. Dianna pushed herself off the chair completely, until she was off the seat and sitting in the scoop created by Jones's crossed legs. She wrapped her legs around Jones's waist.

"Dianna," Jones whispered. She had meant it as a question, but it came out as an oath. Like a prayer to a deity. Dianna. Dianna. Dianna.

Dianna released her neck. The spot she had been kissing felt like it had been plucked from a suction cup.

"Do you want to stop?" Dianna asked. She looked at Jones seriously, like whatever Jones said, she was ready to comply. Jones hadn't realized she had been nervous about feeling pressure, but with concern having settled into Dianna's glance, tension released from Jones's shoulders with quick release.

"No," Jones answered, her voice raspy and barely audible. She cleared her throat and tried again. "No, I just—I've never—I don't really know what I'm doing."

"You've never? Like never, never?" Dianna asked, incredulous. "I'm not judging. I'm just surprised."

"No. I mean I have, just with a man. Only with one man, so not even super experienced there. But definitely not experienced at all with…" Jones waved her finger between the two of them.

"Jones Miller, are you afraid of the word *vagina*?" Dianna chuckled.

"I'm not *afraid* of vaginas," Jones laughed. She pressed her hands into her face and dragged them down. Maybe she could scrub the embarrassment off her face. Or at least scrub off her face itself so that she wouldn't be recognizable as the biggest moment ruiner who ever ruined a moment.

"Jones, stop," Dianna laughed, grabbing both of Jones's hands and clutching them between her own.

"Can you die of embarrassment?" Jones asked. "I think I'm having a stroke."

"I can talk you through it," Dianna offered. "If you want."

Jones watched her. She didn't know how long they had been in this room. She was pretty sure her phone was already dead and she didn't want to ruin the moment any further by asking Dianna to check hers. If they didn't die, they could be free in the next few moments. She didn't know if Dianna wanted to be friends when it was over. This might be her last chance to make an impression, to change her life.

"I want to," Jones said with a nod. She swallowed, a loud gulp filling the space between them.

"Okay," Dianna said.

She released Jones's hands and settled them on Jones's waist. Slowly, she began to lift her T-shirt.

"You're a Rooney fan?" Dianna said, trying to keep Jones just distracted enough to relax, but not so distracted that she wasn't aware of her boundaries.

"Not at all," Jones laughed.

Dianna's eyebrow lifted in question.

"It was my ex-boyfriend's," Jones explained, trying not to laugh at the irony of a woman taking off the shirt she had refused to return to her ex. It was her favorite—she had broken it in just right. And now she was letting a new person remove it. "He's engaged now."

She didn't know why she added that part, but something about getting closer to Dianna, emotionally and physically, made her want to be honest. If you couldn't tell the truth to the person sitting in your lap with your T-shirt gripped in their fingers, who could you tell the truth to?

"Oh," Dianna said, the T-shirt rising even farther with the help of her fingers. "I'm sorry."

"It's no big deal," Jones swallowed again. "I didn't like him very much."

Dianna stilled, and then her body fell against Jones with the heaviness of full belly laughter.

"It's true," Jones said, laughing with her. Dianna's hair was pressed to her cheek, and she rubbed her face into it.

"Oh, I know it's true," Dianna giggled, straightening so that she could look Jones in the eye. "That's what I like about you, J. You don't hold anything back."

Jones was the first to move now, crushing her lips hungrily against Dianna's. They broke apart just long enough for Dianna to yank the T-shirt over Jones's head, before their lips came back together. Dianna threw the shirt somewhere in the dark, caring little for where it landed as she sank her teeth into Jones's bottom lip. Jones moaned into her mouth, setting Dianna ablaze. Dianna used both hands to cradle Jones's face, holding her still as her tongue tentatively slipped through Jones's lips.

They danced, their mouths knowing the choreography with little direction. Dianna lowered her hands down Jones's back, releasing her bra, before slipping the straps off Jones's shoulders. Where Dianna was sharp, Jones was smoothly curved. Dianna drank in the form of Jones's body through her fingertips. She once again released Jones's lips and let her mouth shadow her hands, keeping them fixated to each spot her hands brushed.

"Can we?" Jones asked, nearly breathless. Her words panted into the air as she attempted to catch her breath. She felt as if she had already run fourteen miles of a full marathon. She didn't know how she would keep her heart beating for much longer without exploding.

"Yeah?" Dianna asked, though she continued grazing over Jones's neck and shoulders.

Jones separated just long enough to gesture to the floor.

"Oh, yeah," Dianna responded, scooting backward off Jones's lap. She used the moments Jones took to lower herself to the floor to remove her own shirt.

Jones's eyes followed her every movement. She flicked her tongue over her lips, now swollen and a bit raw to the touch.

Dianna lowered herself beside Jones, dragging her fingers down the space between Jones's breasts and over her stomach. She traced them over the button of Jones's jeans.

"What do you want to do?" Dianna asked. She knew what she wanted to do, but her reference book was probably a lot more stacked than Jones's. She figured they would get through the basics. If they had time, she thought sadly. Please God, let them have time.

"What can we do?" Jones asked, curious. She wasn't so lost that she hadn't watched videos online or ventured into the WLW side of Wattpad stories, but she could only rely on her imagination for what was possible. Unfortunately, she had always had a limited imagination.

But Dianna did not.

"We can do anything," Dianna answered.

Maintaining eye contact to make sure it was all right, she unbuttoned Jones's jeans, pulling her underwear down along with them. Jones stomach stilled its rhythmic up and down motion. She had stopped breathing. Out of instinct, she covered her breasts with her hands, like she had been caught on camera on a nude beach and had suddenly changed her mind.

"Do you want me to stop?" Dianna asked, Jones's jeans midway down her thighs already.

"No," Jones breathed.

Dianna did not respond but continued undressing her. All Jones could think about as her feet were released from the fabric was that she was naked. Even with Warren, she rarely had sex naked. One, or both, of them would always still be in their shirts, just releasing the parts necessary to get the job done. She was surprised at how vulnerable she felt.

Dianna stood up now, taking in Jones's prone body on the floor. She wished the lights were on, the generators now emitting little more than could be achieved with candlelight, so that she could take Jones in fully. Jones was the kind of person who deserved to be drunk in. Dianna moved to remove her own underwear, letting it drop around her ankles, before once again lying beside Jones.

"What now?" Jones asked, her hands still clutched to her chest. She had always done well with clear instructions. She read the full manual before using any appliance, even if it was common sense how an air fryer worked.

Dianna reached for one of her hands.

"Now this," she said, moving Jones's hand to the side. Jones followed suit, letting her other hand fall away.

Dianna placed her hands where Jones's had been, squeezing gently as she brought her mouth to Jones's neck. Jones took in a quick breath, her body lifting with a jerk. Dianna moved so that she was on top of Jones, their chests pressed together. Jones let her hands wander, unclasping Dianna's bra and tossing it to the side. She dragged her fingers over the bumps in Dianna's spine as Dianna kissed her way down Jones's body.

A moan escaped Jones's lips as Dianna positioned herself too far away for Jones to reach. She let Dianna move her legs as Dianna pushed her arms beneath them, cradling her hands beneath Jones's bare butt.

Jones lifted her head to watch, catching the conspiratorial smirk Dianna flashed her before lowering her mouth. Jones's head fell to the floor with a gasp as Dianna circled her clit slowly, with just enough pressure to make stars dance beneath her eyelids as she clinched them closed. She forced her eyes open to watch, wanting to take in as much information as she could. She wanted to be good at this when it was her turn.

Dianna lifted her head, pushing two fingers into her mouth and out again, before inserting them. Jones released a guttural moan. She needed to pee. No, not pee. Pressure was just building up in her stomach. Dianna circled her fingers, mimicking the movements of her tongue. Jones was speaking, maybe, anything but words. Lust-wrapped whimpers spilled from her lips like an ode.

Her legs began to shake, and she pressed her thighs into either side of Dianna's head. Dianna continued, even though Jones had to be squeezing too tight like she was trying to make a melon explode. Dianna moved one of her hands to Jones's stomach, pushing her down into the floor to keep her still. Her tongue was more erratic, the pressure greater as she drove Jones to the edge.

"Please," Jones whispered, before the air shattered open. Her body lifted off the floor as the orgasm ripped through her, her toes so tight she feared they would break off. Her limbs felt separate from her body, far away. She needed to collect them before they got away, she thought, her mind a jumble of kaleidoscope colors. Her heart beat so fast she could feel her pulse behind her eyes.

She felt Dianna crawl back up her body, carrying Jones's scent on her tongue as she kissed her way up Jones's skin. Dianna stroked her face gently, her fingers dipping into Jones's dimples.

"You good?" Dianna asked. Jones, whose eyes were still closed, could not see Dianna's smile, but she could hear it.

Jones smiled, her voice a drawl. "So good." She had never had anything like that happen before. Her body felt elastic.

Dianna lay down beside her, a seductive laugh slipping through her lips. Jones tried to lift herself up, but her limbs felt weighed down. She couldn't control them.

"Hey, hey," Dianna said, her voice soft. She pushed Jones gently back down to the floor.

"It's my turn," Jones slurred.

"How about we rain check?" Dianna said, pulling Jones onto her chest. She held Jones's head like she loved her.

Jones was confused. "What do you mean?" She had never done anything sexual before that hadn't involved any input on her part, though she had had sex several times that hadn't seemed to take her pleasure into account at all. It didn't feel right, taking and not giving.

"I mean, you're tired and you should sleep," Dianna said. She began to hum under her breath, a simple tune that instantly made Jones's eyes feel heavier than they already did.

"I have to," Jones whined, but she was already drifting. Dianna rubbed her back, down and up, down and up. It was soothing. So much so that a tear slipped from Jones's eye and settled just above Dianna's nipple.

Dianna stilled. "Jones?" Jones stayed quiet, silent sobs racking through her. "Jones, are you okay?"

"I'm okay," Jones said with a sniffle. "I just... No one has ever held me before. You know, after."

A deep frown settled onto Dianna's face. Jones hadn't told her much about her ex-boyfriend. She had learned more about him today than she had known prior. And she hated him. Everyone deserved to feel like they were more than just a body to be used up and set aside.

"Well, you're with me now," Dianna said softly, continuing to rub Jones's back.

"Thank my lucky stars," Jones murmured, half-asleep already. Jones's breathing leveled out. The room filled with soft snores once more as Jones slept.

Listening to Jones's rhythmic beating, Dianna slept.

Dianna awoke with a start. Her phone was flashing violently. She had put it on airplane mode to conserve her battery, so she was surprised to see the alert flashing on the screen as three sharp blasts cracked through the air, muffled in their underground room.

She tilted her head to read the most beautiful words she had ever seen on her upside-down phone screen.

"This is an official announcement. Your area is now confirmed 'ALL-CLEAR' from aerial debris. Please exit your shelter safely."

She released a sigh of relief. They were safe. They were alive. They were together. She shook Jones gently, earning a disgruntled groan of a snore.

Reaching for her phone, she turned off airplane mode. The bars were still full, but she had learned that meant little, so she checked Twitter, trying to move as little as possible so as not to wake Jones. She nearly screamed with glee when her home page reloaded with messages from just a few minutes prior.

Jones shifted on her chest. Dianna watched her sleep. She didn't know what would happen when they left here, what reality would look like between them. Would they be enemies again? Would they be friends? Would they be even more than that? That's what she wanted, but she knew it was a big step for Jones.

She checked the time. 6:05 a.m. on Saturday. They had

been here for twelve hours. No one would come in this early on a Saturday. What would it hurt to stay just a bit longer?

So she turned off her phone and slid it to the side. She wrapped her arm tighter around Jones's shoulder, earning a contented sigh in return as Jones burrowed farther in Dianna's chest. And Dianna closed her eyes and went back to sleep.

For now, this was good. So, so good.

★ ★ ★ ★ ★

BUNKER BUDDIES

CHARISH REID

Shea

"Nick, would you like to have coffee with me sometime? I know this great place near campus that has plenty of seating and some nights they have poetry readings. Of course, you're not obligated to participate! I only added it because you're a bookstore man, I mean, a bookstore *owner*. Anyway, the coffee is exquisite—they roast their own beans…" Shea Anderson trailed off with a sigh. "Fuuuuck."

She still stood outside The Page Turner, a bookstore located a few blocks from the University of Chicago, rehearsing her plan of attack. For the last six months, Shea stopped by after teaching just to catch a glimpse at the bookstore owner, Nick Hendrix. Well, more than a glimpse… She actually browsed his collection, pretending to need books she knew he didn't carry. And when she approached his counter for assistance, a bright smile lit his face and creased the tiny wrinkles at the corners of his eyes. So far, Shea had ordered about twenty books just to see that smile.

It was getting out of hand.

She liked supporting a Black indie bookstore as much as the next academic, but her book budget had its limits. Tonight was the night. She'd pick up a book about East German spy craft, but she was finally going to ask him out for coffee. Because coffee was innocent enough. But for now, she just needed to move her ass from the sidewalk to the *inside* of The Page Turner, where the hottest man who ever held books worked. She peeked inside his window and spotted him at the counter.

Shea sucked in a breath as her eyes scanned his body. He was so damn tall…with a lean and muscular build. He could wear anything and his body would make her salivate, but today he wore dark blue jeans and a snug-fitting white T-shirt. His brown biceps stretched at the sleeves, and flexed when he checked his gold wristwatch. Shea fluffed the tight curls of her twist-out and gently exhaled. *Now, or never, bitch.*

As she hitched her purse up her shoulder, Shea pulled open the door. A bell jingled overhead as she passed through the threshold, alerting Nick. His smile popped immediately, bright white against his black beard and smooth dark brown skin. Her heart stuttered in her chest, threatening to stop altogether.

"Ms. Anderson," he said in a low, melodic voice as he stepped away from the counter. "I've got a book for you."

Shea's face grew warm as she stepped up to the polished oak counter with its old-timey cash register. He kept it cleared of extra books and flyers most bookstores might have. In fact, Nick kept his entire store tidy. Not a dust ball or cobweb in sight, and it pleased her immensely. It felt like a little secret she knew about him. Yes, she knew he used to be a photographer and he only took over his grandfather's bookstore a year ago… But she also imagined his clean and spacious apartment, a place where she could slide on polished hardwood floors in her socks.

"Thank you, Nick." She beamed.

He turned on his heel, leaning over his back counter. "You know, I was kind of tempted to thumb through this one," he murmured. "I've heard of the Stasi before, but I didn't know how awful they were. People were really snooping on their neighbors like that?"

He set the book on the counter with a curious expression. It was cute, really. A wrinkle appeared between his thick black brows as he pondered the oppressive regime of East Germany. "Oh, it was terrible," she breathed, excited to talk about her favorite subject. She taught literature, but the Cold War was where her heart belonged. "There's this brilliant movie, *The Lives of Others*. It's about an agent who—"

Brrring, brrring, brrring.

Her phone interrupted her. She fumbled for it, giving him an apologetic smile, and read the phone number. It was her father. "I'm sorry, I need to take this," she said.

Nick waved her off with a gentle smile. "No problem," he whispered.

Shea wandered back to the poetry shelves for privacy. "Hey, Dad, what's up?"

"Nothing much, pumpkin. Your mom and I were just wondering if you wanted to stop by for dinner tonight. She's making shrimp alfredo."

She smiled against her phone. A lovely invitation, but she was on a mission tonight, and could not be deterred. One way or another, she was going to muster up the courage to tell Nick how she felt about him.

Nick

It was hard not to stare at her.

Nick tried to busy himself behind the counter, pretending Shea Anderson's visits weren't the highlight of his week. The incredibly shy professor came by almost weekly, asking for books in that soft breathy voice that always seemed on the verge of an exciting discovery.

All he knew about her was that she was a native Chicagoan, who taught English at U of C. She managed to tell him that much before ordering her books and running away. What he never understood was why a woman who taught English was so obsessed with the KGB, the atomic bomb and the Warsaw Pact. It obviously meant she was a history buff.

And her beauty…well, it was hard not to admire. She usually came to his store wearing a nice blouse and dress pants. But tonight was an exception. Tonight, Shea wore a navy blue dress that kept him staring. The bodice hugged her full bosom, while the neckline was a modest V exposing the top of her nut-brown chest. The wrapped skirt molded the tuck of her waist before draping over her generous hips and down to her dimpled knees. She was a classic beauty, like an actress who shared the screen with Dorothy Dandridge.

Nick imagined photographing her on a warm summer day in Grant Park, beneath the dappling shade of an elm tree. Perhaps she leaned against its trunk, hands clasped behind her back while wearing a coy smile. He could pull dozens of shots of her… He had to shake himself from the fantasy. Focus his attention on his work, what little he had. She was only his third customer that day. Plus, he was no longer a full-time photographer. He'd had to leave the far-reaching wilds of the globe and come back home when his grandfather, Donnie, died. Running The Page Turner wasn't part of Nick's life goals, but he didn't feel right ignoring a be-queathment.

That was a year ago, back when things felt simpler. The world still had climate change, disease and war to contend with. But no one had Imminent Space Debris Hurtling To-ward Earth on that year's bingo cards. When the world dis-covered that a dangerous amount of interstellar projectiles could impact the globe with cataclysmic effects, every world leader had to come together to prepare. This forced America to buckle down and invest in its infrastructure. A jobs bill and enough money to implement a state-of-the-art national alarm system and reopen bunkers from the Cold War.

Nick had read up on it when he left the jungles of Borneo and returned to civilization. While he was lying under swel-tering brush and getting eaten up by fire ants, the world had come up with a plan. When his father, Ike, called him back home to accept the bookstore and the apartment above it, Nick had a jarring moment of confusion. He'd left Chicago, years ago, aching to see the world—to capture its image. Now he was back, stationary and unsure of how to run a business. Also, there might be a day where the world would go up in flames.

That's when Nick made an incredible discovery in his granddad's bookstore.

Actually, below the bookstore.

In the midst of cleaning up Donnie's apartment, he found a key. But neither he nor his dad could find the correspond-ing lock.

"Might wanna check the store," Ike told him after the exhaustive search.

Which was what they did. Behind the counter, the draw-ers in the back office, nothing yielded results. It wasn't until

Nick flopped into his granddad's office chair and tapped his foot beneath the desk, did he hear an odd metallic thud beneath. He remembered that was the moment he and his dad looked at each other with curious expressions.

Together, they pushed the great oak desk, bunching an old oriental rug and scraping the aging wooden floors in the process. Nick had laughed out of nervousness when they found the trapdoor on the floor.

"Goddamn..." his dad murmured, rubbing his chin.

The key fit the lock like something out of an *Indiana Jones* adventure. They went down expecting to find something frightening, but their discovery was much more confusing. A couple of army-issued cots, shelves of canned food, a few lanterns...a tiny bathroom. "Granddaddy was a prepper?" Nick had asked, in awe of the small space.

While Nick quickly learned the ins and outs of running a bookstore, he slowly worked on the upstairs apartment and the bunker. His new living space came together easily. Ordering new cookery and a bed was far simpler than dealing with a subterranean survival room. But there was a benefit to owning a bookstore. Nick was able to order prepper guides and read them while customers filed in and out of his store.

What he hadn't counted on was meeting Professor Anderson.

The first time she walked into his store with those surprised bunny eyes and warm smile, Nick lost his breath. He would have asked her out for a coffee that day but changed his mind when she nervously searched his shelves and stumbled over her words. Maybe she wasn't interested, he thought. Maybe hollering at female customers was a bad idea. But she kept returning. Each book she ordered made her blush, nibble her plump bottom lip and stutter her words.

When she wasn't in his bookstore, he pictured her at the front of the classroom wearing those cute professional clothes, or at home wearing glasses while she graded papers. Possibly wearing an oversized sweater that came to the tops of her thighs, nothing underneath…

"My parents wanted me to come over for dinner." Her quiet voice permeated his lust-filled imagination.

It snapped Nick from his thoughts long enough to blush from embarrassment. "My dad is like that too. Always checking to see if I'm eating."

Did he imagine her eyes darting over his body? She licked her bottom lip before averting her gaze and sweeping a glossy black curl behind her ear. "You look like you stay in shape," she offered, but then her brow shot up to her hairline. "I meant—not that I'm looking at—I didn't mean anything by that!" Shea squeaked.

Nick chuckled, waving his hands. "You're fine, Shea. I appreciate it." He picked up her book. "Did you still wanna browse, or would you like to check out?"

He didn't want her to leave so quickly, but if she needed to, Nick had slipped a message in her book order. He'd wanted to give her his phone number for a while, hoping he hadn't misread her constant visits.

After her twenty-second book order, he said, "Fuck that" and decided to shoot his shot. No harm in trying…

Shea

Now was the moment to ask Nick out on a date. What was the worst that could happen? His bright smile could dim into a pitying closed-lipped grimace before telling her he had a gorgeous girlfriend waiting for him at their home. No big deal.

"I was wondering," she started, eyes glancing between his beautiful face to her book order. "If you had time..." She gestured to his shop. "I know you're busy running a business, but if you're interested in maybe having some coffee, I know a place near—"

Before she could finish her sentence, the lights in the store flickered twice and a deafening siren, from the streets, filled the air. The noise came from nowhere but settled over them like a chest-rattling blanket. Shea screamed in fright as she quickly looked around for the answers she already had.

It was the Global Warning System alerting them that space projectiles would soon impact the Earth. Unfortunately, it was blaring days before the first scheduled drill. Americans had marked next Wednesday on their calendars...so this was something entirely different. This was the real thing. If the event was to occur outside of school hours, Shea's shelter plan involved grabbing her go bag and running from her apartment, near Hyde Park, back to campus. But she was in Nick's store, and couldn't think of Chicago's layout with that roaring siren.

Nick jumped into action, moving from the counter to the front door. From where she stood, she saw people running for cover. She wondered if she should also get going.

"Do you trust me?" Nick shouted from the door, peeking out the window at the scattering citizens of Chicago.

Shea didn't know how to answer. A few seconds ago, she was trying to ask the man out on a date. Now the world was about to end. "I...um..." She checked her phone. What about her parents? At home with their shrimp alfredo? They would be safe in their basement. The house might take a good thumping, but the basement was solid.

"Shea, I can take you someplace safe, but we have to go now."

"Yes." Her voice shook as she nodded, but she quickly squared her shoulders and said in a louder voice, "Let's go!"

Nick locked his door, flipped the Open sign in the window to Closed and extinguished all of the store lights. In the sudden darkness, Shea's heart leaped to her throat as she threw her hands out in front of her. "Nick?"

She felt his muscular chest against her arm. "I'm here, I'm here. Just watch your step and follow me."

His arm wrapped around her shoulder as he guided her toward the back of the store. She turned the flashlight of her phone on and held it aloft as they walked. "Do you have a basement or something?" she asked, trying not to lean heavily into his chest. His warm spiced cologne made that difficult, but she marched on with dignity.

Nick chuckled as he steered her into an office and closed the door behind them. "You could say that. Stand here for a second."

She stopped near the door and pointed her bright white light in Nick's direction. The siren's drone still blaring with the same intensity.

Nick used all of his strength to push the heavy wooden desk at the center of the room. After a couple feet, he paused to squat behind it. When he was out of view, Shea pulled her purse tighter to her body and took a tentative step forward, casting her light over the desk. "Nick…"

A metal door swung upward and Nick reappeared, holding out his hand. "Let's go!"

As Shea rounded the desk, her mouth fell open when she saw the trapdoor in the floor. "Oh my god," she breathed, shining her light down into a black hole. Steep steps led down to more darkness, but she didn't have time to be scared. She trusted Nick, took his hand and carefully followed him down.

Down into a 1960s era bunker.

The temperature grew cooler the farther they descended. Shea took his hand and carefully followed him down. When she reached the bottom, Nick ran back up the stairs and slammed the trapdoor shut.

Her phone beeped. Alerting her that her phone's battery was at five percent. She sighed loudly, surprised to realize that she could now hear herself. The concrete muffled most of the terrifying reality above them, the siren now only a dull tone. Would the walls also mute the crashing sounds that were sure to follow? She tried to shake the awful thought from her mind and remembered that three sharp siren blasts would alert them that the danger had passed.

Before Shea could choose between her phone's battery or its flashlight, Nick was back downstairs and at her side. He flipped the switch nearby, illuminating the subterranean space with a warm, earthy glow. "We're safe," he said in a resolute tone that matched his serious expression. Shea knew he told the truth.

"Okay," she said, nodding. "Thank you." She looked around the space, taking it in, and resigned herself to ride out the storm. But as far as bunkers went, Nick's was quite lovely. The underground dwelling was large enough to hold a plush love seat, a queen-sized bed and a tiny kitchenette that held an incredible amount of nonperishable food...and booze. "This is amazing."

He moved around her, gesturing at the room. "Would you like a tour?" he chuckled.

Despite the strange situation they found themselves in,

Shea had to grin at how proud of himself he was. "Please! How on earth did you get everything down that trapdoor?"

"I got the bed and mattress, the couch and the table set from IKEA. I found some of the small accents from places here and there." He walked toward a door at the end of the room. "I don't know how my granddad managed it, but we have a tiny toilet and sink as well."

"Incredible…"

Nick rubbed his hands on his jeans as he sat on the sofa. "So, I guess we'll just camp out here until the coast is clear?"

Shea looked around for an appropriate place to sit. Like a magnet, she crossed the short distance toward the couch and sat beside him. "I suppose so. I have to assume that my parents are safe in their basement." She sighed, remembering how frightening the threat of space junk had been. "I hope that my students and colleagues have found a safe place too."

Nick leaned forward, resting his elbows on his knees. "I'll bet they have. We've all spent a lot of time preparing for this. My dad is at home watching the game and I know he's got a fridge stocked with the essentials."

"So that just leaves us…" she murmured. "Alone. In a bunker." Saying the words aloud felt scary and exciting, like the evening was full of mysterious possibilities.

"Yeah." Nick pressed his lips together and looked at the floor. "I hope you're not too upset, Shea. This probably wasn't how you wanted to spend your evening."

Boy, oh boy, that couldn't be further from the truth. "Well, no one wanted this—" she gestured to the world above them "—but I'm really grateful that you were prepared. And that your grandfather had some forethought," she quickly added.

His beautiful smile reappeared, melting her heart into a puddle of warm goo. "I'm relieved to hear it." His voice dropped to a low octave. "You sounded like you wanted to ask me something up there."

Shea's breath caught in her throat. Had she imagined it, or did he get closer than he was seconds ago? His body heat and scent seemed to permeate not only the air, but her skin. She opened her mouth, praying that her words would come out in some intelligible order.

Nick

It appeared that the words were on the tip of her tongue.

She worried at the fabric of her dress, wound her fingers around each other and her skin flushed an unexpected dark rouge. Nick desperately wanted her to speak, to say anything that validated what he'd felt for the past few months. He wouldn't normally take this long to approach a woman, but he'd been off his game since taking over the business. His focus was now invoices, taxes and space junk.

Even if she might want to go on a date with him, Nick worried that he didn't bring enough to Shea's table. She was a smart, professional woman who was probably climbing the ranks at her university. While he had plenty of stories about getting lost in some exotic city, that life was now in the past. He was a floundering business owner now.

"Coffee," she finally uttered.

He smiled. "Coffee?"

They locked eyes, and for a moment, Nick thought she might chicken out. But her pensive expression relaxed when her eyes darted to his mouth. Shea took another deep breath, and blurted out, "I've been trying to work up the nerve to ask you out on a date. Nothing too big, just coffee. Before the entire world went to hell in a handbasket, I was going to tell you about this nice coffee shop near campus, where there were poetry readings. If you're into that kind of thing, it's okay—"

"Shea," he interrupted, placing a hand on her arm. She paused to glance at his arm. "I'd love to have coffee with you."

"Yeah?"

The tension in his chest uncoiled as he slid his hand down her arm to one of her busy hands. He gave it a gentle squeeze before letting her go. "I guess I was waiting for you to make a move. I hoped that you coming by every week wasn't just about the books. I mean, I don't mind ordering them, but you spend so much money at my store that I think I might need to start you on a punch card."

She laughed that time, a husky chuckle that shook her shoulders and made his own relax. "You probably think I'm silly." She sighed, shaking her head.

"I think you're very beautiful," he said seriously. "But I'd love to get to know you more."

Shea's smile reappeared. "Yeah?"

"Yes, ma'am. I even left my phone number in your book order."

"Really?"

Nick shrugged. "I figured after fifty-'leven orders, I might need to help you along."

"I think you're really handsome," she blurted out. "As long as we're confessing things in a bunker."

His face warmed upon hearing her admission. "Thank you."

"Oh god," she said, bringing her hands to her cheeks. "I can't believe this is happening."

Nick leaned back on the sofa. "This, being the emergency or what you just said?"

"Yes." She sighed. "I mean—"

He laughed heartily. Shea Anderson was a trip and getting to know her would be a delight. "You're fine. Let's just get comfortable down here, plug in our phones and wait for the all-clear. Although, I never got around to getting a radio…"

"I don't have my phone charger," Shea said with a frown. "It's in my car."

"Don't worry," he said, patting his pocket. "I've got mine."

Little good it would do though. Nick quickly understood the drawback of holing up in a concrete bunker with an already mediocre cell service.

"You've got no signal, right?" Shea asked.

He shook his head. "Nothing," he said. "But I got another charger down here somewhere. I'll hook you up and we'll keep an eye on things. Never know when the danger might pass. We're supposed to hear three blasts for the all-clear, right?"

She nodded, but anxiety furrowed her brow and made her nibble on her bottom lip.

He stood from the sofa and offered his hand to her. "Come on," Nick said with a smile. "We're going to take that tour and I'll show you what kind of amenities you can expect at Hotel Hendrix."

When she took his hand, warmth traveled up his arm and sent a shiver down his back. "This is exciting," she teased.

"Over here, I've got the bathroom, complete with a standard toilet and sink. For as long as the plumbing lasts."

Shea peeked past him and inspected the tiny closet. "Ooh, look at that Dial soap…and all these face towels."

"I keep plenty on hand," he said, steering her toward the kitchenette. "This right here is the breakfast nook/bistro corner." Nick made a big show of placing a hand on the table-top and moving it back and forth. "You'll notice there is no annoying wobble."

Shea nodded with approval while hiding her smirk behind her hand. "You're quite the IKEA craftsman."

"I am. The pantry is mostly full of nonperishable snacks and canned foods. A lot of bottled water and a ton of alcohol." He pointed to the bed on the opposite side of the room. "Past the living room, you'll find the bedroom. A queen-sized bed. The mattress has a long Swedish name that had little dots over some of the letters."

"So you know it's legit."

"I know we were supposed to start with coffee, but would you like a cocktail for now?"

"Yes, please," she said, glancing through his booze collection. She picked up a bottle of Stoli Vodka and presented it to him. "This is probably the best option for a Cold War bunker."

Nick leaned on his incredibly stable table and stared at her. Her dark eyes twinkled with mirth as she bit her bottom lip. He suddenly wished he could kiss that lip, suck it between his own and give it a soft bite. He wondered what sound she'd make.

"Nick?"

He blinked, embarrassed by where his mind had taken him. "Yeah, vodka is perfect," he said. "Lemme get the glasses."

Shea

On her second cocktail, Shea felt comfortable enough to ask Nick about his life. So far, he'd only asked her about herself, which she found delightfully surprising. In the past, she'd had the misfortune of having first dates with men who only spoke about themselves and barely let her get a word in. And since she'd dated men in academia, the chatter was mostly about *their* work, *their* publications, *their* research aspirations.

Because Nick was an engaged listener, she was able to share bits of her life. Stuff she found mundane, but he seemed interested enough. He sat relaxed, facing her with one ankle on his knee and his arm lying on the back of the couch.

"But enough about me," she said, settling into her end of the couch, cradling her vodka tonic. "I've been going on and on about my family and school. I'd love to know more about your photography career. What's it like? Who did you work for? Where's the loveliest place you've been?"

He chuckled as he leaned in for a sip of his drink. "I haven't shot anything in a year, and I don't know when I'll get back into it," he admitted, his smile dipping as he examined his glass. Shea caught the brief change to his expression and wondered what it meant.

A man as urbane as Nick probably missed being on the road and probably found Chicago boring. And she never got to go anywhere... Was she boring too? The instant she'd learned he was a magazine photographer, she worried she was pining for a man who would just leave if the right opportunity arose. Imagining his adventurous life before they met made her hesitant to approach him. What if he wasn't finished traveling the world?

"But to answer your question, I've freelanced for a few cool publications. Have you ever read *Afar Magazine*?"

She nodded. "I have! It's one of my favorite travel magazines."

Nick ducked his head as a grin returned to his face. "Yeah, well, I did a spread for the Orient Express about three years ago," he said. "I'm pretty proud of that one."

Shea gasped. "It's my dream to ride the Orient Express,"

she said in a hushed voice, clutching her drink closer to her chest. "What was it like? What route did you go?"

He tilted his head back as if to recall the trip. "We started in Paris...which was kind of a mess actually. Me and the writer, a guy named Henri, got mad drunk the night before. I mean stumbling-through-the-streets drunk before we fell out in our hotel room. I think I slept on the floor. We woke up late and fled the room, just hauling ass to the train station..."

Shea giggled as she listened, imagining two hungover men running down the cobblestone streets, luggage flapping in the wind.

"When I tell you Parisians were looking at us like we were out of our minds... Man, I didn't care. *Afar* had paid out the nose for those tickets, the assignment was supposed to be for the holiday travel issue and we were on a tight deadline. I just hate that Henri convinced me that another round of tequila was a good idea."

Shea laughed at the foolishness. "I'm assuming you guys made it?"

"Just barely," Nick said, taking another sip. "As soon as we found our train car, we were out like a light again, trying to sleep off our hangovers. Luckily, the trip was four nights because we didn't get to work until the next day. On day three, we ended up in Budapest, where we stayed in a hotel and saw the city. I got some great nightlife shots, didn't drink as much," he said, holding up a finger, "and we headed back to Paris the next day without problem."

"What was the most beautiful part of the trip?" Shea asked.

"The Alps," he answered quickly. "No doubt."

"Do you miss it? Being out in the world like that? The farthest I've ever been was Mexico for a conference," she said, cautiously.

Nick ran a finger along his bottom lip as his gaze slipped back toward his glass. He waited a beat before nodding slowly. "Sometimes," he said in a thoughtful voice. "I don't necessarily miss sorting out visas and customs, or trying to find sim cards so I can call my dad. I guess I just miss the art. Like I said, I haven't shot anything in a while."

"I'm sorry it's been a while," she said. His voice was full of so much longing that it tugged at her heart and made her want to hug him.

But he brightened when he looked up at her face. "Oh, don't feel bad for me," he said quickly. "I'm not in a bad position at all. Because I lived on the road for so many years, I saved a good deal of money. I'm comfortable. I now own the store and the apartment above. I'm back home with my dad, which is good. I like being able to keep an eye on him."

"And your mom?"

Nick nodded. "Yeah, she passed when I was a teenager."

"I'm sorry to hear that."

"Thank you. Dad and I hung in there though. Having a large family outside of us helped."

Shea almost didn't know what to do with her hands. They were itching to cross the space separating them to touch his leg. She was no longer in the position of thirsting over the man from afar, she was now sitting with him and conversing about their lives. The intimacy of their bunker chat was overwhelming, it made her want to snuggle against his arm while they drank.

"And besides, I've met a lot of interesting people while running the bookstore."

She leaned forward. "Oh yeah?"

Merriment danced in his eyes as he looked her over. Shea's face heated up from the Stoli and his intense appraisal. His gaze lingered on her neckline, sending waves of warmth down her belly. If he kept looking at her like that for too long, her panties would disintegrate. "I get the occasional customer looking for this novel or that, which is easy to hunt down. But every week, I get the same beautiful woman in my store, looking for some history book I never have. I'm beginning to wonder if she has very niche reading tastes or if she's ordering hard-to-find books on purpose."

The amusement that played on his smile was just as sexy as his other smiles, sending a wave of arousal throughout her body. Shea no longer wanted to give him a comforting touch; she wanted to settle onto his lap and give him a long, heated kiss. But she also wanted to mind her manners. Just because she was in a bunker didn't mean she got to act a fool. She'd made it this far, but what if this was just a lusty bunker haze? If they were lucky enough to return to the surface, could they continue?

She took a deep breath and searched her mind for something intelligent to say while he watched her with those dark sable-colored eyes. "Um…"

Nick

Nick had hoped she didn't mind a little verbal teasing, because he quite liked seeing her blush. It made him wonder if other teasing was on the table. Did she like her earlobes nibbled on? Was she into scratchy beard kisses along the length of her neck? How would she respond to his fingers and lips dipping farther below?

Never before had he wanted to learn more about a woman.

After years of being on the road and living out of a suitcase, a proper relationship with another person seemed nearly impossible. He had believed his instinct for romance had long disappeared after being a loner. And now, Nick was starved for the intimacy Shea offered under these extreme circumstances. He enjoyed her attention, but he struggled to keep his excitement in check. He still had doubts that he could be the kind of guy who could measure up to her. A guy who had only learned he had to pay property taxes a few months ago…

She pressed her lips together as her eyes darted to her lap. "Um…"

"I'm teasing," he said, trying to release her from any building anxiety.

"No! I know, I just…well, I guess I wasn't as subtle as I thought. You're very—" she gestured at him, her hand moving up and down "—and I'm terrible at saying what's on my mind. So, yeah, books."

"Let's just start with the basics," he said, shifting in his seat, moving a smidge closer to her. "You like ordering books from me?"

"Love it," she breathed, leaning against the back of the couch.

"And you love the Cold War?"

"Definitely." Shea nodded.

"Why?"

She shrugged. "I suppose it started with my dad. He watched all kinds of WWII movies and television shows. But I fell in love with the postwar stuff. The *Mission Impossible* series, the Jack Ryan movies of the '90s, and everything in between. My dad and I share all that stuff."

"Why not study history then?" Nick asked.

"I'm really a literature person. I love teaching students about stories, and I'm incredibly lucky to do it. But I love this other part of my life too, and some things are worth keeping to myself."

"Well, I thank you for sharing the Cold War with me."

Shea grinned. "I have?"

Maybe it was the vodka, maybe it was the cozy concrete structure they were stuck in, but he wanted to share all of his feelings from the past year. Losing his grandfather and gaining this gift was an abrupt change for Nick to deal with, and he often felt like he was still trying to catch up. "I've learned a lot from your books," he admitted. "I read through some of them before I gave them to you, and they helped me with this bunker."

Her face was like the sun shining after a cloudy day. Her smile beamed radiance in their dim setting and made him want to return the favor. "You're serious?" she asked.

He nodded. "I didn't know what I was going to do with this space, but I think those books gave me some historical context to deal with a new version of my life. If I'm going to be stuck here, in one place…why not make a game out of it?"

Shea raised a brow as she looked him over. "A game?"

Nick gestured behind him to the kitchenette. "Okay, so this probably sounds mad corny, but while I was getting my food together, I imagined I was caught by the Russians on the Finnish border," he chuckled, feeling a little embarrassed. "I forget which book—"

"*The Winter War*," she finished. "When the Soviets bombed Helsinki in 1939."

"Yeah, that's it."

She stared at him with dreamy eyes before murmuring, "That's so hot."

Nick raised a brow at the shift in her energy. Shea was now leaning forward, hanging on his every word. Her dark brown eyes glazed with…lust? Or was it vodka? He leaned forward in an unconscious response. "I went to Helsinki once," he said, attempting to impress her with another exotic locale.

"Really? What did you think?" Shea's eyes dropped to his mouth; Nick was certain of it. Her gaze lingered while he spoke.

"I thought it was more fun than Stockholm. The Finns are interesting people. But I want to get back to what you said earlier," he said.

Her intense gaze broke, and her eyes landed on his. "What did I say?"

"'That's so hot.' What did you mean by that?"

Shea licked her lips before pressing her glass to her mouth. "It's ridiculous," she said after taking another sip. "I don't know why I said that."

"But you do," he pressed gently. "I want an idea of how to impress you when we eventually get coffee."

Her face broke into another wide grin as she rolled her eyes. "You're already impressive," she chuckled.

Nick crossed the divide and took her hand; he hoped it wouldn't scare her off. Shea's hand was warm, slightly sweaty, but her fingers tightened around his just slightly. "Tell me," he said.

She pressed her glass against her neck and murmured, "Does it feel warm in here?"

"Yes."

She gave a shaky sigh. "I'm sorry for sounding so nervous, but I don't find myself in these situations, like ever. I've been thinking about you for the last six months. And now that I'm stuck with you—not stuck—now that we're together… I find out you're not only incredibly handsome, but worldly—

and you think about the Soviets capturing you. You're very hot, Nick Hendrix."

He struggled not to squeeze her hand after that admission.

So Nick shifted even closer until they were knee-to-knee on the small couch. No other woman had ever described him like Shea had, and listening to her was a heady experience. "You're gorgeous and incredibly intelligent, Shea Anderson," he replied, pulling her small hand to his chest. "You stay on my mind throughout the week. I have to wait until you come back to my store every Friday, and I *hate* the waiting."

"Oh damn," she breathed. Her face was only inches away from his as her palm pressed against his heart. "I want to kiss you so hard."

"We don't have to wait now," he said, wondering if she could feel how fast his heart pounded. As he tried to keep his excitement in check, Shea nervously licked her lips again. As if she was preparing herself for something big. Nick wanted to give her enough room to navigate the situation, so he waited for her to make the first move.

Shea

Chaos swirled in her mind as Shea held on to Nick's chest. Her fingers grazed what felt like a lump of marble beneath his T-shirt, but under that muscle was a very human heart. Alive and beating hard for her. He'd given her explicit permission to reach out and take what she wanted from him, but Shea couldn't bring herself to act upon it. She stopped right before his face, feeling his hot breath feather against her lips, and seized up. Her brain glitched.

Even while staring into his dark brown eyes, long black lashes and heavy brow. Even while he licked his full lips in preparation…her mind raced with the same persistent doubts.

This is only temporary.
He's a rolling stone.
You're moving too fast.

Shea sat up straight and left his personal space. "I'm sorry," she said, mortified by her indecision. "I don't know what I was trying to do there."

Shea didn't realize her hand was still pressed to Nick's chest until he returned it to her lap. He gave her a devilish smirk as he sat back. "You're being adorable, Shea," he said, standing from the couch. "Would you like anything else to drink? Water?"

She shook her head. "I'm still working on this."

He made a leisurely stroll back to this tiny kitchen. "I haven't had a vodka and tonic in a long time. I'm more of a bourbon man, but this is pretty refreshing."

"Do you ever drink gin?" she asked, thankful for the swift change in subject. Kissing him shouldn't have been this difficult, but Shea was in the middle of a dry spell and was seriously doubting her seduction game. She felt like a kid standing on the edge of double Dutch ropes, trying to find the perfect moment to jump.

Nick's deep hearty laugh came from his belly. "My father is the gin drinker, so no. Nothing against my old man, but I'm still in that phase where I'm not ready to be him or deal with my mortality."

She found his honesty endearing, if not a little irrational. Nick looked and felt virile, while she felt like much of her life had slipped through her fingers. She'd spent most of her twenties trying to earn a terminal degree so that she could work her thirties toward tenure. "How old are you?" she asked as he returned to the couch to place his glass on the coffee table.

"I'm thirty-nine, you?"

"I'm thirty-five," Shea said.

"Oh, so you grown enough to know what's going on in my record collection," Nick said, moving toward an old milk crate she'd missed on the tour. A couple dozen vinyl records filled the basket sitting beside a record player and small flat-screen TV. "I forgot to show you the entertainment center," he said with a cheeky grin.

Shea immediately got up to investigate. "Ooh, Sam Cooke *Live at the Harlem Square Club 1963*?"

Nick slipped the vinyl from the stack and held it before her. "You like Sam?"

"Yes, but I especially love *this* album." She looked up at him and grinned. "You got this from your old man, huh?"

He rolled his eyes. "Alright now, Sam Cooke's an honorary Chicago native. Everybody here loves him."

"You wanna argue or do you wanna listen?"

He faced her with the album in front of him. "I'll do you one better—would you like to twist the night away?"

"You want to dance with me?"

Nick held out his hand. "I do."

Shea didn't think. She tossed back the rest of her drink and set the empty glass on the coffee table. "Okay."

Soon, a liquored-up Miami crowd rose from the speakers as Sam Cooke was introduced. The warm stereo sounds filled the tiny bunker and made her shiver with anticipation. *Girl, get out your head and get into his arms... Let him hold you.*

The two vodka tonics she poured herself were working their magic, but she'd need to do the rest. So, she stepped to him, a little clumsily, but he caught her by the waist. Together, they laughed it off and he held her as they swayed to the first song.

"Alright now," Nick chuckled, drawing her closer. "'Feel It... Don't Fight It.'"

Her gaze flew to his smiling face. "Is that the first song?"

"Is it?"

Shea playfully slapped his muscular chest and rolled her eyes. "Okay, Mr. Hendrix."

"Tell me something," he said in a soft voice. "What does a beautiful woman like you like to do when the world *isn't* on fire? What would you normally be doing on a Friday night?"

"Probably reading," she said, glancing at their feet. Shea's dance skills were a little rusty, and she had hoped she wouldn't step on his toes. "Or watching movies. Something quiet."

"I bet performing for students all week takes it out of you," Nick said as he pulled away and let her spin beneath his hand.

She landed the twirl without bumping into him. When he pulled her back into his embrace, his hand settled on the small of her back, a soft reminder of the tenderness he displayed on the couch. What's more, she was a bit surprised by his reaction to her answer. He sounded as if he understood why she led a quiet life. Her friends often called, begging her to leave her apartment, not understanding how she only wanted to rest.

"It's true," she said, gazing up at him. "After a week of being in everyone's face, I really don't mind alone time."

He nodded. "I get that. I enjoyed that part of traveling too. There's something to be said about solitude. Being alone doesn't mean you're lonely."

Even while deep in thought, Nick's hips kept time with the rhythm of the drums and brass. The more she moved with him, the more her body relaxed and swayed with his. "You're right, there's a difference. I guess I'm mindful of how

I spend my days off. I love a good brunch with my friends, but when I get home, I crawl into my cozy cocoon."

"Ooh, what's in your cocoon?" he asked, spinning her again. "FDR documentaries?"

She laughed as she twirled, feeling a lot steadier on her feet than when they first started. "Maybe a couple documentaries…but mostly soaking in my tub with candles and a good book."

He groaned deeply as he drew her back into his arms. A sexy sound that vibrated through her chest and clenched her pussy. Sam began singing his famous hit "Cupid" when Nick's hand rubbed her back in small circles. "How about the cucumber slices on the eyes? You got those too?"

Shea barely heard his question, as she was too focused on the heat between them. She reveled in the comfort of his large hands holding her. She lost herself in the scent of his cologne, a delightful citrus musk that made her eyes fall shut. "Sure," she said absently as she pulled her hand from his grasp.

She wrapped her arms around his neck, and both of his hands fell to her hips. They danced slower than the music's tempo, but it didn't matter. Soon, the two began dancing in a world to themselves, far away from the Miami nightclub crowd screaming for Sam. Far from the madness of the outside.

No one existed outside of this man.

"Can I tell you a secret?" she asked him.

His full lips quirked into a half smile as he stared down at her. "Of course, you can."

Shea stopped dancing and held him in place. Was she about to make a huge mistake? Possible. Was she drunk with lust, in the arms of a superhot bookseller? Yes, and she didn't want the moment to pass her by. "When you said that you imagined being held captive, it took my mind places. It made me want to ask for something I haven't had."

Nick raised a brow, but his hands never left her hips. If anything, he gripped her tighter. "Where did your mind go, and what do you want to ask?"

Shea took a deep breath and released a torrent of words. "I know we haven't kissed yet, but when we do, I have a certain way I want to be seduced. I've never asked this of anyone, but I'm really into the idea of role-playing. I really, really want to have sex with you. Tonight, while the world is on fire. I hope I'm not being too presumptuous."

Eventually, she stopped speaking, but couldn't bring herself to look up.

Because the silence was too much to bear, Shea opened her mouth to apologize, but Nick beat her to the punch. He took her by the chin, pulled her face upward and said, "It sounds like I need to kiss you now. Because I really want to learn how to seduce you properly."

Perhaps being embarrassingly honest helped nudge the ball forward because Nick captured her mouth in a swift movement. His lips caught her off guard but gave her exactly what she needed. As their tongues met and mingled, Shea couldn't stop the moan against his mouth. She delighted in the sensation of his soft beard brushing against her cheek. The way his hands quickly left her hips to cradle the back of her neck. She melted in his embrace, tempted to grind herself against his hard body.

Their kiss was just as decadent as she thought it would be. And the more she sipped from him, the faster scorching arousal swept through her body, setting fire to her chest. Shea absently wondered if the way he sucked and nibbled on her bottom lip was a preview of what else he could do with his mouth. He dragged her closer to his body and she inhaled as much of his sinful cologne as she could. The spicy citrus, mixed with the cocoa butter on his beard, made the edges of her brain hazy with desire. But before she could collapse into a desperate frenzy, Nick saved her by pulling away from her face.

She wove on her feet in a drunken daze. "You're an amazing kisser," she murmured while her eyes fluttered shut.

Nick's large hands slid down her back before returning to her hips. "And you're a gifted liar, Ms. Perez," he murmured in a soft voice.

Shea's eyes sprang open. "Huh?"

He released her and took a step back. The smirk on his face confused the hell out of her. "You may have fooled our other CIA operatives, but you didn't count on meeting me."

It took a moment for her lust-addled brain to catch up with his words, but when Shea understood, her jaw dropped. *Oh my god, he's really doing this…* Jesus, he was a keeper. Although this was her secret sexy fantasy to rule all fantasies, Shea wasn't great at improvised acting.

But if Nick was trying, she was sure as shit gonna try too.

"Excuse me?" she asked in an indignant tone. She had the feeling that a "Ms. Perez" would deny her identity until she bit down on the cyanide pill in her back molar. But since this was Nick, Shea would probably give up all kinds of national secrets if he kissed her again.

"Don't play dumb with me," he said, walking a circle around her. When he disappeared from view, he leaned down and whispered in her ear, "Was this what you had in mind? This isn't too corny, is it?"

She shook her head. "No, this is perfect, Nick."

"You're also an amazing kisser," he replied in a soft voice. "I wanted to return the compliment before getting too carried away."

Shea fought to keep from giggling, but he was being too damned adorable. "Thank you," she whispered while grinning hard.

"I've been watching you for a while, Vera Perez," he said, returning to his stern daddy voice, which absolutely drenched her panties. "I suspected you were a Cuban national, but what I don't know…is how long have you been spying on the United States?"

Okay, so the addition of *Vera* was a little too much. Nick was interrogating a woman he'd named after "truth"? Every little detail of this game made her silently squee with excitement. She craned her neck to look behind her and said in a haughty tone, "I don't know what you're talking about. My name is… Catherine Parsons and I'm just a secretary."

Nick ran his fingers down her back, leaving a trail of shivers ending at the base of her spine. As good as the sensation felt, Shea remained still, eager to see where he'd lead her in their little dance. "When was the last time you checked in with your handler?"

He still hid from her view when he asked the question. Leaving her to comfortably roll her eyes to the ceiling as she thought. *Would Vera have a handler?* "I don't have a—"

"—not anymore. Mateo was found dead this morning," Nick said as he stepped before her. "Which means you're in trouble, Ms. Perez. Because whoever wanted Mateo out of the picture will soon want to tie off the other loose end."

Shea raised a brow as she stared Nick down. "I'm not a loose end."

Nick's eyes roved over her face before his gaze dropped to her body. His mouth curved at one corner, giving her a slick grin. "You sound sure about that."

Before she could return a witty comeback, he turned on his heel, walked to the kitchenette and retrieved a chair. When he returned, he placed it before her and took a seat.

"I think I'll leave," Shea said, placing her hands on her hips. "You don't have enough to keep me here, Agent..."

"Roberts. You can call me Agent Roberts," he finished, before gesturing to the bed behind her. "And I have more than enough to keep you here. Why don't you just take a seat, Ms. Perez."

Behind her, Nick's bed. Before her, Nick sitting with his back erect, legs astride and looking as severe as any 1950s G-man. *Oh well, I suppose I'm stuck.* Shea smoothed her shirt down as she sat. "You have the wrong woman, Agent Roberts, really," she said, folding her hands on her lap, "this is quite an embarrassment to your nation."

Suddenly, he pulled his chair forward so that he sat directly in front of her. Only a couple inches separated their knees as he leaned forward, piercing her with a glare. "*My* nation?" he asked.

Ah, shit.

"You know what I meant," Shea said quickly, brushing a curl behind her ear.

"And what's your outfit called? Castro's Cuties? Havana's Honeypots?"

"How incredibly offensive, Agent Roberts," she replied, rolling her eyes. "I'd hate to think that's how you view women."

Nick narrowed his eyes as he rubbed his chin. "My apologies, Ms. Perez."

"Ms. Parsons."

"I tailed you to the café where you meet with Mateo."

Shea crossed her arms across her chest. "I don't know what you mean."

Nick leaned with his forearms against his knees, his fingers brushing against the fabric of her skirt. "It was raining when you rushed across Dupont Circle. You wore a dress, not unlike the one you're wearing today, except it was red. Because no matter how much you blend into your new American life, you can't let go of your Communist past, can you?"

Shea's eyes darted back to Nick in fascination as he spun his little tale. He was really getting into this... And she was getting more and more turned on. She imagined herself in Washington, DC, running through the rain, trying to look cool while looking for the next message from her handler, a dead drop under a park bench perhaps.

"You stopped on Connecticut Avenue, under an awning for The Newsroom. You shook out your umbrella and fluffed your curls in spite of the heavy humidity. Mateo chose The Newsroom, didn't he? But you wanted something nicer, more upscale. A place as pretty as you. A bistro to eat small cakes and drink even smaller cups of espresso. But you go where he tells you to go...where the *syndicate* tells you to go. Sometimes he meets you inside with a cold sandwich and stale coffee. Other times, he just leaves you messages in *Le Monde*. But he didn't meet you, or leave a message yesterday."

Fully wrapped up in Nick's story, Shea found herself leaning forward. "What happened to Mateo?"

Nick

Yes, what happened to Mateo, indeed... Nick didn't know where he was going with this diatribe, but he loved how into it Shea appeared. Her expression was full of wonder and curiosity as he described his favorite convenience store in Washington, DC. Years back, when he went to Howard, he stopped at The Newsroom to pick up a number of international magazines and newspapers. And while he didn't read French, he still picked up a copy of *Le Monde* for him and his Senegalese roommate to pour over.

It shocked him how easy it felt to slip into another character. He loved how she just fell into the game as well. After all the books he'd thumbed through, it made perfect sense for Shea to be a Cuban spy. She was certainly gorgeous enough to be a femme fatale moonlighting as a secretary.

"Mateo is dead."

Shea's eyes widened, but he could tell she searched her mind for her next line. She sighed heavily, her shoulders slumping in resignation. "Was it you?" she asked.

Nick shook his head. "No. Believe it or not, Langley didn't take him out."

"But Langley offered him a deal, right?" she asked, leaning forward. "And you're going to offer me the same deal, Agent Roberts."

"Is that a question or a demand?"

"It's reality," Shea replied in a dry tone. "Mateo was a double agent, and apparently not a good one. He had been here longer than I, but got soft and enjoyed the comforts your decadent nation offered. The fact that no one from home has informed me of his now…vacated post, leads me to believe I'm next." She looked him up and down with a shrewd gaze that made Nick shockingly hard.

Goddamn… He could imagine her in some sparsely furnished safe house, going over her options in her head, while inching her way toward a hidden revolver. Nick was so preoccupied with the thought of her trying to kill him for Castro, he almost didn't hear her speak.

"Isn't that what you believe?" she asked, pulling him from his thoughts. "Isn't that why I'm here?"

Nick danced his fingertips along the fabric hugging her thighs. He imagined untying her dress at the waist like a ribbon on a present, unwrapping what he most desired. Shea let out a soft exhale and leaned back on his mattress as his hand moved to the hem at her knees. "You think I have a deal to offer you?"

"I hate repeating myself," Shea said, letting her thighs fall open just a few inches. His hand slipped to the inside of her leg, stroking the soft skin at her knee. "I'll take the same deal, plus the added bonus of citizenship and witness protection. I've been here too long and I can't go back home. Mateo has now made that impossible."

Nick tried not to stare at the way her hem rode up her thighs as she sat on his bed. He was still in character, he was supposed to interrogate her. But even *he* knew that the US government frowned upon an agent caressing the enemy's legs. Try as he might, he couldn't stop touching her. She was too soft, too inviting. "Ms. Perez—"

"—Vera."

He met her gaze and licked his lips. The bunker suddenly felt very warm. He pulled at the collar of his T-shirt and cleared his throat. "Vera. What you're asking for—what you want—is very serious." Nick tested the waters by pushing forward. Sliding his palms upward until his fingers disappeared under her blue dress. "I can't take your demands to my superiors without some assurances."

Shea breathed deeply and let her head tip to her shoulder. Her eyes fell shut as his hands roamed freely. He could tell his touch was pulling her out of her character in a good way. It delighted him to see her loosened up, to hear her soft panting, to feel her warm skin. "How would you like me to assure you, Agent Roberts?" she asked with a sigh.

"Blue passports don't come cheap," he said in a low voice, hands pausing at the tops of her soft thighs.

She peeked at him with a suspicious look. "I assume the price is my body."

Nick couldn't help the startled laughter that escaped him. "Much as I'd love to have you tonight, I know better than to get mixed up with such a dangerous woman." He was about to pull away, remove his hands to adjust his pants, but Shea reacted faster.

To his surprise, she held his hands in place, scooting closer to him and widening her knees between his. "I'm not that dangerous," she said in a sweet voice.

"You could have a weapon on you right now."

"Search me."

His heart stuttered in his chest upon hearing her words. "Well, damn, girl…" he breathed, breaking character.

Shea blinked. "Too much?" she asked. An adorable frown wrinkled her nose.

"No, no." He shook his head. "Hell no, Ms. Perez."

Her smile returned. And that's what Nick needed. The playacting they performed was lovely, quite exciting really, but her beautiful smile was something he desperately wanted to nurture and protect. After six months of learning tiny snippets of information about her, cobbling together her interests, he couldn't believe where they were.

Alone and desperately wanting one another.

He was almost thankful for the Global Warning System, for the space debris hurtling toward the Earth.

Without thinking too hard, Nick gently pushed Shea back against the plush mattress and climbed the foot of the bed to kneel over her. She let out a small squeak as she grabbed him by the shirt. "You know what? You might be right. A careful search might not be a bad idea."

"You'll see that I'm not hiding anything," Shea said with a bright smile. Her fingers splayed against his chest as she arched into his touch.

He ran his finger up the outside of her thigh, to the edges of her panties before chuckling. "You're a Commie spy, my dear. Hiding is what you do best."

Shea

Oh my god, oh my god, oh my god…

Shea wasn't sure how long she could keep the Vera Perez act up. Not while Nick's body covered hers. She could barely think of her next line when his large hands trailed up her hip, fingers slipping beneath her panties. They were finally in his bed, she was horny as hell and ready to give up anything just to get him out of his clothes. Thank god she wore the flimsy wraparound dress to his store. It tied off at the waist and all he needed to do was give it one swift yank.

Beneath Nick, she felt small and delicate and protected. She leaned into his gentle touch and urged him with her eyes to continue. But it did occur to her that she might need to give him more verbal cues to get the ball rolling. After all, this was only the first night they'd admitted their feelings to one another. Normally, some arbitrary amount of dating would have to occur before she invited someone to her bed.

Now look at her. It was the end of the world and she was a Cuban spy trying to seduce a federal agent.

Who could be this lucky?

"No weapons to hide," she clarified. "Go ahead, Agent Roberts. Undress me if you must."

Before he could respond, Shea quickly untied her dress. As she pulled it open, revealing her lacy black underwear set, she held her breath. Even as turned on as she was, a small bit of anxiety made her bite her lip. She may have been comfortable with her large breasts, stomach rolls and dimpled thighs...but Nick was new to the game. Shea hoped he appreciated her body as much as she did.

Nick rested on his side, right next to her, and let his hungry eyes rove down her body. "My, my, my, Ms. Perez. The United States appreciates your transparency."

Shea narrowed her eyes. "Well, actually, the United States was never transparent while meddling in the progressive governments of Latin America—"

"No, no, Shea," Nick murmured against her neck. "We're not in the classroom right now. We'll do that fantasy next time."

"Oh, sorry!"

"Tonight, we're blindly loyal to our nations," he said, peeling her dress down her shoulders. "We're seducing one another for state secrets. And I'm searching your gorgeous body for weapons."

She grinned while pulling her arms out of her dress. "Right."

As she shimmied the fabric down her waist, Shea realized she had nothing to worry about. Nick's lusty stare seemed to do most of the undressing, leaving her short of breath and very hot. She inched herself away from him, moving closer to the headboard of the bed. Left in her underwear, Shea felt like a sex goddess summoning her most ardent devotee.

Nick quickly undressed, tossing his clothes to the floor as

206 · CHARISH REID

he went. When he was completely naked, he slowly crawled up the bed to meet her. Giving Shea enough time to admire how the taut muscles of his chest and arms flexed as he moved. The dim light of their setting cast shadows along the strong ridges of his belly. As her eyes drifted lower to the deep V at his hips, pointing directly to a long and thick erection, she fought to keep from trembling. The anticipation of riding him overwhelmed her too much, and pulled her right out of their game.

"Okay, I think I'm ready to fuck," she said, unhooking her bra and yanking the straps down.

Her declaration didn't slow his steady crawl toward her. "Are you sure?" he asked, chuckling. "You don't have anything else in your character file?"

Shea shoved her panties to her ankles and kicked them to the floor. "We're helping the Russians develop a bomb and our intended target is Kansas City."

Nick took her by the back of the neck and pulled her into a crushing kiss, groaning against her mouth. "Jesus, that's oddly specific."

"It's the first city I could think of," she murmured as he pressed her against the headboard. His hands traveled all over her body, hoisting her thigh around his waist and squeezing her ass.

"We'd just destroy Cuba," he said, grinding his hips against her.

Shea hissed from the pleasure of his dick sliding along the seam of her pussy. If she angled her hips just right, he could—oh god, there it was... Her clit sang in delight as she rubbed against his veined shaft. "Mutually assured destruction," she gasped.

Nick continued thrusting while palming her breast,

squeezing and stroking her stiff nipple. "God, Shea, you're about to become my destruction."

"I want you inside me right now," she begged.

He pulled her away from the headboard and settled her onto his lap. It had been a while since she'd had sex in this position, but she was relieved that she'd been in control of how fast and deep Nick could penetrate. "How long have you been wanting to ride this dick?" he asked with a smirk.

"Longer than I'd like to admit," she said, taking him in her fist.

He drew a shallow breath and closed his eyes while she stroked the length of him, teasing a restless groan from deep within his chest. "Shea…"

She'd put him out of his misery soon enough.

Raising herself above Nick, she sank onto him. The intrusion nearly unraveled her. Even a drenched pussy needed easing, and Shea was not in a hurry. Every inch she lowered herself on, stretched and rubbed the right spot, sending electric spirals of bliss throughout her body. Once she made it safely to the hilt, she felt Nick twitch inside of her, and rested her forehead against his.

"You feel like a dream," he whispered, hooking a strong arm around her back. The movement pressed her breasts into his muscular chest and shifted her hips to take him even deeper. Shea almost came when he licked the tip of his thumb and applied it directly to her already wet clit. The small circles he rubbed pulled a ragged breath from her chest as she kissed his collarbone and up his neck.

Eventually, Shea rocked her hips and slid along his hardness. The sensations of his hands, lips and dick made her close her eyes and drift into a beautiful rhythm of up and down. She bounced on him until her thighs burned and her orgasm teetered on the edge. Shea reveled in his tight embrace, his firm thighs beneath hers…his dark brown eyes boring into hers as he thrust to meet her. He held her gaze even as his lips found her nipple. His tongue thrashed the sensitive bud until she shuddered.

"I don't know—" she panted through the joyride on his lap "—how long I can last."

"I've got you, baby," Nick said, pushing her to her back.

When her head hit the pillows, she let out a content sigh. "Thank you."

"I've got you," he said, holding her knees apart, "and this pussy."

She believed him. If ever there was a guy who would take care in pleasing her and her pussy, it was Nick. Shea felt desired and safe in his hands. His long strokes were steady, not erratic. While he loomed over her, he took his time and caressed every part of her, one hand planted beside her head while the other traversed a slow path from her neck down to her hip.

"Do that thing again," she breathed.

He must have understood what she meant immediately because he licked his thumb again and pressed it to her throbbing clit.

"Yes," she cried. "You fucking get it!"

Nick chuckled above her, still stroking her vagina lovingly. "I'm a photographer," he said, leaning down to kiss her shoulder. His full lips traveled toward her collarbone so he could lick the hollow of her thrumming pulse. "I know how to watch and learn."

She barely heard him over her own gasps and moans. His every thrust was a new shock to her system, pushing her closer to her own explosive release. She tried to grab at the edge before being shoved over the cliff, but Nick's insistent tempo made it difficult to catch her breath, much less her orgasm. Shea hooked her ankles behind his back and met each thrust. "Yes, right there…"

She trailed off, once the pressure of an expanding universe felt like it bloomed within her womb, sending infinite gyres of pleasure throughout her body. She cried out and arched away from the bed, eyes squeezed shut and head thrashing about. Shea cried his name in a reverent prayer knowing that no one could hear her beneath the ground, in a concrete bunker. She had the freedom to unravel and come as loud as she wanted.

While she breathed through her lusty haze, Nick picked up speed, chasing his own pleasure in a series of short staccato thrusts. She opened her eyes and watched him assail her body with his passionate strength. The beautiful gleam of his sweat-soaked skin, his flared nostrils and corded muscles mesmerized her. This was not the mild-mannered man who stood behind the counter of The Page Turner bookstore. Nick was a man possessed by hunger. With her legs wrapped around his waist, she met the rapid rise and sink of his hips as best as she could. She held on to his thighs, following him toward his own powerful release.

He buried his face into her shoulder and he growled his surrender against her ear. The rumbling moan was like another welcomed vibration traveling through Shea's body. "I'm a lucky man." He sighed, settling his dead weight against her.

Shea wanted to agree with him, but she was too preoccupied with his heavy frame pressing her into the mattress. She hesitated to ask him to move because he felt like the greatest weighted blanket.

She felt lucky.

Nick shifted against her, pulling out and lifting his body away from her. She immediately felt his absence and it was kind of awful, but she didn't protest. She lay in his bed wondering about what came next. After the drinks, after the games, what would be next for all of them?

Nick

Cuban spy.

College professor.

Vera Perez.

Shea Anderson.

It didn't matter which version of the beautiful shy woman who special ordered his books was in his bed…she was there. And she contained multitudes. Nick wasn't sure if she'd heard him when he said he was a lucky man, but he meant each word.

Even now, as he watched her lie beside him with one arm tossed over her head. Strategically shrouded in his sheets like a Black Venus, Shea rested serene and devastatingly gorgeous beside him. "You're staring."

It was true. He was. Unabashedly watching her through the viewfinder of his mind. Clicking away at her different positions. Her bare thigh, the top of her chest. All of her exposed walnut-brown skin contrasting against his crisp white sheets. Shea was a work of art he wanted to frame…or fuck. Nightly.

"How can I not?" he asked, running his fingertips along the curve of her breast. When he hit the peak of her stiff brown nipple, he rolled it around in a circle just to hear her moan. He took it between his finger and thumb and pinched to see her squirm beneath him and felt like he was finally in control of this night. "You're so fucking beautiful, you know that?"

Her dark brown eyes connected to his and she smiled. "You're not just saying that because the world is ending?"

Nick shook his head. "The world isn't ending. I would have felt something by now."

Shea frowned. "What do you feel now?"

"Hope."

From the moment she descended into his bunker, he felt that hope. Knowing that he wouldn't be alone at the end made a difference. But after making love to Shea, Nick knew there was more. There were weeks, months and years of being by her side. He held her loosely because he knew there was time.

Shea shifted to her side and faced him. "You think everything outside is okay?"

"I know it is," Nick said confidently. "In the morning, we're going to go upstairs where we'll call our parents and I'll make you pancakes. Do you like pancakes?"

Shea nodded. "I do."

"I want to make love to you aboveground, in the sunlight. I want to play more games with you."

"I can't believe you're real," she murmured with a strange expression on her face. Her lips tightened into a straight line as her eyes narrowed. Nick watched her burrow half her face into her pillow and close her eyes with a sigh. "I can't believe we're here."

Nor could he.

As he stared at her, he felt he'd hit the jackpot with Shea.

Shea

Sharp pings of technology stirred Shea from sleeping in an awkward position. She winced as she lifted her head, a sharp pain stabbed the side of her neck. Following the chirping sound to her left, Shea found her phone. Blue light signaled a message from *outside*.

The phones worked?

As she extricated herself from Nick's firm hold on her thigh, she carefully twisted around to grab her phone. It was around 7:00 a.m. and dozens of missed text messages flooded her locked screen. Most of them from her parents, some from her girlfriends, a couple from university colleagues. What she gathered from the messages was that the danger had passed. Everyone she knew was safe. The United States was in the clear. Shea sank against the pillows with a sigh, relieved that her world could go back to normal.

But after last night, she wasn't sure she wanted to return to a world without Nick. Oh jeez…that felt a bit dramatic. Shea turned to face him, to watch his profile in the dark. His smooth forehead, strong nose and full lips came together to form a beautiful picture, one that she didn't mind kissing again. Of course, she'd wait until he woke up. And when he did, would the magic disappear? In the safety of the bunker, with the threat of nihilism looming over them, he gave her the fantasy she'd been pining for.

Nick shifted in his sleep, reaching toward her body. A hand landed on her thigh and pulled her against him. She couldn't help the giggle that escaped her. He grumbled deep and shifted closer. "What are you laughing at, Ms. Perez?"

"Nothing," she whispered, scooting next to him. "The emergency alert is over. We're safe."

"Thank God," he said, gathering her into his strong arms. She heard him breathe deeply against her hair before sighing. "I'm so damn glad to hear that."

She smiled against his chest, placing a whisper of a kiss

to the firm muscle. "I suppose we should get ready for the day…greet the outside." Her suggestion was tentative as she waited on his response. She didn't want to leave, but she didn't want to overstay her welcome. He'd been so accommodating and gracious during her stay, offering her amazing sex, but doubt nagged at her.

"What's your hurry?" he asked. "We're supposed to have pancakes."

Shea looked up at him, making out his features in the dark. "That still stands?"

As an answer, Nick took her by the face with both hands and kissed her deeply. The familiar pleasure of last night's exploits unfurled in her chest and spread throughout her body as she kissed him back. When he pulled away, his hands remained. "Please come upstairs with me, Shea. Let's keep this going. My weekend, and hopefully every other weekend, belongs to you."

The doubt dissipated like mist against morning sunrays. Sunrays she was now anxious to see. It was a new day with a new chance at romance, and Shea was thrilled to see where it could lead. "Okay, well, I'm hungry now," she chuckled.

He reached down and gave her ass a love tap. "Say less, baby. Get on up and get dressed."

After a short time of getting ready, they ascended the stairs, leaving behind the cozy bunker. The bookstore was safe and secure, just as they had left it. Nick kept the closed sign hanging in the door before letting Shea out and locking up.

Outside was the same as any other day. People on the street, opening shops, buying newspapers. A few cars rolled past the store, moving to their destinations without fear. The morning sun warmed her face and made her feel alive.

Shea watched the scene with Nick standing beside her.

Without thinking, she took his hand and squeezed tightly. "Thank you for last night."

Nick slung an arm around her shoulder and kissed her temple. "I should be the one thanking you," he whispered in her ear. "Maybe later this weekend, we hit up that coffee shop?"

Ahh, yes...the other reason for her showing up yesterday. She laughed at what now felt like a distant memory. "Of course we can, Agent Roberts."

★ ★ ★ ★ ★

INTERLUDE

SARAH SMITH

The most important lesson I've learned as a songwriter and jingle writer is this: have something to write with on you at all times. Always.

Even when you think you won't need it, like when you're taking out the garbage or in the bathroom, you will. Because that's usually when inspiration strikes—whenever the hell it wants to, at the most random and inconvenient moments.

That's what's happening to me right now as I sit on the toilet emptying my bladder after guzzling an entire thermos of tea on my drive back home from an impromptu trip to the vet. You see, today my cat, Mango, decided to crawl into the trash can and devour three discarded muffin wrappers. I, of course, panicked and sped him straight to the vet. Thankfully all was well. Because they're paper, they'll dissolve in his digestive tract and he'll pass them in a few days.

But today's chaos has thrown me off completely. I haven't eaten or showered and I've got a late-afternoon Zoom meeting to prep for. And this is why I'm humming the melody that just popped in my head over and over as I relieve myself because I'm so off-kilter that I broke my own rule and didn't bring anything to write with me.

The bathroom door squeaks as Mango nudges it open with his face. He plops his chunky body next to my feet, then slow-blinks at me before letting out the quietest mewling sound in the world.

My heart melts instantly. I reach down and pet his impossibly soft orange fur. "You're lucky you're adorable. You're forgiven for earlier today."

I hop up and wash my hands, all the while humming the melody, then dart down the hallway to my office, grab my phone and record myself singing for thirty seconds. I save it and breathe a sigh of relief. Not sure what I'll use it for yet. Maybe it'll be the catchy hook for a song I can pitch to a producer. Or maybe I can use it in an advertising campaign. Those thoughts halt instantly when I check the time and see that I've only got twenty minutes until my first Zoom meeting. I still need to eat something. And shower. And put on makeup. Shit.

I dart back to the bathroom, toss my glasses aside onto the counter, flip on the hot water, shed my T-shirt and yoga pants, and hop in the shower. Under the hot stream of water, I quickly shampoo my hair and soap my body. As I rinse off, I force myself to take a breath. Yeah, today has been a mess so far, but I can't go into my meeting stressed-out, which is with a jewelry company. It's a lucrative contract—they want something moody and seductive for a Valentine's Day jingle. If I nail this pitch, this gig will pay in the mid five figures. I want this contract *bad*. It would be the biggest single contract I've ever gotten, which would be a huge professional boost—

not to mention a fat chunk of money that I'd love to see in my bank account. This high-end jeweler isn't going to want to hire a frazzled hot mess to take on their Valentine's Day campaign. I need to exude confidence during this meeting, like I didn't just have a ridiculous pet emergency—like I totally, unquestionably have my shit together.

So I do the one thing I always do when I need to calm down: I sing. I choose one of my favorite pump up songs: "Don't You Worry 'Bout a Thing." It's one of my favorite Stevie Wonder songs, but I'm also a huge fan of Tori Kelly's version, so that's the one I bellow under the stream of steamy water. It only takes a handful of seconds before the nerves dissipate and I'm swaying my hips and head as I sing and groove.

By the time I turn off the water, I'm feeling slightly less frazzled. I dry off, wrap the towel around my hair, slip on my fuzzy bathrobe, then throw on a sheet mask before heading to the kitchen for a snack. Ojai is beautiful and I love living here—it's got that quiet, small-town charm but it's only a couple hours from LA, so I can commute to meet with clients when needed—but the desert climate is hell on my skin. I look like the crypt keeper if I don't moisturize my skin intensely at least four times a week, and I definitely want to look my best for this meeting.

Mask in place, I sprint to the kitchen and scarf down two leftover lumpia along with a green smoothie while going over the client info in my head for the meeting.

The sound of my doorbell going off interrupts my thoughts. I groan while chewing, tempted to ignore it as I've now got only ten minutes to pretty up so that I'm camera ready. But then it sounds again, meaning I'll need to get rid of whoever's at the door.

When I answer it, I'm greeted by a tall, broad man, I

think? Because I'm sans glasses and squinting through a face mask, the person standing in front of me is blurry.

"Hi, Jocelyn? I'm Caleb, from Pop Pop's Desert Paradise Remodeling."

My eyes go wide. Today is the day I scheduled to have a contractor come over and give me an estimate to replace my kitchen cabinets. In the chaos of today, I completely forgot.

"Oh! Shit!" I cup my hand over my mouth. "Sorry for swearing."

Blurry man chuckles. "It's okay. I've been known to mutter a curse or two."

"Um, right…" I step aside to let him inside, too flustered to laugh at his joke. "Look, I'm really sorry about this, but I have a work Zoom meeting in, like, ten minutes, and I still have to get ready, so is it okay if you take a look at the cabinets without me?"

I move to shut the door and point in the direction of the kitchen. "Promise as soon as I'm done with my meeting I'll check back in with you."

"No worries, take your time."

I yell a thanks before darting back into the bathroom and start swiping on my skin care. When I check the time and see that I've only got four minutes till my meeting, my nerves start to crackle. But I close my eyes and make myself take another breath.

"You've got this, Jocelyn," I say.

I start singing "Don't You Worry 'Bout a Thing" again. I belt out the lyrics, smiling to my reflection in the mirror as I stand up taller. I've already come up with a few melodies and lyrics, and I'm planning on singing them to the jewelry store marketing head during our meeting. This song is the perfect warmup for my voice. I reach for my glasses so

I can see clearly when I put on my makeup, chaotic day be damned. I've got this. Just like Tori and Stevie say, I don't need to worry about a—

The door flies open.

"Jocelyn?" the contractor booms.

I yelp, dropping my glasses on the counter. All I can see is a blurry form in the doorway.

I clutch at my robe. "What the— Caleb? What the hell are you doing?"

"I—I know, and I'm so sorry, but I hear the warning siren blaring. Didn't you hear it? Your phone probably has the text alert too." I'm dizzy as I try to process the information Caleb is sputtering at me. Text alert...siren... I start to wonder why I didn't hear it until now. Was I that in my own head? And my phone should be on the bathroom counter, but I don't see it. A high-pitched wail is emanating from outside, and Caleb's own phone is just a fuzzy black rectangle in his slightly less fuzzy hand.

Fuck.

"We need to take shelter. Now."

Caleb's booming voice sends my heartbeat racing.

"My basement. We can go down there."

Caleb makes an affirming noise before moving toward the door.

"Wait! My cat! I don't know where—"

"I've got him."

My heartbeat eases the slightest bit, but it's back to thrashing against my rib cage as the siren wails louder and louder. I swipe my glasses from the counter, dart in front of Caleb, then run toward the kitchen, which is where the door to the basement is. I shove on my glasses, throw open the door and run down the darkened steps as fast as I can.

Even as my heartbeat drums in my ears, I can hear the sound of Caleb's heavy footfalls behind me. I register the slam of the door and Mango's indignant mewl.

My feet hit the carpet and I smack the light switch on the wall. I do a quick glance at the space, quietly thankful I finally hired a contractor to finish the basement this summer. It's a small space, only about four hundred square feet, but it's carpeted with a cozy pull-out couch along the wall, flat-screen TV and a fully stocked small refrigerator. There are worse places to ride out a natural disaster.

When I spin around to check on Mango and Caleb, I promptly freeze. Because standing in front of me is the hottest man I've ever seen in my life, his chest heaving as he catches his breath, holding my cat in his massive hands.

A stammer lodges in my throat. He looks like an extra from a TV series about Vikings, except instead of fur pelts, he's clad in worn jeans, work boots, a flannel and a hoodie. Dude's gotta be at least six foot three, maybe four? Even though his clothes are loose fitting, it's clear he's jacked. I'm one hundred percent certain that if I grabbed his forearm, my fingers wouldn't touch by a solid few inches. And his thighs... holy Jesus. My eyes go wide for a long second before I remember that it's rude to stare. I blink and aim my gaze back at his face, but I know without a doubt that I won't be able to get those thighs—those thighs that resemble tree trunks more than actual human legs—out of my mind anytime soon.

Golden blond hair falls in shaggy waves around his face and a pair of warm hazel green eyes gaze at me, unblinking, like he's trying his hardest not to let his eyes drop any lower than my face.

Probably because I'm standing in front of him in just a robe. I glance down and notice the belt knot has loosened.

The top of the robe is open enough that my cleavage is on full display, and my legs are fully exposed all the way up to my upper thighs. I clutch one hand to my chest, pulling the fabric together. My other hand grips the fabric shrouding my crotch.

"Um…" His Adam's apple bobs as he swallows, his gaze glued to me. Then he presses his eyes shut and shakes his head. "Sorry, um… I didn't mean to barge in on you in the bathroom. I am so, so sorry about that."

"It's okay," I mumble, gripping the fabric even tighter around me. "It was an emergency."

He nods, eyes still closed. "I swear, I didn't see anything."

I didn't think I could burn any hotter than I did seconds ago when I first took in Caleb's male model appearance. But as it turns out, I can. My face is currently engulfed in flames at the thought that Caleb glimpsed even the tiniest bit of my naked body. I haven't shaved my legs in a week. My bikini line? Even longer.

I quickly readjust my robe and tighten the belt, shuddering at the thought that maybe he did actually see me and he's just saying this to be polite since we're stuck together for god knows how long. A full-body cringe starts to make its way through me, but I tense up and ward it off. No. I can't let my brain go there. If I do, I'd die of humiliation, and I need to maintain some level of composure if we're going to be stuck together in this small space.

"Again, I'm really, very sorry…" His hands shake slightly as he speaks, eyes still pressed shut, and that softens me the slightest bit. Because it shows he's just as nervous as I am right now.

"Caleb. It's fine. You don't have to keep apologizing."

He finally opens his eyes, the worry lines in his forehead

smooth away. His hazel eyes flash relief as he gazes down at me.

He scrunches his lips, like he's too nervous to smile. Mango squirms slightly in his hold. "Is it okay if I set…"

"Mango. And yeah, you can set him down."

I take in Caleb's slow, steady movement as he lowers his tall, broad frame to the ground, places Mango on the carpet and stands back up. He shoves his hands in the pockets of his worn jeans and steps back until he almost hits the wall behind him. All the while he keeps his gaze lowered. When he stops, he hunches his shoulders, instantly shrinking himself by a few inches. And that's when it hits me: he's trying to maintain space between us, trying to make himself less physically imposing to me.

I soften even more. The nerves lingering inside of me ease from fiery to tingly. That is so considerate of him to do that. As a smaller woman, I've been around my fair share of hulking dudes who either don't know or don't care just how disruptive and intimidating their size can be. But even though Caleb is nearly twice my size, I don't feel uncomfortable in his presence. Yeah, I'm nervous, but not nearly as much as I was a minute ago—and I wasn't nervous because of how big he is, more because of the awkwardness of this situation combined with how freaked out I was at the sound of the warning siren.

"This, uh, might be a weird question, but…do you want to wear my clothes?" he says after a quiet moment.

"Um, what?" I almost laugh.

He clears his throat, his peaches-and-cream complexion igniting to a fiery hue along his neck and cheeks. "I can give you my hoodie or my flannel to wear. If you—I mean, if you want…if it would make you more comfortable."

"Oh. Um…"

I glance down at my bare legs. Goose bumps prick up against my still-wet skin. The thought of wearing just a robe for the next however many hours makes me want to crawl out of my own skin.

"Actually, that would be great," I say, hugging my arms around me.

He nods once and spins around, facing the wall as he begins to shed his hoodie. I quickly spin around too to give him privacy. That doesn't stop my brain though. Instantly I picture what naked Caleb looks like. It happens like a reflex. In my imagination, he's flawless. Rugged and ripped with a healthy dusting of dark blond hair on his chest that trails down all the way to what is most certainly an impressive, thick…

I bite down so hard on my tongue I have to muffle a yelp. I try to swallow, but there's so much saliva pooled in my mouth that I almost choke. What the hell is wrong with me? My contractor, who is a total stranger, is standing four feet from me, about to give me the literal clothes off his back to help me feel more comfortable, and here I am mentally violating him.

God, I am such a cavewoman. A heathen. A literal deviant.

The sound of fabric rustling halts before he clears his throat again. I wonder if he does that when he's nervous.

"Here you go," he says softly.

When I turn back to him, he's holding a balled-up mound of fabric in his hand, which is stretched toward me.

I smile and say a quiet thanks as I take the hoodie from him, barely able to maintain more than one second of eye contact with him after the way I just ravaged him in my brain.

"It's clean, I swear," he blurts. "Just did a load of laundry this morning. So, um, you're good."

He frowns like he's annoyed with himself for what he said before scrubbing a hand over gold-blond scruff along the sharpest jawline I've ever seen.

I bite my lip, but it's no use. I burst out laughing anyway.

A smile splits his ruggedly handsome face, and for a moment I'm breathless. This guy is downright gorgeous when he smiles.

"Wow. That was a really weird thing to say." He chuckles. "It's okay. I appreciate the heads-up. Clean clothes are always a plus."

We share another laugh before I spin around. A half second later I hear the sound of Caleb turning around too, and I take that as my cue. I quickly dress and unwrap the towel from my hair so it can air dry.

"Decent," I say when I turn around.

Caleb turns and flashes one hell of a boyishly handsome half smile before glancing down at the floor for a second. It almost comes off like he's shy, which is endearing as hell.

I shrug, the collar of his navy blue hoodie so wide on my frame that it nearly falls over my shoulder. I zip it up all the way to the top and smooth my palm down the front of the hoodie, which nearly hits the tops of my knees.

"Not a perfect fit?" The hint of teasing in his tone goes far to lighten the mood even more than when we shared laughs together just a minute ago.

"Weird, isn't it? I mean, I could have sworn we were the same size," I joke.

Another shared chuckle has me feeling even lighter. I can tell Caleb is too. He's standing at nearly his full height now and his arms are resting at his sides instead of shoved into his pockets.

"Wanna sit?" I point at the nearby couch, where Mango is currently curled up.

He nods, and gestures for me go first. I take the far end, pulling Mango into my lap while Caleb plops onto the opposite end.

"Here." He grabs the plushy blanket that's draped over the back of the couch and hands it to me. "So you don't get cold."

"Thanks." I smile at him and drape the plushy material over my legs.

A few quiet moments pass, and the reality of the situation starts to sink in. Something big is hurtling toward the Earth. When it hits, how bad will the impact be? What will life be like when we're eventually able to go back out into the world?

A mix of dread and nerves settles in the pit of my gut.

"You okay?" Caleb asks.

It's then that I realize I'm frowning. "Yeah. Actually, no. I guess I'm just a little freaked out. I mean, a meteor is going to hit us."

He nods and looks away, his expression solemn. "We're safe though in here," he says when he looks at me a second later, his mouth curved in a slight, reassuring smile.

"I hope everyone was able to get to shelter okay." I hug my knees to my chest. All the muscles in my body are tight with tension.

"I read a while back that the alarm system is pretty sophisticated," he says. "It's designed to alert everyone hours before impact. It'll be okay."

He sounds so certain in his soft tone. It's the most surprising comfort.

He pulls his phone out from his pocket and swipes his finger across the screen. "Is there someone you need to call or text to let them know you're okay?"

I start to say I'm good, I'll just text from my own phone, but then I remember that I don't have my phone with me. In my hurry to get ready for my meeting, I must have forgotten in it my office upstairs.

"Actually yeah," I say. "I should probably text my parents and check on them."

He hands me his phone and I type out a quick message to my mom's phone number, explaining that I don't have my phone, but that I'm safe and sheltering in my basement with a friend. Before I can even text again and ask if they're okay, she texts me back.

Oh that's such a relief, anak! Thank god y

Ah darn it I hit send too soon! Thank god you're okay. Your dad and I are safe at home sheltering here with your apongs. We love you!

I text Mom "I love you too," then hand the phone back to Caleb.

"All good?" he asks.

"Yup. They're safe at their house sheltering with my mom's parents." When I smile, I notice the muscles in my neck and shoulders loosen. At least my family's okay.

But Caleb frowns and taps the screen. "Damn it," he mutters.

"What's wrong?"

"Not sure." He taps his phone screen once more before bringing it to his ear. "I must have lost service. I keep trying to call back, but nothing. Straight to voicemail. Oh wait..." He's quiet for a few moments before putting his phone on speaker. "...cannot be reached at this time. Please try again later. Good-bye," an automated voice recites.

"That's so weird, you were just talking to..." Then it hits me. "Maybe all service is down because so many people are trying to call their loved ones."

"Ah yeah, you're probably right." He starts typing out a text just in case but then his phone rings. "Hey, Larissa... Yeah, I'm okay, just taking cover in a client's basement, we'll be fine. How are you?...Oh that's good...Yeah, actually. That would be nice." He chuckles softly before pausing and touching the screen of his phone.

"Toby is gonna miss you tonight. Aren't you, boy?" A woman's voice sounds from the speaker of Caleb's phone as he holds it up. They must be on an app that doesn't require cell service.

He shifts slightly and I can make out the face of a yellow Lab on Caleb's phone screen. When he barks, Caleb chuckles.

"Miss you too, buddy. I'll be home soon though. You be good for Larissa, okay?"

I hold back the "aww" I'm dying to make at witnessing Caleb have a phone conversation with his dog.

When I realize that I've been gawking at his conversation, I turn away slightly to give him some privacy.

"You stay safe, honey, okay?"

"You too," Caleb says. "Just hang tight. I'll be by as soon as this is all over to check on you both. Love you."

"Love you too. Be sure to—"

The woman's voice cuts out. Any kind of service must be down now. He sets his phone on the arm of the chair.

"That was the sweetest thing ever by the way, you checking on your dog. I would have done the same if I didn't have Mango here with me." I glance over at Mango, who, after jumping off my lap a minute ago, is now curled in his cat bed next to the couch, licking his front paws.

Caleb's cheeks turn pink as he flashes a flustered grin. "I just needed to make sure Toby was okay."

"Your girlfriend's okay too?"

"Girlfriend?"

"Yeah, the woman on the phone. She's the one watching Toby, isn't she?"

Caleb stares at me for a long second before chuckling. "That was my stepmom."

"Oh!"

I let out an embarrassed laughing noise. "I don't know why I thought... I guess I just assumed since you said her name and 'I love you'..."

He waves a hand. "No worries."

The half smile he flashes makes my stomach do a tiny flip. I don't know why... I barely know this guy... I definitely shouldn't feel as giddy as I do to find out that he's single.

"She's retired so she offers to watch Toby most days during the week so I don't have to leave him home alone when I go to work," Caleb says.

"That's really nice of her," I say. "Toby is an excellent dog name, by the way. It's really cute."

"That's actually his nickname. His full name is Toby-Wan Kenobi."

I burst out laughing. "That is ridiculously adorable."

"I let my niece and nephew name him when I got him a few years ago. My sister, who's their mom, got him for me as a gift for my thirtieth birthday. My nephew was really into *Star Wars* at the time so he wanted to name him Obi-Wan, but my niece thought Toby was better. So Toby-Wan Kenobi was my idea for a compromise."

I swoon even harder than when I did while he was on the phone talking to his dog. Because the fact that Caleb seems to be so good with kids *and* is into animals is my romantic kryptonite.

I swallow back the thought and remind myself to keep it together. We've known each other for less than an hour. On top of that we technically have a professional relationship, since he's my contractor. And I definitely shouldn't be having daytime fantasies about the guy I hired to redo my kitchen cabinets. That's beyond creepy.

I push those thoughts aside and notice Caleb glancing down at Mango.

"So what's his name origin story?"

I reach to give Mango a chin scratch. "It's not that interesting. Mango was his name when I adopted him from the animal shelter a handful of years ago. I thought it suited him perfectly because he's an orange tabby."

"It's still pretty cute." Caleb winks at me and I try my hardest not to choke on the air in my lungs.

"He's cute for sure," I finally say, relieved that my voice sounds mostly steady. "But also a handful."

"Really? He seems so laid-back."

I scoff-laugh before giving Caleb a quick rundown of my frantic day taking Mango to the vet.

His eyes widen. "Whoa, I didn't know cats ate stuff like muffin wrappers."

"This guy does. He's a garbage disposal. I have to be careful about leaving food out on the kitchen counter or the dining table. He'll hop up and devour anything and everything."

I give Mango one more chin scratch and he slow-blinks

at me before nuzzling the plushy edge of his bed and falling back to sleep.

"That's why I was running around like wild when you first came over," I say. "The surprise vet visit threw off my whole schedule today and I was scrambling to get ready for a Zoom meeting. Not like that matters now."

Caleb nods like he understands. "I've been there. Toby has a habit of chasing after bees and he's been stung a couple times. Had to cut work to rush him to the vet."

I make a sympathetic *aww* sound.

Caleb shakes his head while aiming a smile at a now-sleeping Mango. "The things we do for our little guys."

He glances at the karaoke machine sitting under the TV.

"Karaoke fan?" he asks.

"Big-time. It's in my blood."

The corner of his mouth hooks up. "That must be why you sounded so good in the bathroom."

I cover my face with a hand and attempt to muffle an embarrassed laugh. "Crap, you heard me?"

He nods.

I lean my head back and groan. "Bad habit I guess."

"Not even close to a bad habit. You have an incredible voice. You should be a singer."

"I am actually. Well, I'm a songwriter and jingle writer, but I sing a lot when I'm pitching and recording."

Caleb's brow lifts like he's intrigued. "Damn, really? What a cool job. Have you written anything I've heard of?"

"Maybe? Do you listen to Top 40 radio? A song I co-wrote earlier this year is getting a lot of airplay right now."

When I tell him the title, those hazel eyes practically bulge from his beautiful face. "Hell yeah, I know that song. I was singing along to it on my way here. You wrote that?"

I chuckle a "yes," amused and the tiniest bit turned on at the image of this ruggedly handsome Viking grooving to a pop song.

"Man, that instrumental part between verses, with the piano? That was genius. So catchy."

"Aww thanks. I'm all about writing a killer interlude. It's kind of my signature."

"What other songs have you written?"

I name a half dozen more that have been released over the past couple of years, all of which he admits to knowing and loving.

His hazel eyes are wide as he looks at me and stammers, "Holy crap. This is awesome. Like meeting a celebrity."

I blush, giddy at the fanboy vibes Caleb is giving off. As a songwriter and jingle writer, the bulk of my work is done behind the scenes. I've never been someone who craved the spotlight, so this job is a perfect fit for me. Even though millions of people listen to my songs and jingles, they have no idea who I am, and I love that. I can be creative, earn a good paycheck and maintain a private life. But it's admittedly satisfying to hear Caleb's praise.

"What about jingles?" he asks.

"Okay, well, do you remember that soup commercial last Thanksgiving with the little kids building the snowman that comes to life? I wrote and sang that."

His brow hits his forehead. "That's my favorite soup. I buy it from the grocery store all the time."

I giggle. "Oh and that jingle for the organic grocery chain that just opened. And that radio ad for that new amusement park outside Santa Monica. And that local shoe store ad that started airing a month ago."

I name off a few more.

Caleb's mouth is half open in a shocked smile. "Wow. It's like you wrote the soundtrack for what I listen to in the car when I drive between jobs. That is pretty damn cool."

"If I hadn't grown up singing karaoke at every holiday and family gathering ever since I could talk, I probably wouldn't be doing this for a living."

"That sounds like a blast. My family gatherings usually consist of us bickering and fighting over who gets the last of the spinach and artichoke dip."

"Oh my family does that too, except instead of fighting over dip, we're usually fighting over the last lumpia. And it's all going on while someone is belting Celine or Whitney in the background."

Caleb licks his lips before a rumbling sound echoes from his stomach. He claps a hand over his middle.

"Sorry," he mutters, glancing down at his stomach like he's embarrassed. "I guess today wasn't the best day to skip lunch, especially since who knows how long we'll be sheltering in place."

"You haven't eaten much?"

"Just breakfast, and that was right before I headed to my first remodel job." He waves a hand. "It's my own fault. That'll teach me to skip meals. My parents always told me not to. I should have learned by now," he jokes.

"Well, my mom always taught me to offer food to people the moment they walk in the door, so she'd be pretty embarrassed of me too since I didn't do that for you."

I hop up and walk over to the fridge right as Caleb starts to say it's no big deal. I pull out a massive Tupperware container of leftover pansit and a foil package of fried lumpia.

I swipe some plastic cutlery from the top of the fridge and

walk back over to the couch. Caleb's eyes practically light up as I move to hand the food to him.

"Interested in some leftovers?"

His stomach rumbles again, this time louder.

I raise an eyebrow. "I'll take that as a yes?"

He laughs and reaches out both arms to accept the container of pansit and plastic fork from me, practically growling thank you before digging in. I sit back down on the couch and rip into the lumpia. Before I can even take a bite, Caleb has eaten nearly a fourth of the savory rice-noodle dish with shredded carrots, cabbage, celery, ground pork and shrimp.

"Holy...this is so freaking good," he says around a mouthful.

I open my mouth to say thank you, but the words lodge in my throat. I'm too mesmerized by how the muscles in his jaw flex as he chews, how each swallow glides slowly along the thickness of his throat, how he moans softly between bites...

My mind starts to wander to a filthy place it has no right to be... I wonder if he makes the same noises when he's in bed...or if the sounds he makes are rougher, if they sound more like growls...

I clear my throat, press my eyes shut and shake my head slightly to refocus on the moment. I shift slightly on the couch, pressing my legs together as I dole out a silent warning in my brain.

God, Jocelyn. What is wrong with you? Are you really getting turned on watching your contractor eat? Your contractor, who you've known for an hour?

Apparently that's exactly what happens after ten months of go-nowhere dates and no sex.

I stand up from the couch, grab a plastic bowl from the top of the fridge and fill it with bottled water from the fridge, then set it on the floor for Mango in an attempt to focus on something, anything, other than how attractive I find Caleb in this moment.

"Seriously, this is the best meal I've had in a while," he says, jerking me back to tamer thoughts.

I order my brain to stay rooted in the moment. "My Apong Meena's recipe," I say, my voice slightly higher pitched than usual. I clear my throat. "I'll be sure to tell her you like it."

I sit back down and scoot closer to him on the couch so I can deposit a half dozen lumpia into his now nearly half-empty container.

"You don't want any?" He points his fork to the container.

I shake my head. "I'll be good with the lumpia. Besides, there are two smaller containers of pansit in the mini fridge and some leftover pork adobo if I get hungry…or if you need more food."

He takes a bite of the lumpia and frowns slightly.

"I know, it's not as good as when it's freshly fried—"

He holds up his free hand, finishes chewing, then swallows. "What do you mean? Jocelyn, this tastes incredible."

I laugh. "Swear it's better when it's hot and crispy, straight from the fryer."

He shakes his head, smiling. "If you say so."

A minute later, the entire container is empty. Caleb leans back and rests both his palms on his stomach, a satisfied smile tugging up at the corners of his mouth, while I silently order myself not to gaze at the sliver of muscly flesh that peeks between the hem of his shirt and the waistband of his jeans.

I start to offer him more food, but he shakes his head.

"I couldn't eat more even if I wanted too. That was a lot of food, and it was delicious. Thank you again."

He starts to cough.

"Oh! You probably want something to drink."

I hop back over to the fridge despite his protests that he's fine. As I reach for the bottle of water in the door compartment, I spot a half-full bottle of bourbon on top of the fridge, hidden behind the stack of disposable plates and utensils.

I grab it along with the water and stand in front of Caleb, holding one in each hand. "Pick your poison," I tease.

"Wow. You've got the best-stocked basement I've ever seen."

"This is what I always wanted, a basement that is essentially a second living room. My one upstairs is for show with the all-white aesthetic and completely impractical Pinterest-inspired decor. This one is where family and friends can come over and party."

He laughs and reaches for the water, thanking me again. I move to put the bourbon back but he stops me.

"Actually. You feel like having a drink with me?"

There's a shyness in his eyes. It sets off what feels a lot like butterflies swarming in my stomach. Why does it feel like he's asking me on a date? And why does it excite me more than any other offer for a date I've had recently?

I eye the amber liquid swishing around in the stout bottle before looking at Caleb again.

A drink with my hot Viking contractor who I'm trapped in my basement with while the world is ending around us? May as well.

I grab two paper cups from the top of the fridge and pour us both doubles.

I sit back down on the couch and raise my cup. "To one hell of a workday."

That crooked smile I've already decided is my favorite appears, and I fight the urge to swoon. "Indeed."

★ ★ ★

"No way. I don't believe you." I nearly choke on a sip of bourbon, I'm laughing so hard.

"Believe me," Caleb says. "I was sixteen and very, very foolish. And not very smart."

"So sixteen-year-old you thought it would be a good idea to mail a naked Polaroid of yourself to your high school girlfriend while she was studying abroad?" I have to stop twice while speaking to catch my breath between giggles.

Mango peers up from where he's been sleeping in his bed, clearly irritated at the loud noise. I reach down and give him a pat.

"I'm not proud of it," Caleb says. "She was studying in Mexico City, so that meant we were going to be apart for Valentine's Day, and for some reason, my teenage self thought it would be romantic. Her host family didn't think it was very romantic when they saw the picture."

Caleb explains that his girlfriend was so shocked to receive the surprise nude, she screamed and dropped the envelope on the ground in full view of her host family, who then called her parents and ratted him out.

"At least I had the sense not to include my face in the photo. So it was just my scrawny torso and naughty bits," he says. "What a lucky girl she was to get that."

I clutch my aching stomach as I cackle. Bourbon was a great idea. We're three drinks deep, which has loosened us up to the point that now we're exchanging embarrassing stories of when we were teenagers. It's only been a few hours of chatting, but it feels like I've known Caleb for longer. I realize I'm comfortable around him in a way that I've never felt around any guy I've known for just a few hours.

Maybe that's a product of the strange circumstances we're

in: sheltering from an impending meteor impact in a small space after he saw me nearly naked. That forces you to get to know a person *real* quick.

But then I realize that the reason doesn't really matter to me. I genuinely like this guy—I like talking to him, laughing with him, drinking with him, just being around him. Hunkering down in my basement with Caleb is a better time than most dates I've been on. That's gotta count for something.

"Believe me," Caleb says when he catches his breath. "I wish the most embarrassing thing I did as a teenager was dye my hair the wrong color."

"You do not." I run a hand through my now-dry hair, swiping it over my shoulder. "My normally jet-black hair did not take to the blond grocery store hair dye. At all. It was orange for two solid weeks until I could earn the money to go to a salon and have it dyed properly. So I walked around school my freshman year looking like a troll doll. My mom was livid and refused to help me pay to go the salon. She said it was the perfect opportunity for me to learn from my mistake."

"Yikes. She's hard-core."

"She is. Good thing my dad's around to soften her."

"They sound like quite a pair."

"They are. He's this tall, menacing-looking white dude, but he's a huge softy on the inside. And there's my mom, a tiny Filipino woman who looks so sweet, but will rip your throat out if you cross her."

"Sounds like my grandma and grandpa. My grandpa was this burly homebuilder who was a total softy for my grandma. He wrote her poetry. And he'd bring her flowers every Sunday before they went to church together."

"That's so sweet." I notice Caleb's glass is nearly empty

and lean closer to refill it. "So you took after your grandpa then when it came to your career?"

His smile turns wistful. "Yeah. When I was a kid he'd let me help with projects around his house. When I got older I'd go to job sites and help him. He taught me everything I know about home construction and remodeling. I named my business after him, actually. To honor his memory."

I recall that the name of his company is Pop Pop's Desert Paradise Remodeling.

I make the corniest *aww* sound ever and lean forward, gently gripping his arm. "Oh my gosh! 'Pop Pop' is what you called your grandpa? Of course! Pop Pop Remodeling! That is so cute, Caleb. And so beautiful. Your grandpa would be so proud."

Caleb glances down at my hand, which is gripping the thick flesh of his forearm. And that's when it hit just how inappropriate I'm being. I'm lunging at the poor guy.

"Sorry," I mutter, quickly pulling my hand away and scooting back.

I down more water and quietly decide to cut myself off from the bourbon.

"It's okay. You don't have to be sorry."

The soft growl of his voice compels me to glance up at him. He flashes a small smile, like he's trying to comfort me. What a guy. Here I am tipsily clawing at his body and he's being such a gentleman about it.

A beat later his smile turns more relaxed and his gaze lingers on me. "Being felt up by a hot woman has been the highlight of this day."

His words have me stammering. I go quiet, cupping a hand over my mouth and lean back, sinking deeper into the couch. Caleb shakes his head, his expression twisting like he's tasted something bitter.

"Crap, I'm sorry. I—I shouldn't have said that. That's so inappropriate given the situation."

I pull my hand away from my face. "The situation?"

He rakes his fingers through his gold-blond locks and huffs out a breath. "Yeah. We just met. We're stuck together for the next...who knows how long, and here I am making comments about your looks. It's because of all the alcohol I've had, but still, that's no excuse. What I said was creepy."

A pink flush makes its way up his neck and cheeks.

"I'm so sorry, Jocelyn—"

A sudden boldness, likely from all the bourbon I just consumed over the past few hours, powers through me. I lean forward and cup Caleb's deliciously scruffy face in my hands.

"It wasn't creepy. Not even close."

"It wasn't?" he mumbles, a dazed look in his hazel eyes.

I shake my head. "No, because I think you're hot too."

He quirks an eyebrow. "You do?"

I nod. "That's why I was so stunned and speechless when I first saw you with my glasses on. I was so taken aback at, um...how hot you are."

"Oh. I thought you looked that way because you were freaked out about the siren."

"Well, yeah, I was. But I was also freaked out by your hotness."

The worry melts from his expression as he grins. He reaches up and gently wraps his hands around my wrists, my hands still cradling his face.

"Are you still freaked out?" he asks, his voice a low rumble.

"No."

He shifts slightly; we're nearly nose to nose.

"How do you feel now, Jocelyn?"

His hot, wet breath skims my lips.

"I feel like I want to kiss you."

And then I do exactly that. I press my lips against his, relishing the feel of his soft, warm skin against mine. We move slowly at first, our mouths barely opening, our tongues lightly touching and teasing, like we're testing out how exactly we want this to go. It's soft and slow for the first minute, but soon I'm straddling Caleb's lap and his hands are gripping my waist.

I moan into his mouth and feel him smile against me. When he shifts slightly, the couch cushion dips and I slide an inch toward him. The weighty presence of his body is the biggest turn-on. I bet I'd feel even smaller and more delicate lying underneath him, his physique a shield of muscle over me.

As our kisses gain in intensity, I get handsier. He does too. Now I'm tugging at his hair, which he loves judging by the way he moans every time I do it. The sound of rustling fabric mingles with our pants and groans. It manages to drown out the nerves popping off inside of me. I was confidence incarnate when I grabbed his face, called him hot and started kissing him. But even now as we go at it, it's almost too much. Never in a million years did I ever think I'd ever live out such a fantasy scenario. Here I am, trapped in my basement having the hottest make out of my life with a sexy contractor I've known for a handful of hours. Straightlaced, rule-follower me has never, ever done something so bold, so sexy. I can hardly believe it. My brain can barely process this too-good-to-be-true scenario.

Leaning back, I rest my hand on his toned chest and break our kiss.

Our gazes lock as our chests rise and fall with each breath we take.

"Are you okay?" he asks.

"Yeah, I just need to catch my breath."

Eyes closed, he leans his forehead against mine. "Good idea."

I have to close my eyes too. Even looking at him for very long has my nerves crackling. He's too handsome, too sexy, too sweet, too perfect, and if I think too hard about any of this, I'll freak myself out or...

Just then he leans away, but only enough so that we can make eye contact.

"What's going on in that head of yours?"

"I guess I'm just kind of blown away. This isn't how I thought the day would go, with me making out with my super handsome contractor. But hey, I guess I'm down to get a bit wild when the world is ending." I wince. "Sorry, that's kind of morbid."

A throaty laugh falls from his thick lips.

"I get what you mean. I don't do this sort of thing either. But we can just go with it though. We don't have to think about anything other than how good this feels—as long as we both want it."

With his softly spoken words, every warring nerve inside my body halts. Warmth hits. It's as soothing as it is arousing.

"Do you want this, Jocelyn?" His thighs tense under my own thighs, and I nearly whimper. I nod.

He cups his hands over my cheeks and I take in his cloudy gaze, how his inky pupils have doubled in size ever since we started touching and kissing, how his breath is so ragged it sounds like he's sprinted a 5K.

"Do you want me, Jocelyn? I want to hear you say it. Please."

His rasped words make me ache. I flex my thighs, relishing the way my clit is already pulsing.

"I want this. I want you, Caleb."

The corner of his mouth hooks up. It gives his half smile a naughty gleam. "I want you too."

Soft fingers land under my chin, pulling my lips back to his and we resume that breathless kiss from a minute ago.

"I've been trying not to stare at you this whole time," he says against my lips. "You're just so stunning."

I smile, glowing from the inside out. "I've been trying not to mentally undress you this whole time."

He chuckles.

"It would probably freak you out if you knew the filthy thoughts I was having about you hours ago," I confess.

"Try me."

There's a faint growl in his voice, like he's trying like hell to keep his voice under control. He shouldn't though. That's exactly what I want: his guard down and his inhibitions gone.

I shake my head against his, and he opens his eyes. "I don't know if I can say. It's too embarrassing."

He lowers his face to my neck and presses a feathery, lips-only kiss to the spot of skin that meets my shoulder. I moan through a shiver.

"Well, now I really want to know."

My breath catches when he slides a hand up the back of the sweater I'm wearing. When he scrapes his teeth over my shoulder, I gasp. He returns to my neck. This time, there's tongue with his kiss. I have to grip his shoulder to steady myself, it's disorienting in the best way.

"Tell me," he growls against my skin. "Please."

I nod and press my eyes shut in an attempt to focus against the heat and pleasure flashing across my body.

"When you were undressing to give me your hoodie to wear, I was picturing you naked, how your body looked," I admit in a shaky voice. "My, um, my mouth was watering at the thought of kissing you and doing other filthy things to you."

His lips stretch against the side of my collarbone. My stomach does a double flip.

"You think I'd get upset that a beautiful woman was fantasizing about me?"

He dusts one last kiss on my collarbone. Then he leans back to look me in the eye. "That's one of the hottest things anyone has ever said to me."

Hearing him admit all that is instant comfort. I bite back what I'm sure is the cheesiest grin on earth and begin to unbutton the top of his flannel. He follows my lead, quickly taking the bottom buttons. When I push the fabric off his shoulders, I nearly choke. His actual body puts to shame the body I've been fantasizing about. Hard lines run the length of his broad torso. It's all firm, unyielding mass. I tally six ab muscles before running my fingers through his chest hair.

"Whoa." I cover my face with my hands when I realize I've said it out loud.

Soft, firm flesh encases both of my wrists. Gently, I'm pulled away and meet his amused face.

"Um, your body is…just…holy hotness," I say.

I stammer as I try to blame all the bourbon I've consumed for my inability to form the necessary words, but Caleb just shakes his head and smiles.

"Stop. It's sexy when you talk like that."

He slides me off his lap, then stands to unzip his jeans.

When he steps out of them, I'm greeted with tree trunk legs and the impressive length between them.

My mouth falls open even as I'm smiling.

"Hopefully you're not disappointed," Caleb says above me.

I jerk my head up to look at him. "Are you kidding me? You're gorgeous."

That familiar pink flush appears on his neck and cheeks again, a perfect complement to his adorably shy smile.

He reaches down and pulls me up to stand with him, then kisses me. This time, it's so slow, so sweet. He parts my lips open with his tongue and in no time we fall into a teasing, filthy rhythm, just like before. Our tongues play and tangle. He leads with an urgent rhythm I can just keep up with. Smiling against his mouth, I have to remind myself to breathe.

Soon I'm clawing at the hoodie I'm wearing like a rabid animal. I need to be naked with him, I need to feel his skin hot and slick and writhing against me.

The vibrations of his chuckle tickle my mouth.

"Here." He takes over, gently yet quickly unzipping it.

As I stand totally nude in front of him, my heartbeat picks up. It's been a long while since I've been naked in front of someone and the nerves inside of me are starting to crackle.

But then I take in Caleb's hungry stare, how he looks giddy and shocked at once. Those hazel eyes drink me in in a slow gaze that starts from my chest and falls all the way to my feet. He stammers at first, which makes me feel like a goddess.

"You're stunning, Jocelyn."

I reach up, tug my hand at the back of his head and pull him down to me. Our lips crash together, and I can barely breathe. His grip falls to my waist, leading me to sit on the couch.

"Oh wait!" I step out of his embrace, then lean over the couch, yank away the cushions, then pull out the sofa bed. I toss the blanket over it along with the fuzzy throw pillows, then hold my arms out. "Ta-da!"

He grins at the bed before turning back to me. "That's perfect for what I have planned."

"And what's that?"

Instead of answering me, he leads me to sit on the bed before gently pressing his massive hand against my stomach.

"Lie down for me?"

I do what he asks. When I see him kneel in front of me, my legs quiver. Oh hell yes.

He moves his hands to the tops of my thighs, but before he even makes contact, he looks at me. "Is this okay?"

"It's more than okay."

He grins before bowing his head down. A second later, light kisses and even lighter teeth scrapes spill across the insides of my thighs. Already I have to steady my breathing to keep from losing it.

"We should have done this sooner. Like, hours ago," I yelp as he inches closer to the apex of my thighs.

"You're right. We should have. Now I gotta make up for lost time."

Giggles fall from my mouth. But when his breath ghosts over my clit, they morph into gasps. Then his tongue hits, my jaw falls open and I moan. He starts with slow swirls, eventually picking up speed. He stops and sucks. The light pressure has me seeing stars. It's not even a minute, and I'm about to plummet off the edge.

"Caleb." Running my hands through his hair seems to spur

him on just the right way. He returns to a slow pace, then speeds up, then slows once more. God, this guy. He picks up right away that this variation of speed drives me wild.

Heat builds, along with the pressure. Thank goodness I'm lying down because I'm dizzy at just how incredible Caleb is. His hands are better than my own. His mouth and his tongue are the best I've ever had.

Both of my calves begin to cramp, signaling that the incoming crash of pleasure is close. When I bury my hands in his hair to hold him in place, he takes the cue. He keeps that steady pace, that gentle pressure, and I explode against his tongue.

All of my limbs convulse around him, but his lead pipe arms hold me in place. Rapid breaths help ease me as I come down.

He crawls up to the sofa bed next to me and slides a pillow under my head. Finally my heartbeat steadies, and I glimpse over at him. When I grab him in my hand, he shivers. He's hard as steel.

"Do you have a condom?"

He grins and says yes before rolling over and hopping off the couch bed to where his jeans are on the floor. He curls up next to me again, condom in hand.

I immediately push him down flat on his back with my forearm. He must find my pitiful show of strength amusing because he chuckles.

"No laughing." I swipe the condom from his hand, rip it open with my teeth and spit the wrapper out. A groan rips from his throat when I slide it on him. "Just let me ride you."

When I lower myself onto him, I have to go slow. It's not just our size differences, it's that I want to savor every single moment of this fantasy come to life.

"Easy," he grunts, digging both hands into the fleshy part of my hips.

I press my palms against his chest. "I'm not some delicate little thing." My head falls back as I moan. "I like it hard and fast."

He holds me steady to keep from thrusting and I look down at him. "Fuck, that's hot," he rasps. "But if you go too hard, too fast, I'm going to lose it, Jocelyn. And I want this to last."

Leaning down, I run my tongue along his bottom lip. I jerk back up before he can capture me in his mouth. "I saw the other condoms in your wallet. There's always round two."

With that, I thrust up and down in a slow rhythm, using his chest to steady myself. His eyes roll to the back of his head.

A low growl rips from his throat. "Jocelyn." He lets out a frustrated chuckle, then exhales. "You can't keep going like this. I'm going to blow."

"Good."

The up and down rhythm I employ delivers pleasure to both of us. With each thrust I'm stretched even more, reaching a pleasure peak I haven't hit with another man in ages. It's not just Caleb's size doing me in. It's the pleading look in his eyes, the way he tries to hold off for me, even when I tell him it's okay to let go. It's the way he holds on to my body for dear life, like he can't believe this moment is happening either.

Licking my fingers, I start to circle my clit. Caleb's brow shoots all the way up to his hairline. "Fuck, Jocelyn. I can't take it...watching you do that... I can't—"

An animal-like yell falls from him, blasting through the room. He presses so hard into my hips with his fingers, I'm certain I'll bruise. Good. I want a memento from this wild and impossible moment together.

A lightning bolt of heat and pleasure hits my clit, and I come soon after. My pitchy cries accompany the last of his deep grunts. I fall on top of his chest, which is just as sweaty as mine. His thick arms wrap around me, and I nuzzle into him. The frenzied beat of his heart is the only sound I hear.

When we finally catch our breaths, an exhausted laugh falls from his lips. "That was…"

"Fuck."

He responds with a proper throaty laugh. "Absolutely."

Hugging me tighter into his body, he presses a kiss on my forehead. "Are you thirsty? Or hungry?"

I gaze up at him. "Only for you."

Burying my face in his chest is the only way I can think to hide the burn consuming my face. Could I possibly sound more desperate?

I can't help it though. It's more than just the mind-blowing sex we just had. There's something else between us. Comfort, connection, genuine emotion. I want to wrap myself in that feeling as long as possible.

And sex. I want to have more sex with him too.

When I glance up at him, a playful smile tugs at his lips. "So eager. I love it."

With his response, I relax the tiniest bit. Seconds later I feel him start to harden against my stomach, and I grin before kissing him.

"How much longer till you can go again?"

The sound of sheets rustling wakes me. When I open my eyes, I'm treated to the sight of bare-naked Caleb walking the few steps from the couch-bed to the refrigerator. I'm quiet as I take in the visual of his beautifully muscled body while he moves, reaching and grabbing items in the fridge. I have to bite my lip so I don't make any noise. But good god, is he hot. Watching all of those muscles in his back arms and his legs bulge with every move he makes is mesmerizing, but it's his ass that has me salivating. Despite how intimate we've been with each other the past few hours, I haven't yet gotten an up-close, unobscured view…until now. Just…wow. I wonder if he does a lot of squats in his workout routine—it sure looks like it judging by the ample swell of his rock-hard ass. I've never seen a backside as perfect as Caleb's.

I could get used to this view, to seeing Caleb again so we can have a repeat of the last few hours. Even just chatting and laughing with him would be a blast. Being with him has been the best time I've had with a guy in ages…

I catch myself the second that thought materializes in my brain. What am I doing? I shouldn't be making future plans with this guy. Yeah, he's amazing, but we hooked up because we were stuck together during a natural disaster, there was chemistry, and we acted on it. I don't even know if he'd be interested in anything more than this little interlude we're currently enjoying.

Maybe I could ask him…

I stamp out the thought instantly. Whenever I brought up the "what exactly are we/where is this headed" topic to guys I've dated in the past, I was almost always told I was coming on too strong—and that was from guys I'd dated for weeks, sometimes months. Doing that now with a guy I've known for less than a day would definitely come off as too much.

The thought sends a tinge of disappointment through

me, but I push it aside. I just need to focus on enjoying the moment.

When Caleb twists around and catches me staring, I bite my lip.

He grins, quirking an eyebrow. "Enjoying the show?"

"Very, very much."

He walks back over, sits on the edge of the bed, and sets the plate down by me. "Thought you might like some breakfast in bed," he says, while reaching down to give Mango a pat while he snoozes on his cat bed.

My heart flutters at the makeshift platter he's put together: clementines, strawberries and cherries.

"If I had access to a kitchen, I'd have whipped up something more elaborate," he says.

I sit up and grab his face to kiss him. "Don't. This is the sweetest breakfast in bed ever. Thank you."

I try not to fantasize about him doing this every morning for me. That's ridiculously clingy given how we've known each other for less than a day.

He swipes a strawberry and holds it up to my mouth. I take a bite, then he takes a bite. I notice he's refilled Mango's water bowl and set a plate down with a few morsels of meat from the pansit for him too. My chest aches at how sweet it was for him to think of my cat.

I beam up at him. "Amazing in bed and amazingly thoughtful."

After our first round of sex, it didn't take long for Caleb to bounce back for round two, then three. I was blown away. He possesses a stamina I've never experienced in all my dating and relationship history.

I drain the bottle of water he hands me. "What kind of exercise do you do? You were…"

I still can't believe just how hard the two of us went at these past few hours. Caleb had a total of three condoms in his wallet, and we wasted no time using all of them. But even after we ran out, we didn't stop, using our mouths on each other until we were both sweaty and panting and shaking all over, completely wrung out from the pleasure we had given each other.

I glance around the room as flashbacks from earlier rotate through my mind. The arm of the couch he bent me over. The wall he pinned me to. He took the reins with confidence the entire time, but always made sure to check in and see if I was okay with it all. And I was. It was the best sex I've ever had.

He chuckles while peeling a clementine. "I do a bit of everything, but really, my job is what keeps me in shape. It's pretty physical with all the lifting and hauling I have to do day after day. But I try to run and lift weights on my days off. And I play basketball with my friends a few times a month too."

"Wow. You're an Olympic athlete compared to me. If I make it to the gym twice a week, I count that as a win."

I skim a hand over the ample curve of my thigh, feeling the slightest bit self-conscious about my body even though I know I shouldn't.

Caleb's massive hand lands gently over mine. "Hey. You look incredible. Whatever you're doing, keep doing it."

And with those words, that tiny moment of insecurity is stamped out instantly.

He captures my mouth in a kiss, turning the flutter in my heart to a full-on flip. This guy. God, he's amazing.

The intensity of our kiss picks up. Grabbing me by the hips, he hoists me onto his lap and runs his hands all over me. Heat and goose bumps flash across my skin at once. He gives a slight thrust with his hips, and I giggle as my knee knocks into the paper plate that's sitting next to us.

"Mmm, what about breakfast?" I mumble between kisses.

When he leans back slightly to look at me, there's a flash in his eyes. "Oh I still want breakfast."

In one smooth move, he lays me on my back and positions himself so his face is between my legs.

I start to chuckle as he wags his eyebrows at me. But the moment his tongue laps at my clit, my head falls back and I groan. Just like our first time together, he starts slow, like he's taking his sweet time, savoring each second that he's making out with the most sensitive area on my body. It's enough to have me convulsing after barely a minute of his mouth on me.

Heat and pressure collide in my core. My legs start to quiver so hard around his head that he wraps both arms against my thighs.

I can barely think, barely speak, barely breathe.

"Caleb...please..."

They're the only words I manage for a solid couple of minutes. The pleasure is too intense, too strong.

Soon it consumes me, and I break. Climax hits like a wave, pulling me under so quickly that I barely have time to react.

I shout so hard, so loud, my ears rattle and my throat goes raw. My thighs are a vise around Caleb's poor head. But I can't help it. He's just so good—with his mouth, his cock, his hands, his words, everything. Everything about this guy gets me hotter than I ever thought I could get.

When I start to come down, my body loosens. Slowly, Caleb straightens up, not once breaking eye contact with me. When he winks and runs his tongue along that gloriously plump bottom lip of his, I swear I could come all over again.

"Yum," he growls.

I let out a breath and laugh at the same time. "God, you are something else."

"As long as you let me keep doing that to you, I'll be whatever you want."

I reach up to pull him down next to me. Three sirens blast outside at the same time that Caleb's phone sounds with an alert, jolting us both. He twists around and grabs his phone from the arm of the couch. His brow shoots up as soon as he studies his screen.

"Huh."

I lean up. "What's the matter?"

"Looks like it's safe to go back out again. No need to shelter anymore." Caleb's eyes cut to me. "We're free to go."

"Oh. Great. That's really great..." I guess that means our little interlude is over.

I bite my tongue to keep from asking him where we go from here. I don't want this to be the end. I like Caleb a lot. And I don't want this to be the last time we see each other.

I open my mouth to speak, but quickly stop myself. We've known each other for a total of twelve hours and I already want to have a "so what are we/where is this going?" chat. That'll probably send Caleb running for the hills.

"So, um, you're probably gonna go check on your stepmom and Toby, right?" I say quickly.

"Yeah." He runs a hand through his hair, glancing off to the side.

"So I guess our little interlude is over," I say, mostly to myself.

"Interlude?"

When I look up, Caleb looks amused.

"Music terminology. It seeps into real life sometimes."

"This doesn't just have to be an interlude, Jocelyn. I'd like it to last a lot longer."

"Really?"

I don't even care how eager and hopeful I sound in this moment. We're on the same page and I'm freaking ecstatic. I should probably tell him that.

"Really," he says with a smile.

"Good, because I know that things kicked off kind of weird with us given that we hooked up in my basement while sheltering from a meteor. But I like you, Caleb. I'd like whatever this is between us to last too."

He grabs me by the hips and pulls me back onto his lap. I grip his broad shoulders to steady myself. Biting my lip keeps the squeal I'm aching to let loose at bay. With his hands around my waist he scoots me closer till we're nose to nose.

"I'm not in a hurry to leave you anytime soon," he rasps. "Unless you want me to?"

"No, don't leave." I say it so quickly, he chuckles. "Stay. As long as you want."

Caleb kisses me. "Promise I'll whip up a hot breakfast in bed for you tomorrow morning. Whatever you're craving."

My stomach does a somersault at the thought of Caleb staying for breakfast tomorrow...and every other day.

We engage in a feverish kiss that leaves me light-headed

by the time we break apart. I tug my fingers through his hair, shivering when he groans in satisfaction.

"Make any breakfast you feel like," I say. "I just want one thing."

"What's that?"

"Serve it to me naked."

He rumbles out a chuckle. "You got it."

★ ★ ★ ★ ★

ANYTHING YOU CAN DO
I CAN DO BETTER

DENISE WILLIAMS

1

PIPER

Friday Evening, Edison, Iowa

Hale's breath was hot against the back of my neck, his voice on the razor's edge of a groan. "You're better at chemistry than me." His nose slid to my nape, sending a delicious kind of tingle down my spine. "You're better at biology. I don't think I'll ever truly best you in the classroom."

I shivered as he placed my palms on the smooth surface of the podium and then stroked his hands back up my arms, his unexpectedly soft skin leaving a trail of goose bumps in their wake.

Staring out at the empty lecture hall, I couldn't see his face, but the hard planes of his chest pressed behind me, and he ground his length against my backside. "You're the smartest person on campus." His lips grazed my ear as he continued the slow grind, driving me to the edge. "And I'm going to make the smartest person on campus come so hard, she forgets basic addition."

I parted my lips, whether to moan or to prove I could recite the quadratic equation even in this quivering state, I wasn't sure. But his hand was dipping lower and his voice was in my ear again, palm pressed against my back, guiding me to bend lower as his fingers dipped between my thighs. The empty auditorium was in front of me as he worked my body, the rows and rows of gray seats the only witness to my unraveling. Hale's low voice was a tease and a promise as my climax began to crest. "You're the best, Piper. The best."

Ding.

The ancient elevator's echoing alert pulled me from the fantasy I'd had since I was eighteen, the first time I outperformed Hale Edison III on an exam and realized the intense thrill I felt at his cool expression, poorly hiding his astonishment. I'd mostly outgrown my need to prove myself through academic achievement, though being in this building again took me back to the days of believing the only way I could make my family proud was to become a doctor, to become the best doctor. I grew up in the real world, though. I knew as a Black woman, I'd see hurdles every step of the way and there would be a lot of people making sure those hurdles were hard to get over. I'd arrived at Edison University ready to fight. On the first day of classes, I knew he was the one I had to best. That was before the fantasy started, the fantasy no man had ever lived up to.

The elevator creaked as it began its descent toward the basement and I questioned if it was safe. Being late to the awards ceremony where you were being honored because you got stuck in an elevator during a misguided attempt to relive your college days wasn't the best way to make a splash in the alumni newsletter.

The building smelled the same. I hadn't been inside West Hall in at least fifteen years but the memories of lab reports and exams, of complaining about our professors in hushed voices, and then begging those same professors for letters of recommendations, it all swept over me with a single inhale. Well, those memories along with the thigh-clenching, belly-dipping fantasy of my college rival earning an A-plus in G-spot stimulation. I bit the side of my lip and pushed the thought away. I'd get plenty of real-life Hale Edison III this weekend and nothing about it would be pleasurable.

The car bounced a little on arrival at the basement level and I made a mental note to take the stairs on the way up. The fluorescent lights overhead cast industrial gray walls in a slightly green tint. Built in the fifties, the walls still had bomb shelter signage from the Cold War. The institutional gray of the painted concrete-lined hallway was the furthest thing from a comfortable homelike color, but that's what it had been. I'd found my passion and my calling in that basement. I'd felt more myself in that basement competing with Hale than I did anywhere else. Now I dragged a manicured fingernail along the cinderblock walls.

On a bulletin board, the poster for the Alumni Awards Banquet was pinned next to a reminder about lab safety and a flyer with missing fringed pieces along the bottom advertising a roommate needed. I fiddled with one of the pieces at the bottom that included a phone number and email address. Hale's face on the Alumni Awards poster looked on. Dr. Hale Edison III, BS Biology and Biochemistry '08. Foster Award for Alumni Excellence. It was the top award given to alums and I swallowed my bitterness that Edison was receiving it before me. My face was next to his. Piper Drake, BS Biology and Education '09. Edison Award for Young Alumni Excellence. The second most prestigious award an alum, at least a young alum, could win.

"Looking for a roommate, Drake?" The voice was low, but not like the whisper I fantasized about. It was a voice that sounded like a smirk looked. He didn't used to sound like that, though. He used to barely speak at all unless it was to goad me.

On the first day of college, I'd raised my hand first, prepared to show the roomful of who I assumed to be entitled rich kids that the girl here on scholarship could cut it. More than that, I could best them all. Despite my hand in the air, waiting to answer the question about taxonomic rank and provide relevant examples, the professor's gaze swept over me to call on a bewildered-looking boy whose hand wasn't up. *Mr. Edison. Good to see you, and clearly your family legacy of academic excellence continues. Do you have the answer?* I wished my roommate was with me in the class—at that point, she was the only person I had any kind of relationship with and what I would have given to have been able to share an eye roll with someone.

Now, all these years later the university founder's great-grandson strode toward me in a tailored gray suit, his hair just long enough to need sweeping from his face and his brown eyes dancing. "I know you decided not to become a physician, and educators are woefully undercompensated, but surely you could do a little better than this." He tapped a finger on the edge of the flyer where the apartment was described as *close to campus* and *mostly not bad.*

"Edison." It had always taken a split second to reconcile my immediate annoyance with him, the fantasies of how his bare chest might feel under my fingers and my grudging respect for his academic abilities. He'd known the answer in that first biology class, but the examples hadn't been as good as mine. At least in my opinion. "Don't you have some puppies to be sacrificing to the gods of career success and haircare products?"

His smirk shifted into a grin, the shape of his smile still so familiar all these years later, and a low chuckle escaped his lips. "I have people to do that for me now, Drake." He leaned against the bulletin board at an angle such that his photo from the poster hung over his real-life shoulder. The smile in print looked plastic, if not devastatingly attractive. The man in front of me looked human and only a little like he'd be good at bending me over a lecture podium. "Who has the free time to do their own sacrificing anymore?"

"Not you. Congratulations, by the way." The words were sour in my mouth. Yes, I'd googled him and read that he was one of the youngest and most talented physicians making waves with medical innovation and, yes, his work to tackle maternal morbidity for women of color was laudable, impressive even. But our relationship was cemented on day one when he became the personification of my urge to prove to anyone watching that I deserved my spot at Edison University. I don't think he even noticed me that day, but he did once I made it my mission to outperform him.

"Thank you. And to you. I read about your advocacy for increased accessibility in STEM education." He nodded toward the poster behind him before looking back to me. "We've come a long way since first-year bio."

"I suppose so." The building was quiet, which was to be expected for a Friday evening. I'd been pleasantly surprised when the side door was still unlocked and I could visit my old academic home before heading to the ceremony. A handler from the Alumni Association had offered to escort me, but I begged off. I didn't want to have to schmooze in this building. I wanted time to remember and reflect on how far I'd come. I'd hoped to do that alone. "What are you doing here?" I tried to make the question casual, but it came off slightly accusatory.

"Don't worry. I'm not here looking for an apartment. I won't fight you for this one." He crossed his arms across his chest, which—dammit—was more developed now than in college, and his stupid muscles bunched under the jacket. He snagged one of the dangling corners of the flyer and handed it to me.

"That razor-sharp wit is still intact, I see." I fought the urge to cross my own arms, and instead slid my palms down the front of my dress, a red fitted number I'd made my best friend photograph me in from every angle.

"It is." I didn't miss the way his eyes followed my movement. "It's what you always liked about me." He grinned again, a wolfish expression he probably thought was cute. "That I'm witty and I'm a gracious winner."

"It happened so rarely. It's hard to remember if you were gracious about it."

"You didn't always win, Drake."

I gave him my sweetest smile, my teacher smile that, when used correctly with a certain kind of man, drove him nuts. It was condescending as hell but it felt appropriate for Hale Edison III in the biology department hallway. "No one *always* wins. I just usually bested *you*."

"You know—" The rest of his sentence was lost in the deafening alarm that blared from the speakers.

Whoorl whoorl whoorl.

As the alarm continued to blare, their phones signaled an emergency notification. This is an official announcement—aerial debris detected. This is not a drill. Please find immediate shelter in an underground bunker or interior parts of a building away from windows. Remain sheltered and wait for an all-clear.

Whoorl whoorl whoorl.

Our eyes met, even while our bodies were frozen in place—him leaning against the wall, cocky, and me standing every inch of my five foot eight in heels with my stunning red dress. I imagined the look on my face matched the look on his as realization took hold. The time I'd spent applying the deep red lip color and perfecting the shape of my brow didn't mean much now that Hale Edison III was the last person on earth I was ever going to see.

2

HALE

The alarm had finally stopped, the sudden silence jarring after fifteen minutes. Fifteen minutes where Piper Drake and I communicated through shouting and hand gestures and managed to take shelter in an unlocked office. We'd done that before, the shouting and gesturing, anyway, but they were never productive hand gestures. The room we'd slipped into contained mismatched furniture with spots covered in duct tape and a couch that looked like it survived several decades. I knew this office. When Piper and I were teaching assistants, we'd shared a desk in this cramped space and it looked like the furniture might not have changed since then. I watched Piper rub a palm over her chest and my medical training kicked in before my long-standing desire to rub her chest myself. "Are you okay?"

"Yeah," she said, absently looking around the room, pacing between the spot on the wall where she'd been leaning and the desk nearest where I was perched. "You?"

"Other than it being the end of the world?" I shrugged and nudged a chair toward her with my foot, trying to ignore the way the curls had fallen from her swept-up hair and framed her face. Instead, I motioned around the Spartan room. "I guess I thought I'd go out in nicer surroundings."

She looked at the chair like it might be covered in hot fudge. It certainly wasn't clean, but none of the stains looked fresh. She'd always been like that. I'd read it as pretension early on, but I'd decided it was her being more careful than the rest of us. Knowing what I knew as an adult, about how Black women were viewed and treated in society, she probably was right to be careful. Still. It was just a chair.

"Might as well have a seat. I think we'll be here awhile."

"My dress will wrinkle," she said, sliding her palms down the front of her dress again and dammit, that was distracting.

"I'm pretty sure it doesn't matter."

I thought she'd scowl, and it looked like she was starting to, but it fell from her face and she sat delicately in the chair. "Figures I would finally break down and buy a nice piece of clothing and this happens. I saved for months to buy this and you're the only one who will see me wear it."

"It's a nice dress. I can look at you a lot if you'd like." That was a joke. I'd never not looked at Piper Drake when we were in a room together. "I could randomly applaud if that would make you feel better."

"It would," she said, a tiny grin turning up her lips. "It's really what you should have been doing this entire time, anyway."

I let my gaze trail down her body. "You never dressed like this in college." Not that I'd minded the tank tops and tight jeans she'd worn. "I would have applauded. You look hot in the dress, Drake."

She snort-laughed. It was at the same time completely sexless and the sexiest sound that could have come from her mouth. "Were those the romantic lines you used to win over your wife?"

"They were the romantic lines I tried before she divorced me." It had been a few years and so it wasn't the mention of my divorce that caught my interest, but the fact that Piper Drake knew I'd been married. "Have you been keeping tabs on me? Casual social media surveillance?"

"It's the end of the world and you're concerned if I've spent time focused on *the* Hale Edison III? Might be thinking a little highly of yourself."

Her words hit me somewhere primal, maybe because she was right. It was like Piper Drake had always known where to aim the arrow for maximum damage when it came to me and she hit the bull's-eye more often than not. When I started college, I assumed everyone knew what they were doing better than me. They knew how to dress a little better, to talk to girls a little better, to make friends a little better. I knew how to do school, to be good at science, but that was it. I knew what an Edison was supposed to do and I tried my best, but standing next to Piper again, some of that old doubt crept in. No matter how confident I felt as college went on, when I was with Piper, I always felt like she saw through me, but in a way that made me feel naked. Almost like she preferred what was under the mask.

I didn't tell her that, though. I just shrugged and smiled. "What better time to think highly of yourself?" I pulled my phone and keys from my pocket and tossed them on the desk. The device was a glorified paperweight now with no cell or internet service once the alarms sounded. "And I did agree to think highly of you, too, at least about you and how you look in your dress. Hell, I'm a generous guy—I'll think highly about how you look out of the dress, too, if it makes you feel better."

Piper shot me a withering look, but her cheeks tinted darker. "How do your patients not punch you in the throat?"

"I'm in obstetrics. Some of them have tried, but they usually aim for a father if there is one in the room." I glanced at my phone again. There were ten patients I wanted to check on, there were emails I wanted to respond to and there were research findings I wanted to peruse, but I couldn't and it probably wouldn't matter even if I could. I tried my best to compartmentalize and shake off the thoughts. All of that sobered my response and I stood, pacing. "I'm sorry for what I said. This is serious. I will take it seriously. Are you sure you're okay?"

She sank her teeth into her lower lip the way she'd done all those years ago when she was thinking, moving some big piece of information through her brain that always moved just a hair faster than mine at getting to the conclusion. She raised a hand and I worried it might be shaking, but instead she pointed one manicured finger at me. "There's a sticky note stuck to your butt."

I swiped at my backside and my hand brushed against Piper's as she stretched across the small space to pluck it off and hold it up for my inspection. It read, *Don't touch this, Josh. It's mine. —Brenda.* We both stared at it, the loopy blue handwriting in sharp contrast against the light yellow slip of paper.

"Well," I finally said. "Josh is gonna be disappointed."

"Can't fight dibs, though." Piper tossed the note on a nearby desk. "Your butt belongs to Brenda."

"Here I was hoping you'd fight for me." I flashed her what I knew was a charming grin. My ex had said it was my best and worst feature because I knew it usually went a long way in getting what I wanted. Piper didn't take the bait, though.

She laughed. Piper laughed hard. The giggle burst from her lips and grew into a belly laugh, the sound echoing off the concrete walls. It was so unexpected to hear her laugh like that and see her beautiful and strong features split into such a joyful look.

"It wasn't *that* funny," I interjected once she'd regained most of her composure.

"It was." She fumbled around on the desk behind her until she found a box of tissues to dab at her eyes. "I mean…" She waved around at our surroundings. "You once pushed me down a flight of stairs when we were racing to get to a research opportunity first and now we're back here together for the end of the world. And you're—what?—hitting on me? It's funny."

She looked young in that moment, dabbing at her eyes. She looked young in a way I know I used to look, too.

"I wasn't hitting on you." That was a lie. Kind of. I hadn't intended to hit on her, but when the words left my mouth, I knew I wanted her to play along or volley back. "And you tripped. We were racing and you tried to jump in front of me on the stairs and you tripped. I didn't push you. I would've never done that."

She cocked an eyebrow and narrowed one eye. She was wearing makeup, dark shading around her big, brown eyes, and I couldn't remember if I'd ever seen her in makeup.

I learned a long time ago it was never my place to comment on a woman's appearance, or anyone's appearance for that matter, but I thought she didn't need it. The rich color on her lips, though, that drew my eyes to her mouth in time to see her lips part to speak. "No. You're about to twist the truth, but I came back to help you and you still tried to beat me to Dr. Hart's office, hobbling along."

"I got there first."

My phone buzzed on the desk and a calendar reminder flashed on the screen. *Reminder: Edison Alumni Awards Banquet, one hour.* In fifteen minutes, everything had changed and my laugh wasn't as raucous as Piper's but I chuckled. "I let you win."

She sat back in her chair, crossing one shapely leg over the other. "Still counts."

I let my eyes fall to her strappy heels and wander over her ankles before meeting her gaze. "You're pretty cocky for someone in the wrong shoes for a rematch."

She bounced one foot, the buckle on her shoe catching the light. "It's not being cocky when you're the best." She glanced around the office. "I guess we should make a plan. We're supposed to shelter in place but we could try to get somewhere."

I walked to the door and looked up and down the empty hallway. Everything was unnaturally still. It was unsettling to be in a place you always felt teemed with so much life and energy, and have it feel so still. "I don't know where we'd go. We're in the middle of rural Iowa. Should we see if anyone else is in the building?"

I glanced over my shoulder and watched her rise to her feet, again smoothing her hands down the front of her dress. "Good idea. Maybe someone is working late and will save us from being alone together." Piper bent to fix something on

3

PIPER

We'd searched the top three floors of the building and hadn't found a single soul. "It's ironic," Hale said, trying the last door on the hall, even though we could see the lights were off. "But you have to give it up for their commitment to work–life balance. Friday night and no one working late."

"Self-care is so important," I returned, trying the doorknob nearest me. It twisted slightly left and right but the door was locked. This old building, constructed in the fifties, was all concrete and the fluorescent lights gave everything an eerie hue. In college, we'd joked how vampires would be at home in this fortress so guarded from the sunshine and natural light. I wondered what we'd see if we looked out a window. We'd somehow both silently decided we didn't want to know.

"I guess we should try to find some food," I said walking back toward the elevator. All this preparation for the day the sirens would go off and I hadn't thought to put even a granola bar in my purse. "You probably have a fully stocked blast shelter at home, huh?"

I was ready for a witty comeback as we stepped into the elevator. *Huh. Are we supposed to be taking elevators?* I tried to remember the guidance we'd all gotten nonstop for months, but Hale's lack of a comeback pulled me into the present. "Is that a yes?"

He shrugged again. "My ex has one. She got the house."

Well, don't I feel like a jerk. It was easy to forget Hale wasn't the same soft-spoken boy I'd met freshman year. He'd been married and a pang of jealousy I didn't like hit me. Of course, never one to lean into emotions, I kept going. "You should have fought for half of the canned goods and toilet paper."

"Oh, thanks to my great lawyer, I got all the supplies, just no shelter." He snapped his fingers. "But if a robber was in my apartment when the sirens went off, he's in luck."

"Could be she, or they. Don't be so provincial, Edison. The worlds of thieving and squatting are not just a man's game anymore."

"Sisters and siblings are out here doing it," he said, leaning against the wall of the elevator car as we descended to the floor below. "Don't worry. I heard you put enough entitled white boys in their place in college. You don't need to remind me."

I met his eyes. "Entitled white boys like you?"

"Hey, I may have been entitled and a white boy, but I always appreciated the power of women." His smirk was annoying and sexy and annoying. I couldn't decide which and the conclusion ping-ponged in my mind, even when his eyes dipped from my eyes to my lips in an exaggerated way. "Always." In the time I knew him, Hale adopted a confidence that bordered on cocky, but it always seemed like an act to me. Between classes and research and work, I might have spent more time in college with him than anyone else. Still, I'd imagined what would happen at the intersection of that confidence and my body.

I didn't want to react to the way his expression changed ever so slightly and just for a flash, but I did, the familiar heat moving up my spine until me shaking my head was one part waving off his ridiculousness and the tail end of a body shudder. "Anyway. I guess the robbers in your house will be okay."

Hale nodded, looking around without meeting my eyes. "Is there…anyone at home with your supplies?"

"Not that I know of." I didn't tell him I'd always lived alone, never finding someone who challenged me enough to risk taking a relationship to the next step. No one who challenged me in the way he had.

"Ah." We stepped out of the elevator and he glanced down the part of the hall we hadn't explored. His booming voice made me jump. "Is anyone here?" It sounded like the man with the searchlight at the end of *Titanic,* which was so darkly in line with our current situation, I didn't even give him a hard time for yelling near my ear, just a raised eyebrow when he turned back to face me. "What? It's faster," he said, shrugging one shoulder. "And we have four more floors to check."

"We could divide and conquer," I suggested, already eyeing the path to the stairwell and deciding if I wanted to get a jump on him while in these heels.

"You seriously want to compete about this?" The tone of his voice said *let's be mature adults, here* but he was clocking the exit, too.

"It would be more efficient and it's not a competition." I

braced against the nearby wall to slip one heel off. The aging and discolored tile was cold when I lowered my foot to take off the other shoe.

"It's not?" Hale was behind me, the heat of his body radiating against me, or maybe that was just the lingering impact of the fantasy.

I'm going to make the smartest person on campus come so hard, she forgets basic addition.

I clenched my thighs together at the memory and stumbled, but Hale's hand was there, against my spine. It took a moment to regain my balance, a split second where I realized how long it had been since I'd had great sex. By the time I straightened, Hale's hand was still there at my back until I was steady on my feet. "No, it's not a competition. It's two adults looking for other people in an old science building and when you finish your floors, I'll be waiting for you downstairs having already finished."

He grinned, this crooked grin I remembered. "I'll take two and three and you take four and five," he said, nodding toward the stairwell and walking that way, glancing over his shoulder. "Best snack foods, wins!"

He was through the door before I realized the vending machines were on the floors he was taking. *Dammit.* I pushed the button for the elevator and the doors creaked open. The first time I'd talked to Hale was in that very elevator early in our freshman year. He'd been getting preferential treatment in our bio class for a few days and we were the only two people in the car. I knew who he was by then, the latest in the long line of Edisons attending Edison University. He didn't exactly match the image I had. He was dressed in just a T-shirt and jeans, but he didn't smell wealthy—he just smelled like a slightly sweaty, when-is-the-last-time-you-washed-that-hoodie first-year dude, like most other guys I'd gotten to know. He didn't sound like I expected either, his voice quiet and soft. "You're in my bio class, right?"

I'd nodded. I knew I should have said something but I was tired. I worked two on-campus jobs to afford school, which meant sometimes studying had to go late into the night and I resented the hell out of anyone I assumed had it easy. And Hale Edison III certainly had it easy from my vantage point.

"That quiz was rough. How did you do?"

I'd gotten nineteen out of twenty questions correct and that was steaming me, too. All in all, I was in a bad mood. "Fine, you?"

He's pushed his fingers into his hair. "I got all twenty, but I wasn't expecting to. I want to study more next time. I was wondering if maybe you'd like to—" The door had stopped on the ground level, the ding cutting him off, and I'd hurried out with a wave. I didn't want to acknowledge that he'd outperformed me our first quiz of the semester.

Now, all these years later, the doors opened on floor four and I stepped off onto a different shade of discolored cold tile. I never knew what he was going to ask me. I'd rushed out of the elevator determined he'd never beat me again and by the time I slowed down enough to think about the interaction, it was too late to ask. I'd wondered for years, though. Now, the hall was deserted and I looked up and down before copying Hale, yelling into the dimly lit space, "Is anyone here? Hello?" I was met with stillness and silence—the fifth floor was abandoned and I wondered if Hale would find anyone on the lower floors. Part of me hoped he did. It would slow him down, but this was the kind of thing where more people were better. *Right?* Another part of me—the part me of who'd had to clench her thighs when he touched me, hoped it was just him and me.

I knocked on a few doors nearby and called into the darkness again, but found nothing except aging posters of anatomical structures staring back at me. The one showing musculature looked a little like Hale. Well, if Hale had no skin. It was what I imagined his muscles looked like, though he seemed to have more now than in college. I was softer, rounder and hotter. Hale was hotter, too, and I was too smart to be thinking about that, especially under the watchful gaze of that poster. *Judgmental skinless asshole.* I put everything into my job happily, but I'd never made time for marriage or kids. I'd barely made time for dating and I was usually the only one getting familiar with my own anatomy.

A door slammed below. I heard the pounding of feet and I hurried to the stairwell. Grown, mature, self-anatomy-studying woman or not, I was not going to let that entitled white boy win and I remembered something important about the fourth floor.

4

HALE

*D*on't think about her naked. *Don't think about her naked.*
Don't think about her naked. The mantra was a fool's errand. The girl who drove me crazy in college, who filled
my fantasies in med school and who was always in the back
of my mind during my marriage was here with me in that
tight, curve-hugging red dress. The idea of her body bare
and on top of me was all I was thinking about. Well, or her
body below me, or bent over, or any number of other con-
tortions. I pushed on a door I was surprised gave way to a
break room of sorts. The motion sensors caught me and the
lights flickered on, the vending machines coming to life.
They were newish and looked sturdy, like I could back Piper
up against one and rattle loose some snacks... *Fool's errand.*

The first time we talked in that elevator, I'd had the same
urge, to back her against a wall and feel her warm body
against me, to taste her lips. I hadn't had the first clue of

how to do that at the time. I think if I'd tried to even step closer to her, I would have started tripping over my words. Touching her or letting her touch me would have been out of the question. It had been a moot point, anyway. I'd started to ask her to study with me and she'd walked out, leaving me with my flashcards in my hand and my face hot from humiliation. For the kid whose family started the university, my peers oscillated between ignoring me completely and assuming I was getting preferential treatment because of my family. Nowhere on that continuum felt great and Piper seemed to be the only one who didn't care. In a weird way, she was the only one I really cared about proving myself to. So, I ignored the other people and tried harder because of her. Because of Piper's unstoppable drive to push harder and do more. Piper's sometimes condescending tone when she knew more than someone who didn't realize it. Piper's ass in those jeans she used to wear that guaranteed she'd outperform me on an exam because I was too busy willing my hard-on to go down to fully focus on the questions.

Above me, she yelled to get the attention of anyone who might be in the building and I flicked my eyes around the lounge, looking for something to use to break into the snack machine after realizing there was no credit card reader. I hadn't carried cash or change with me in years. Spotting a departmental award from 1987 on the back of a shelf, I considered using the pointed end to break the glass as I brushed dust from the surface. As I wrapped my hand in my jacket and swung it, I thought about my grandfather's lecture about what was expected of an Edison when I first arrived on campus and laughed. The glass, or maybe it was acrylic, spiderwebbing but not shattering into a billion pieces, and it seemed the old man's hopes for me had been fully dashed in that moment. He was rolling in his grave at the image of me vandalizing campus property to impress a woman, but I couldn't bring myself to care too much.

I heard the pounding of footsteps in the nearby stairwell and grinned, making a grab for snacks when I nudged the unshattered glass away. My jacket made for an excellent makeshift bag that looked like the grocery haul for two twelve-year-olds—chips and candy, cookies and anything else I could wrestle into the bundle. I had no idea how long it would take or how long we'd be trapped, but we wouldn't go hungry. There was something oddly fulfilling about knowing I could provide comfort or sustenance for Piper, even in this small way.

I strode into the office space a moment later.

"What took you so long?" Piper's chest heaved. *Dear God, her chest.* As a doctor, I sometimes felt I shouldn't be so stirred by the human body and I usually did have some objective distance, but not with Piper, not at the curve of the tops of what I imagined were full, soft breasts I could get lost in.

"You just got here and you know it," I said, walking toward her. "Your chest is heaving."

"Are you admitting you were looking at my chest?"

I set my jacket on the desk near her, unfolding the sleeves I'd used to secure it. "Are you going to admit you were looking me up on social media?"

She sucked her lower lip into her mouth and grinned. "I withdraw my question."

"Same," I said, showing off my haul. "And ta-da."

"Damn, Edison. Did you rob a vending machine?"

I snatched a bag of peanut M&Ms off the top and tossed them to her. "Yeah. Figured if robbers can enjoy my place, I guess we all might as well turn to a life of crime."

She caught the bag gracefully and tore it open. "These are my favorites."

"I know." I was looking down at the snack pile. "I mean, you shoveled them in your mouth like they were oxygen when we studied for the MCAT."

"You remember that?"

She'd show up to the library for our study group with her hair wrapped in a silky scarf sometimes and I'd imagine what it felt like as I'd peek at the way the color offset her brown eyes. Her eyes would dance and that's when I knew she'd figured something out or overcome a hurdle. I'd been worried someone else in the group would notice me noticing her so thoroughly, but no one ever did. "Seriously, you ate them all the time. It's not that weird that I remember," I said defensively.

She didn't respond and when I finally braved a glance up, her expression was skeptical. "Forget the M&Ms," Piper finally said, reaching into the pile of snacks. "Why did you grab these?"

I was a double board certified specialist in obstetrics, on the surgeon general's national task force on maternal and birthing people health, former president of the homeowner's association for the home I no longer owned, and I destroyed the cockiest teens you've ever met in rec league basketball every weekend. I was a mature, confident adult with my life together, and yet, one look from Piper Drake had me wanting to sink into the floor, the second I saw what she was holding.

Between her fingers was a small box of condoms and my brain short-circuited.

"It must have been in the vending machine..." I stammered. "You know, college kids. I just grabbed things without looking." I tried to snatch them from between her fingers and she pulled back. "Give them to me," I insisted, stepping toward her to take the condoms and...well I wasn't sure what I'd do next, but get rid of them.

"Why? Do you need them this instant?"

I took one quick stride and was in front of her body leaning against the wall she'd backed against. "Just give them to me," I said, making a grab for the package, but she hid it behind her back, blocking me. "Why are you acting like such a child?"

"I'm not the one who brought condoms and M&Ms for dinner." She tried to duck away from me, but I pressed one palm to the wall by her head and reached behind her to try for the box again with my other. Instead of saying something else, she let out a sigh, a heavy breath near my ear that made me freeze and combust at the same time. Piper's lips were parted and her chin tipped up. Our mouths were so close, I could see the tiny chip in her front tooth. I'd catch myself staring at the teeny, tiny imperfection across the lab table for years, during study groups, and now here she was. It was a perfect imperfection and one of the only few she ever willingly showed me.

"Just like old times," she said on a soft exhale that felt like a moan.

I hadn't meant to pin her like this, hadn't planned that our thighs would touch. "One old time," I said, mirroring her soft tone. "It only happened once."

She met my eyes and then lowered her gaze to my mouth. "Just that one time." It felt like an eternity that we stood there, bodies together, heat growing between us, but she shook her head finally and handed me the box of condoms, ducking under my forearm.

"I didn't find food, but I brought something better," she said, shaking off whatever just happened and walking toward the desk. "Remember Dr. Scroner?"

I'd called him Dr. Boner in my head until well into my thirties. "Sure. Worst professor I ever had. It's like he was drunk."

She pulled two bottles of Scotch from under the desk. "Probably was because his office was stocked and unlocked. I'm guessing his teaching hasn't improved."

"Drake, you're my hero." After feeling her against me, the cold wall at my front had been a sharp contrast and I didn't know how long it would be until the world ended, but I was certain being a little drunk on Dr. Boner's stash would make it go easier.

She handed me one of the bottles of Scotch, the scent of the liquor hitting my bloodstream before I even took a sip. "To the end of the world," she said, holding her bottle out for me to clink mine.

"To the end of the world," I said, taking a swig. The liquor burned going down in a deeply satisfying way. The only sound around us was the HVAC system rumbling, that and the years of things unsaid.

"Did you imagine the end being like this?" Piper stared into her bottle, now back in her hand.

I shook my head and thought about her question. "Honestly, I assumed I'd be at work, taking care of people. The hospital is where I've spent most of my adult life." I took another swig. "Just before we divorced, I told my ex that. She wasn't even surprised, just…resigned, I guess." The alcohol was a good distraction from that memory. She'd been hurt that I didn't expect to be with her, but I knew she wanted honesty. Still, I hated the disappointment on her face and expected to see that in Piper's features when I looked up, but she only nodded.

"Me, too. I just always assumed I'd be at work, probably working late grading papers. Like you said, it's where I spent so much of my life." I watched her tip her bottle up, taking a sip and cringing at the taste of the cheap liquor. "It's always been hard to find someone who understands that, or who makes me want to find better balance."

"To unhealthy work-life balance," I said, raising my bottle in her direction. "Dr. Boner's hooch was kind of therapeutic, huh?"

"I guess, so. Though a little late." Piper slid off the desk and went to the small coffee maker in the corner, returning with two mugs. "Can't say there's much need to unpack our workaholic tendencies now."

"I don't know…" I poured a few fingers of Scotch into a mug that read PHDelusional. "Maybe if nothing else, we'll go out in the company of someone who fully understands our love for the work. That's something, right?" I'd meant it as a joke, but as the words left my mouth, they felt true. It wasn't the Scotch—well, it wasn't all the Scotch. I felt my muscles relax and my anxiety calm and I desperately wanted her to know me again. I didn't expect Piper to respond in kind, but she was again quiet for a moment before her voice filled the room.

"And if you want, we can pretend you didn't want to kiss me a minute ago," she said, before tipping the bottle to her own mug. "I'm sure that might have been embarrassing for you."

The old me might have denied it. The kid would have. The academically confident but romantically inexperienced college junior who'd had a flash of a chance with Piper would have, too, but I had a lot of years between now and that kid and couldn't give in to the urge to tell her all my secrets, but I could give in to a different kind of urge. "Don't act like you didn't want me to do a helluva lot more than kiss you. Now or junior year."

5

PIPER

Junior year

Outside, the April sunshine made the budding flowers and newly green grass look like a brochure designer's dream, but no one in our premed cohort was enjoying it. We were all in the basement of West Hall, glued to computer screens and hitting the refresh button. Five of us sat silently, the stench of nerves probably wafting into the hallway and Hale Edison sat across from me, his brow furrowed in a way I pretended wasn't cute as hell. There were so many things I pretended I didn't think were cute or sexy or irresistible about my academic rival. I didn't think the way he pushed his glasses up on his nose was adorable and I definitely didn't notice how his forearms flexed when he worked his fingers over something delicate in the lab. I'd go to my grave before admitting how often I imagined those forearms flexing while his fingers worked over me.

"I'm in!" Someone shouted from across the room and the sound of hurried typing followed as we logged in to see our MCAT scores after waiting for over a month. I stared at the screen, digesting what was in front of me before looking up. One student groaned, another swore and two women gave each other a high five. Across from me, Hale remained glued to his screen, but a smile slowly spread across his face and he pushed his glasses up on his nose. He met my gaze and looked instantly concerned, but before he could open his mouth, I closed the browser window and walked out of the room, needing to find somewhere dark and quiet.

I wasn't sure how long I'd been in the storage room at the end of the hall when the door creaked open. The light from the open door illuminated the rows of supplies, the light from the hall reflecting off a beaker on the top shelf.

"Drake? You in here?"

I planned to stay silent—I was still in the shadow of the door, but a sob escaped my traitorous lips and he found me, walked inside and crouched down.

"Drake? What's wrong? Your score?" His hand brushed mine and it was such a soft touch that I cried harder, emotion welling in me. "It's okay," he murmured, continuing to brush my hand. "Talk to me."

I'd never cried in front of Hale—if you'd asked me the person I least wanted to break down in front of, it was him and his stupid chiseled jaw and expensive shoes. I never cried in front of anyone, and my only response was to suck in a breath because I wondered if he might be the only one who might understand.

"Drake, c'mon." His hands moved up my arms. "It's okay. A low score is not the end of the world."

He had no idea and I couldn't explain it, but he didn't let

go of my arms, he didn't move from in front of me. If anything, he moved a little closer, awkwardly crouching next to me in that cramped space, and then he shocked me. When I still didn't say anything, he pulled me into an embrace, his arms wrapping around my back and my face sinking against the crook of his neck where he smelled good and felt warm. His lips were near my ear, murmuring, "It's okay. It's okay."

"It's not," I finally said into his shirt. He stood for everything I wanted to be better than, but he was also the only person who might understand. "I'm not going to be a doctor."

He pulled back from me, his arms still around me but falling to my waist, and our eyes met. "What are you talking about? Of course, you will." His hand flexed at my waist when the door behind him clicked shut, the air-conditioning in the ancient building pushing it closed without assistance. We were in the dark, bodies pressed together which made it easier to voice.

"I'm not." I let my own hands slide up his sides and heard the sharp intake of his breath. I'd spent three years next to Hale in classes, labs and volunteer work but I'd never touched him, not like this, and the hard lines of his body, and curves of his muscles, and the soft cotton of his shirt under my palms was a welcome distraction. When my fingertips were against his shoulders, I tipped up my chin, and repeated more definitively, "I'm not."

"Drake." His hand flexed again at my waist and then his other palm was on my shoulder, moving to the back of my neck, clumsy in the dark. "Piper. You're the smartest person I know. The best prepared. You're still going to be a doctor."

"But I'm not. I don't want to talk about it," I said, stroking the side of his neck and once again hearing the sharp intake of breath. There was no light in the closet and it felt like our own little world.

Hale was quiet. For an entire minute as we stood there with only our breathing and the brush of fingertips against skin. "You're touching me," he said finally.

"You started it."

I couldn't see him smile, but I was pretty sure I heard it in his voice. "Do you want to stop?"

I shook my head, then added, "No. Not unless you want to." I shifted closer to him, bringing my hips to his body, and feeling him rigid against my belly. His breath was against my cheek and we were so close in this confusing moment.

"I don't." His face was closer to mine and his nose brushed mine, his aquiline, Edison family nose just like the one on the statue in the quad. "What do you need, Piper?"

"I can't handle everything right now. I need a distraction."

He gulped audibly, like a cartoon character. "Okay." His hand slid from my waist to my hip and I moved my fingers into his hair to pull me to him. Hale's voice was almost a whisper. "What kind of distraction?"

"Piper? Hale? You down here?" Two of our cohort members shouted from outside the door and we both leaped apart, the spell broken in the dark.

Hale took another swig from his mug after dropping that little challenge and I sipped thoughtfully from my own, shaking off the memory of that closet all those years ago. He'd stepped into the hall and told the others I needed space. The next morning, I'd changed my major, but I didn't forget what it was like to touch him in the dark. The grad student office suite wasn't dark, but it still felt like being back in that closet and I rolled his cocky words in my head. *Don't act like you didn't want me to do a helluva lot more than kiss you. Now or junior year."*

"Maybe while we were standing there I had a fleeting thought that the last orgasm I'd ever experience was from my own hand in the shower before I rushed to the airport. Don't take too much credit." If Hale's little jab had thrown me into the throes of old memories, mine made him sputter and cough on his Scotch. I took the win.

He pounded at his chest. "Come again?"

"Well, I would if I could. Catch up, Edison."

He nudged his finger along the top of his nose, though he wasn't wearing glasses and I wondered if he'd gotten LASIK recently. There was something so endearing about the gesture.

"Have I scandalized you?"

"Scandalized? No." He took a small sip and set his mug aside. "But you did want me to kiss you a few minutes ago? Or...do more than kiss you?" His bravado was gone, the confident air of a doctor I'd seen on him tonight that I didn't remember from college. "Because I would." He sat forward in the chair. "I mean, end of the world and all. It would be better if your last orgasm was provided by someone with extensive knowledge of the human body." When he shifted in his seat, his pants legs drew up and I saw the colorful socks with yellow smiley faces on them.

It was such an unexpected sight and I smiled to myself. "*I have extensive knowledge of the human body,*" I said, crossing one leg over the other, enjoying the squeeze of my thighs. "I teach anatomy and biology and have been exploring my own body for a very long time." I took one more small sip, catching the heated look in Edison's eyes.

"Drake," he said, rising to his feet. "Imagine what we could do with our combined anatomy knowledge."

His hand hovered over my knee, the tips of his fingers barely grazing the skin there. "Can I touch you? Because, cards on the table, I've wanted to touch you since the last time we spoke. Since the first time we spoke, really."

The touch sent a shock wave of anticipation up my thighs and I nodded. "This can't happen," I said, guiding his hands.

"Why not?" He nudged me to uncross my legs. "I can't in good conscience let your last orgasm be a rush job alone in the shower."

I bit the corner of my lip before studying his face. "I never said it was a rush job. I take my time with important work."

He let out an appreciative hmm. "I remember that. Well, you're the teacher." He swiped the cushion from the cracked vinyl seat he'd been sitting in and dropped it to the floor in front of me before falling to his knees and toying with the skirt of my dress. "Instruct me. I've wanted to taste you for a very long time."

All those years ago, I'd enjoyed the sharp intake of breath from quiet Hale Edison, but it was my breath now, sharp at his words even as my thighs spread. "Yeah?"

He nodded, working my dress up my thighs and smoothing his warm palms over my skin. "Yeah." He tucked his fingers under the edge of my panties and raised an eyebrow. "I know you won't pass up the opportunity to show me how to do something."

"Pull them down," I said, leaning back on my outstretched arms. "But if we get in trouble with Brenda, it's your fault."

"I'll take the hit," he said, shoving my panties into the pocket of his slacks. His lips grazed my thighs and his breath was hot against my folds, already wet from our tête-à-tête,

294 · DENISE WILLIAMS

a blessing since that vending machine probably didn't have lube. "Here, Drake?" He dragged his knuckle up my sensitive seam and around my clit with a barely there touch.

"Your tongue," I said, watching his face in this surreal moment. "And harder."

His tongue traced the same path, the flat side surface sliding over my wanting flesh and then the pointed tip swirling around my clit with a delicious slowness. I groaned at the slow-building sensation and slid my fingers into his dark hair. He kept that swirl going as his finger teased my opening, moving in and out but not deep, not like I wanted.

"Give it to me," I groaned.

"Say, please." His voice was garbled against my skin but I grinned.

"Now," I said. "Who is instructing who here?"

He laughed against me. "True. And I'm a good student. Always have been." His finger slid all the way in, then was met by a second. He pressed against my G-spot in no time, the delicious pressure building onto the pulsing sensations in my clit. I was going to come on Hale Edison's tongue at the end of the world. "Lay back, Drake."

I lowered myself onto the surface of the desk, awkwardly at first, but then Hale pressed gently on my lower stomach and my back bowed at the intensity of that added pressure at the core of me. I squirmed and wriggled against his fingers and his mouth, his tongue still working my clit as if we'd been like this together for years. My muscles tensed, body coiling and coiling and coiling like the most dangerous kind of spring.

Despite the buildup, and the way I felt every inch of my body tense, ready to fall like dominoes, the orgasm took me by surprise. "Oh, God!" I cried out, my nerve endings lighting up like fireworks as Hale pulled an explosive, lingering climax from my body. "Oh, God," I repeated, melting into the surface of the desk.

He kissed my sensitive skin gently and looked up, meeting my eyes. "They say doctors have a God complex, but you can just call me Hale."

I should have had a snappy comeback but my body reeled with too much pleasure. "Edison, you're really good at that," I murmured on a languid exhale.

"You've never said that to me before."

I placed my palm over my pounding heart. "Well, we never studied like this."

"That's a shame." He wiped his mouth with the back of his hand and raised from his knees, holding out a hand for me. "You want to study more with me, Drake?"

I took his hand and rose to a sitting position, the world swimming around me for a moment as I returned to an upright state, my thighs still spread with my dress up over my hips. "Bring it on, Edison."

"Let me do this first," he said, his mouth crashing down onto mine, our lips and tongues mingling. He tasted like me and Scotch and I fell into the kiss. "Wow," he said finally pulling away and sucking in a breath. "I've wanted to do that since I first saw you, too."

I didn't tell him how long I'd wanted that, too, how many fantasies he still starred in. Instead, I said, "What are we—"

A startling creak sounded from down the hall and then a door slammed. We both froze.

"Is someone else here?"

6

HALE

I stared at Piper who had already jumped to her feet, skirt still bunched on her thighs that were still streaked with the evidence of her arousal. "What are you doing?"

"Looking to see if someone is out there," she whispered.

"Um…" I nodded to her exposed skin and motioned to my pretty obvious erection.

"Ugh. So what?" She pushed down the hem of the dress waved her hand to me. "Get your priorities right."

I stood, grumbling and adjusting myself. "I thought I had."

The hallway was still, the fluorescent lights casting eerie light over empty corners and the painted concrete walls. "Hello?" Piper called out and I tried to step in front of her, an urge to protect her from whatever or whoever had slammed the door.

"Stop walking in front of me," she hissed, nudging me out of the way.

"I'm trying to be a gentleman. We don't know who is out here." I took a bigger step and braced my arm to the right to keep her behind me as we crept down the hall in the direction of the sound.

Piper tried to maneuver around me. "And you're—what?—an MMA fighter?"

"Listen, Drake." I glanced around and then turned to her, my palms against the surprisingly warm skin of her biceps. In the cool light of the fluorescents, she was warm with the red dress like a spot of heat. "You might be smarter than me and tougher than me, but at the very least, I'm bigger than you and since I can still taste you and I would very much like you to remain unharmed so I can taste you a few more times before this is all over. Will you just let me go a little caveman and stand in front of you in case we run into a nut-job running early for the postapocalyptic street fights and wielding a machete?"

Her stare was steely, jaw set in the way I remembered. But she finally relented, touching the pad of her thumb to the side of my lower lip and swiping it over my skin. It was such a soft gesture in the shadow of that hard expression. "Fine."

"Thank you," I huffed, wanting to strangle and kiss her in equal measure. I turned back toward the closed door to the classroom, the room I'd been poking around when Piper showed up. That felt like years ago, even though it was just a few hours. I wrapped my fingers around the doorknob and twisted, glancing over my shoulder where Piper was basically stuck to my back and looking pensive. "You okay?"

"You said I was smarter than you," she whispered.

"That's what you took from all of that?"

Piper shrugged, her eyes widening. "It just seemed worth noting!"

"You're impossible, I don't know why I even—" She nudged me from behind and the door creaked open like it was auditioning for a WD-40 ad.

The lights at the front of the room were still on, illuminating the low podium and table on the small stage. Piper's fingers dug into my sides and her chest was against my back. "Hello? Anyone here?" We stepped together into the room and I knew her heartbeat matched mine in intensity. The space was cool, making me think the air-conditioning worked better in this classroom than the little graduate student suite we'd commandeered for M&Ms, scotch, sex and waiting out the end of the world.

"Is someone down here?" Piper called from behind me and we looked left and right. I had no idea what I was doing so I channeled every police procedural I'd ever seen, feeling a need to yell, "Clear!" No one stirred or spoke as we made our way along the cinder block wall toward the stage, Piper holding on to me. I liked that part despite the mild uncertainty and fear. I guess that was one way to lose the erection I didn't particularly want to share with a stranger.

"There's no one here," Piper said, loosening her grip on me. She took a few steps from me, padding up the short staircase for the stage in her bare feet and putting us at eye level. "Do you think they went into another room?"

"Maybe… I liked it better when I knew we were alone."

"Me, too." She glanced around and I admired the curve of her neck; I couldn't help it. The curve of her neck was part of every memory of every premed class I took. She'd rub her neck with the tip of her index finger when she wasn't sure about an answer. It didn't happen often, but those were the only times I had a chance of scoring higher or doing better.

She touched that soft fingertip with the red-painted nail to her neck now and I was lost in the motion.

In an instant, there was a loud crash and Piper was against me, or maybe I was against her. Our arms were tangled and it took a moment to shift my brain from that fingertip to the crash to Piper in my arms. The door had slammed again with no one in sight.

"Damn air-conditioning," she muttered, her face against my chest. "How could I forget that after four years of doors slamming?"

I willed my acute stress response, my fight-or-flight instinct, to slow. "You're right. Shit." I lowered myself to the top step, awkwardly since Piper's arms were still around me and she was draped across my lap once we were seated. I stroked the spot on her neck where she'd been rubbing.

"Guess that little moment of…whatever in there didn't calm us down much," she said, settling against me. Piper would not acknowledge that she was willingly cuddling with me. She would deny it was happening if I brought it up so I didn't mention how her weight on my thighs made me feel safe and surrounded and how she smelled so good.

"That moment of me giving you the best orgasm of your life?"

"I never said it was the best of my life." She rested her head against my shoulder.

"But it was, right?" I fiddled with the zipper at the top of her back. "I guess I'm okay if I take second place to your own ministrations. How about that?"

"You can have second place." Her fingers toyed with the buttons on my shirt, exploring each one as we both came down from the high of adrenaline. "This was our Biology 101 classroom. It's where we first saw each other."

"Not exactly," I said tugging on her zipper, seeing how easily it would slide down.

Piper smacked my stomach with the back of her palm. "Are you challenging me because I gave you second place? Fine, it was, hands down, the best orgasm of my life."

I tugged the zipper a little lower, rubbing the space between her shoulder blades. "Yeah, I already guessed that, but that class still wasn't where I first saw you."

"It was the first day of freshman year," she insisted, pulling back to meet my eyes. "The professor should have called on me—I had my hand up—but they called on you instead because you're an Edison."

"Yeah. That happened, but I'd already noticed you." I tugged the zipper another inch down her back and I noticed how she squirmed against me when I did. I loved how Piper reacted to me. "It's why I sat near you in that class."

"I'd never seen you. I don't think we ever even spoke until a few weeks after that in the elevator after that first quiz." She searched my face like I might be trying to pull something over on her. "Where had you seen me before that class?"

"There was some mixer in the dorms. All the new students were there and I didn't want to go. I didn't know anybody, but my dad said I should as an *Edison*. Whatever that meant." I had a single room so I didn't even have a roommate to tag along with. By the time I'd arrived, everything was in full swing in the lobby.

"I vaguely remember that. I don't remember you, though." She squirmed against me, teasing I was pretty sure, or maybe just not super comfortable on this old wooden staircase, but I tugged the zipper another inch lower anyway, sliding my palm up her spine, memorizing the ridges of her vertebrae.

"I hung out against a wall," I said with a chuckle. "I was

about to leave and go back to my room, but I saw you laughing with some people." When I trailed my finger down her spine, toying with the clasp on her bra, she shivered under my touch. "And you had this great laugh. You still do." I twisted the first hook on the closure, which took two tries. I'd never been able to get a bra undone with one hand so I wasn't sure why the skill would come to me smoothly at the end of the world. "There was some kind of makeshift dance floor. I wanted to ask you to dance with me, which I'd never done before because girls kind of scared me."

"Because our underthings are so complicated?" She sat up and swatted my hand away before reaching behind her back and unhooking her bra in one swift motion.

"Show-off," I said, stroking my fingers down the middle of her back and pushing the straps aside. "Because I was a science nerd who was awkward-looking and I knew what people would think when they learned who I was." I hadn't even wanted to go to Edison, but I didn't have a choice. "And you looked...so gorgeous and cool."

"My high school students tell me no one says *cool* anymore." She wriggled against me, her palm settling again on my stomach.

I squeezed her round ass playfully and tugged the zipper down another inch. "Well, we're old, so it's fine." Teasing her was fun but my body had shifted back to its previous state of wanting all of Piper Drake and I fought the urge to rip that dress off her.

"But you didn't ask me to dance," she said, bringing the conversation back to my story.

I shook my head. "'Yeah!' By Usher, Lil Jon and Ludacris came on and everyone got excited and your group of friends started dancing around you, but I didn't know how to dance. I watched you a little longer—you wore this blue T-shirt that dipped low in the front and you had this smile that just made me…"

She raised her head again, meeting my eyes.

I wasn't embarrassed exactly, but I looked into her eyes, the curve of her brow and the shape of her lips. I remembered her crying against my shoulder after we got our MCAT results and the different feel of her against my shoulder now. It was ridiculous that I felt a stronger pull toward Piper than I had to anyone else in my life. I could blame the circumstance or the fact that I was turned on or even the nostalgia of being in this room, but it wasn't any of that. It felt like I'd missed a lot over the years, but had suddenly found everything I needed. "I went back to my room and watched that music video on repeat until I could do all Usher's moves, just in case the opportunity to dance with you ever came up again."

"Wait…wait. I need to see this."

"No way. Since one drunken night in medical school, I've never shown anyone." I tugged the zipper the rest of the way down and slid my palm down the back of her dress, palming her ass and squeezing, continuing my teasing. "In retrospect, I don't know why I assumed that same song would be playing and it was before I knew you were the most competitive person I'd ever meet. If I wanted to catch your attention, I probably should have challenged you to a foot race instead of to dance." I stroked a thumb over the L4 and L5 vertebrae at her lower back. "I didn't think someone like you would ever notice someone like me, so…I studied, just in case. Anyway, doesn't that earn me one of your stories?"

"No," she said, shifting on my lap so she was straddling me, the dress inching up her thighs and her warm, wet center over my dick through my pants. She began undoing my buttons while I palmed her through her dress. She giggled when I gave her a light pinch and the vibration of her laughing made me groan.

"C'mon," I said, raising a hand to slide the dress down one shoulder, kissing the skin there and sweeping the bra strap away. "I'll go down on you again if you tell me."

She laughed again and pulled her arms free from the dress. "You'll go down on me again regardless."

"Probably." I wanted two more hands so I could hold both breasts and keep my hands on her backside, but I had to split my efforts and Piper's breast was warm and heavy in my hand, her brown nipple pert and responsive against my fingers as I rolled one and then another between my thumb and forefinger. "Tell me, anyway. Tell me something embarrassing."

She rolled her eyes but grinned and her breath caught when I added more pressure to my roll. "Fine," she murmured when my lips met her neck. "I had a fantasy of you..."

I continued toying with her nipple. "Had or have?"

"Had. And have. Can I finish?"

"Please."

"Fine," she said on a gasp when I gently pinched. "I have a fantasy of you bending me over that podium and fucking me in this classroom."

"That sounds doable," I murmured against her neck, pulling her against my cock.

"While saying I was better at chemistry and biology."

I smiled against her neck because of course that would be Piper's fantasy. "We haven't been students for years," I said as she finished with the buttons on my shirt and rolled her hips against me. "When did that fantasy start?"

"I've been having it for...a while. And I know, I'm a classic academic overachiever with a slight praise kink. I can't help it."

I thought of the lyrics to that Usher song that lived rent-free in my head and kissed up her throat and spoke into her ear. It had to be fate we'd end up here together and I wouldn't pass up my chance to dance with her again. "Stand up, Piper. And walk to the podium."

7

PIPER

The cool air in the room was jarring when we pulled apart and I stood on the stage, my dress at my waist and Hale stalking toward me, his shirt open and revealing the sculpted, lean frame and the thin line of hair running from his belly button. "Will the praise alone do the trick," he said, reaching me and pulling my back against him, "or am I going to need to find some gold stars?"

"The gold stars are obviously a plus." I groaned as his palms slid from my hips to cup my breasts and then back down, pushing the dress down my thighs so I was bare, standing on the stage of this lecture hall.

"Of course, they are," he said into the back of my neck, his lips brushing my nape. "God, you're gorgeous. Did you always look luscious?"

I did my best Lil Jon impression. "Yeah!" Hale swatted my ass, making me laugh and then moan when his hand traveled lower to between my thighs to stroke me. My brain could not catch up to the level of upside down this night had gone and I didn't want it to when his finger made one long pass and dipped inside me.

"At what point should I say you were better at chemistry?" His finger worked in and out and I squirmed, wanting more. "Or do I just keep repeating it?"

"You don't have to limit it to chemistry. You can mention biology, physics—" I sucked in a breath when he added a second finger and his thumb brushed over my other hole, just a swipe but it sent shivers up my spine. "Any class, really," I added when I caught my breath.

"Ah," he said, flattening a palm on my back. "I see. So just, decimate my own pride."

"If you don't mind," I said, backing against his hand. The podium was cool against my chest but was a perfect height to grip. This was so close to my fantasy I worried I'd wake up at any moment.

"Can you come again like this?" He pumped faster and I felt the jut of his rigid cock against me. "Probably not able to, huh?"

"Are you reverse psychology'ing me into an orgasm?" My body was already coiling as he pumped against my G-spot and teased. "It doesn't work that way."

"Yes, it will. You like to prove me wrong." He pumped harder and pressed my back with the flat of his hand. "You like to prove everyone wrong."

I wanted to roll my eyes and deny him this small victory, but with each thrust of his fingers I was teetering on the edge, with fifteen years of this fantasy behind every stroke and thrust. The fantasy and that he knew me so well.

"Good. Good, Piper." His voice was a murmur at my

back as I tensed, his hand holding me in place as I squirmed against him, so close and so ready until I squeezed my eyes shut against the pleasure racking through me, and everything happening outside the classroom was gone, forgotten. There was my body under Hale Edison's touch. "So good, Piper."

I liked hearing him say my name, that always felt more right to me than "good girl" or something like that. He'd always called me by my last name and I liked the way it sounded coming from his lips.

I heard his belt and his pants hitting the floor, then the unexpected, "Oh no."

"What's wrong?" I straightened, looking over my shoulder.

"I don't have a condom. I left that box in the grad office." He looked longingly at the door leading to the hallway and I glanced down to where he held himself in his fist, a drop of pre-cum already beaded at the tip.

"Edison, the world is ending. Who cares? For what it's worth, I have an IUD." One of his palms was at my hip and I squeezed it. "Will you do this now while we still can?"

His lips crashed down on mine at that awkward angle with him still behind me, but it was perfect—hurried and frantic but still soft in the frenzy. Hale kissed me like it was a relief, like the kiss was the breath he'd been needing, and maybe I was just projecting, because that's what it felt like to me, too. "Bend down," he said into my ear when breaking the kiss, his cock at my backside. "Let me tell you the ways you're smarter than me." His fingers spread me for a moment and then the head of his cock was there, the head wide and stretching me in the most delicious way.

I closed my eyes again, cataloging every feeling as he pushed in deeper, the way he filled me, the weight of his hand at my back and his fingers digging into my hip. "You don't have to say it." I groaned as he pulled out and pushed back in. We fit together at this angle like we were meant to be joined like this. "This is so good."

"You *were* the best," he said. "For what it's worth." He squeezed my hip, thrusting into me while pressing his palm gently but firmly against my back as I lowered my fingers to my clit. "The smartest, the sharpest." His words were short punches between each thrust and I gripped the podium with my free hand. "I always knew it."

My body craved each shift, the pressure in the right spots and my own fingers circling my sensitive clit. His words draped over my skin like silk. "Hale," I panted. "Hale. Hale."

"I always saw you," he said on ragged, stuttering breath. "Always. Let go, Piper. Give me another one." He thrust again, the control in his pace maddening, but just what I needed as my orgasm built to a peak and I crashed around him, the pulse of my core moving through my whole body. "Good. So, Good."

His thrusts grew shallower and more erratic and then he pressed deep into me and let out a low shuddering groan with his own release.

It was a moment before he gently lifted me to him, his hands pressing against my belly, his mouth at my shoulder and my neck. "You made me better, Piper. You made me want to be better."

I turned in his arms and kissed him, this time slowly with our bodies against each other, touching everywhere we could until we had to pull apart to breathe. "You made me better, too." We kissed again and we kept kissing, making up for all the years we didn't kiss and somehow erasing all other kisses that filled the space before this moment.

"This is romantic," I said, cupping his jaw and shifting from foot to foot.

"But it's freezing and uncushioned?" He finished my sentence for me. "Want to go back to our other hideout? There's a couch there." He slid his arms out of his shirt and draped it over my shoulders. "And M&Ms."

"You read my mind," I said, sliding my arms into the sleeves and involuntarily inhaling his scent on the fabric. "Maybe *you're* actually the smartest."

"I like you so much," he said, taking my hand, "that I won't even make you repeat that later."

8

HALE

Saturday Morning

I stroked Piper's bare back in the makeshift bed we'd created, pulling the cushions and pillows off the ancient couch. A lamp on one of the desks was a soft glow in the room and the shadows around us were soft. We'd devoured each other like we had no time other than now, which I guessed was true, and Piper was everything I wanted at the end of the world. The night before, we'd cuddled together after another round, both drowsy and warm against each other, the chaos of what was happening aboveground recessing into the shadows. In this lulling sleepy murmur she'd asked me why I got divorced. My parents had asked me that, colleagues and friends, too, and I'd always said I let work get in the way. It wasn't a lie, but Piper's soft murmur pushed me to say more. I'd pulled her closer and admitted, "It was too easy. We never disagreed or fought or anything. It was easy and then it was…unfulfilling. We never pushed each other to grow."

Piper had given a soft *mmm* sound against my chest as her finger traced lazy circles over my skin. "She didn't get it."

"I didn't get it," I'd corrected. "I was content, but I was never happy. I was never…excited. It's hard to admit you're still chasing the high of a beautiful girl risking a fall down the stairs to defeat you. That that's what you truly want."

Piper had been quiet and I wondered if she'd fallen asleep until she said, "I, on the other hand, always told men up front I was that woman. Most of them wanted easy."

"We should have found each other again sooner." I stroked up her back, fingers tickling the nape of her neck, bracing for the response because I meant it.

"We have each other now," she'd said against my chest, before drifting off to sleep, the cadence of her breathing changing to a slow, steady rhythm while my thoughts whirled.

Hours later, I stared at the ceiling, counting the tiles, and making and remaking patterns out of them as I rolled her words around my mind.

She stirred under my fingers. "It's morning?"

"Yeah," I said, tracing circles on her shoulder. "After five."

She sat up, rubbing her eyes. "Good morning." There were a few sweatshirts hanging on the back of the door to the graduate suite and she'd pulled one on along with my boxers sometime in the night to trek to the bathroom. She looked sleep rumpled and I linked my fingers with hers because I couldn't not touch her.

I hadn't slept, but staring at the ceiling I'd had one recurring thought. I don't want to be without this woman and her words had taken up residence in my head. *We have each other now.* The idea of that, even as we sat on the precipice of the end of the world, felt warm. It made me feel right in a way

I never had and I took in her sleepy expression, brushing a piece of hair off her forehead. "Marry me, Piper."

Her hand fell from mine and she stared at me with an owlish expression. "Are you drunk? Did you finish that bottle of Scotch while I was asleep?"

I laughed, the laugh of the exhausted and content. "Marry me," I repeated, picking up her hand again.

"Edison, there are so many things about that statement that I don't even know where to start."

"Start here." I placed her hand on my heart. "I know it's too fast and also we're waiting for the world to burn down any minute and I know we can't actually get married in this concrete basement."

She let me place her palm on my chest and kept it there, the warmth of her hand through the fabric of my shirt even as she nodded. "Yes, those are a few good reasons. Also, we've spent twelve hours together after fifteen years of not speaking and in college we were enemies! You can't ask me to marry you."

"To be fair, though, they've been a good twelve hours. And we were rivals, not enemies. Marry me."

Piper let her hand fall from my chest and looked around the room as if for an explanation.

"And I knew I wanted you from the first moment I saw you and I think I knew I loved you on some level since the first time you competed with me for a grade and I knew for certain I loved you on *every level* when you let me be with you after the MCAT results came back. You let me see you cry and hold you when, for once, you weren't the best at something. When maybe you felt like you'd failed." I had never forgotten the way she'd melted against me, the way her crying sounded, so hopeless, and when I hugged her how she'd leaned into me.

She rubbed the side of her neck with her index finger. "It was dark. You didn't see me."

"Well, I saw for a minute. It was something and you trusted me." There was silence between us for a few moments, the unmistakable sounds of birds outside the painted window where I knew a group of trees sat. The birds chirping was such a life-affirming sound and so out of place with the moment. "I know it's ridiculous, but marry me."

"You can't keep asking me that," she said.

"Technically I haven't asked. They've been more declarative statements."

Her laugh was short but real and she took my hand again, placing our linked fingers back over my heart. "You made me better, too." She took in a breath, releasing it on a slow exhalation.

I opened my mouth to speak but she pressed a finger to my lips.

"I couldn't afford to go to school here. I didn't go to a fancy private school—my parents didn't have money. I felt the need to prove myself from day one. To be the best and prove to everyone that I deserved to be here."

I nodded and squeezed her fingers.

"And I was going to be a doctor. It was my lifelong dream, prestigious for my family, and hopefully well paying. I was going to break the cycle of poverty in my family. I wanted my community to be proud of me. So, I made sure I was the best, but then I realized it might not be what I wanted to do after all."

"And then you got your MCAT score?" I scooted closer so I could stroke my hand over her bare knee.

"And then I got my score." She let go of my hand again and brushed her hair off her face. "And I knew I wasn't going to be a doctor. I switched to education the next day. But what you saw wasn't me feeling like I failed. It was me coming to terms with my plans changing."

"Plans…change. I thought I'd stay with my wife forever and then we divorced after six years. Now I'm here with you. Sometimes changing plans is good. Sometimes the changes take you back to what and who you wanted in the first place."

"It is and this change was good. I don't worry about proving myself anymore and I realized that when you hugged me in that closet. So, you made me be better, too."

"So, mar—"

"I swear to God if you say it one more time, Edison."

I bit my tongue harder than I meant to. "I get that…but I don't care if you got a low MCAT score or changed your career plans, Drake. I never cared."

"I didn't get a low score." Her voice was low, almost inaudible. "I got a forty-one."

My mouth fell open; it actually fell open on its own. "Drake, that's in, like, the top one percent of test takers."

"Top half a percent," she corrected because of course she did. And she was right. "And even with that score, I still didn't want to go to medical school, so I didn't."

"Shit," I said, leaning back against the couch. "You *are* smarter than me. I'll hand you that all day long."

"I know. But it's a standardized test and I've been in education long enough to know that's not a perfect indicator." Piper grinned and this time, she reached for my hand. "But I'm not the same person I was in college. I'm not worried about deserving to be anywhere anymore. I'm a grown-ass woman now who makes grown-ass woman decisions. So, you can't propose based solely on one night of, admittedly, fantastic sex." She kissed my fingertips. "Even at the end of the world."

She looked up, her dark eyes meeting mine. "Even if there's no one else I would have rather spent my last hours with."

"Okay," I said, reluctantly, tucking her against my side. The silence of the room and the ambient sounds from outside surrounded us for a couple minutes. "Forty-one?"

"Are you intimidated now?" She was so soft against me. For having so many sharp, witty, motivated edges, Piper always felt soft against me.

"Completely."

"Will that stop you from doing that thing we did at two this morning? Because I'd really like to try that again."

"No," I said. "I think being intimidated by your test score might help me do that again. That and stretching first."

Piper rose to her feet and I dragged my palm down the side of her leg. "I'm sorry I won't marry you, Edison. No hard feelings?" She slid her fingers through my hair.

"None. But if you change your mind…"

"You'll be the first to know." She nodded toward the hallway and I listened to the click of her heels on the tile as she walked to the bathroom at the end of the hall. Proposing was ridiculous and, on some level, I knew she'd say no, but something about asking her to be with me felt so right. I rose to my own feet, stretching after a night on the uncomfortable bed and full of aerobic and slightly acrobatic activity. I thought I heard the birds still chirp outside the covered window and I looked at my phone, knowing service was still out.

I flipped mindlessly through the apps and then I got an idea. I scribbled a note on a Post-it and stuck it on the door to the grad suite before I walked out.

9

PIPER

The heels in combination with a stranger's University of Kentucky sweatshirt and Hale's boxers was a look, but I wasn't about to walk through a public bathroom with bare feet, even at end of days. *He asked me to marry him.* "Some kind of psychosis must be settling in." My side comment to no one ricocheted off the walls as I washed my hands and studied myself in the mirror. The bananas thing was, I'd wanted to say yes because the thing I hadn't said, the thing I should have said, was that competing against him had cemented for me that I belonged at the school, which was what gave me the courage to leave the premed track. Over the four years, I'd gotten the sense Hale had pressure on him to succeed, too. Only everyone in his life assumed he would do it, while I always felt like I was having to defy society's expectations of me. But he never treated me like that. He always treated me like a worthy adversary and I was. I took that for granted back then—I took the confidence, but I didn't let myself see how much Hale had to do with my newfound self-awareness. I sighed, nearing the door, our little love nest until a meteoroid shower plummeted the world into chaos and destruction. It was a silly idea. *Marry him.* He'd said he was in love with me back then and my ridiculous heart, the soft part in the back I hid from everyone, hoped he still was.

There was a yellow Post-it on the door when I got there. Brenda's butt note was crossed out and in its place, in Hale's tiny, serial killer handwriting, was *Meet me in the bio classroom —H.*

I hustled down the hall. Maybe he heard something or maybe he just wanted to do the 2:00 a.m. thing back on the stage, but either way, I didn't want to lose any time. Only, when I got close, a familiar song started playing through the speakers and Hale was standing at the front of the room as the beginning of "Yeah!" filled the room.

"What is going on?" I had to yell over the opening beats as I hurried to the front of the room. "What is this?"

"Don't marry me," he said, holding out his hand and tugging me close.

"Yes, we already agreed on that." I let him pull me in and he was swaying to the music. "What are you doing?"

"I missed the chance to dance with you all those years ago. If you won't marry me, will you dance with me?"

"You're losing it," I said, dancing with him in a beatless shuffle. "You're genuinely losing it."

"I know." Hale started singing along near my ear. "Go with it."

"Will you show me the dance you learned?"

He grinned and sang along, looking like nothing was wrong in the world. For the second time that morning, I wondered if he'd had Scotch for breakfast. "Will you agree to marry me if I do?"

"No."

"Date me?"

"Date you?"

"Date me."

"Yeah, okay. Show me the dance and I'll date you for as long as we have left." I stepped back and watched him twist his body in the throwback of the early part of the century. He was good—really good—and I clapped and hooted, enjoying it most when he'd start laughing and messing up the steps.

"Okay," I said, standing from the desk. "Okay. I relent."

He did an impressive rockaway and I pulled his face down to mine. "You're still a nerd."

Hale's arms wrapped around my waist. "Joke's on you, forty-one. You're dating me, now."

"That my new nickname?"

"It will remind me you're smarter," he said, brushing his lips over mine. I sank into the kiss and his hands moved under the sweatshirt to rest against my bare back. The song had ended, throwing the room into a startling silence.

"For what it's worth, you're pretty smart, too." I cupped his cheek. "I wish we had more time."

"The 2:00 a.m. thing is going to take at least thirty minutes if done right." He leaned against my touch. "If we survive this, I'm going to ask you to marry me again eventually."

I opened my mouth to tell him how ridiculous it was to keep bringing it up. I'd braced both hands on his biceps and looked him straight in the eye when a deafening alert sounded, once, twice and then a third time. Our expressions matched because if we survived this, I might be tempted to say yes. "That was three alerts. That's the all-clear sign, right?"

His phone buzzed on the stage where he had it hooked to the speakers and we ran to it together and he grabbed for it. His eyes widened and he read it out loud, "'This is an official announcement. Your area is now confirmed "ALL-CLEAR" from aerial debris. Please exit your shelter safely.'"

"We're safe!" I yelled. At some point I started crying and then we were in each other's arms again.

"We're safe," he repeated, kissing me hard, but when he pulled away, he looked stricken.

"What's wrong?"

"I vandalized a vending machine. Like, I really destroyed it." He ran a hand through his hair. "And we had sex on a stranger's desk. A presumably underpaid and overworked stranger."

"A few times," I added. "They're definitely going to take away our alumni awards for that."

He grinned and twirled me around, dropping a soft kiss on my lips. "That's okay. This reward feels harder earned."

"I think you're right."

"I've waited fifteen years to hear you say that," he said, before kissing me again.

★ ★ ★ ★ ★

EPILOGUE

TAJ McCOY

One Month Later

"Griff, this thing is happening in less than a minute. Can you hurry up please?" Halley called from the main floor of their new town house. Griffin's lease was up when they arrived home after the siren snafu, and he fell in love with the property that Halley had moved to after their breakup. Halley's leasing manager allowed them to transfer from her studio into a town house unit—a spacious two-bedroom currently loaded with boxes.

"I'm coming, Hal, I just couldn't forget our Luna-Toons." Griff scooped up the cat, kissing the top of her head. "If the siren goes off before we grab her, we'll never get her out from under the bed."

Halley reached over and scratched beneath Luna's fuzzy chin, the cat stretching her head upward to expose more of her neck. "Come on, sweet girl, we're headed to the basement."

In the month since the incident, Halley's team gained recognition for their foresight to plan such a massive emergency test without the knowledge of the executive administration. Chief Henry took credit for his team's ingenuity, of course, but he acknowledged each member of the team at a NASA project debrief. After submitting one hell of a report, Halley had been promoted to project manager, and she pulled the same group for several quick missions back to Colorado to beef up the system and fit the station with a landline to HQ.

"I love that we have our own basement." Halley sighed as Luna nuzzled against her cheek. "No need to be stuck in tight quarters with a crowd of people..."

"Me—" The sirens started before Griff could agree. Loud and whirring, the familiar sound shocked Luna, who buried her face in Griff's neck. "Come on, babe, let's head down."

"I mean, do we really need to do this since we actually know there's no threat?" Having second thoughts, Halley craned her neck at Griff, who gently pushed her toward the stairs. "We haven't even had time to make the basement comfortable."

"Don't worry, I spent some time down there and set up some space for us for tonight." They thudded down the wooden stairs, Halley turning to wink at Griff, laughing at Luna gripping Griffin's shirt with her claws—the sirens still blaring.

The test was scheduled to run for two hours, so they wouldn't be uncomfortable for too long, and their finished basement had a full bathroom. Eventually, they planned to put a cozy modular couch and a movie projector down there, but the frequent trips to Colorado hadn't given them much time to get settled and buy new furniture. At the bottom of the stairs, Halley turned to look at Griff, who winced as Luna pounced out of his arms and ran toward her cat tree.

She had one on each level of the house, all configured differently, with multiple condos for her to hide.

Halley's eyes followed Luna until she was distracted by a string of lights shaped like stars, their warmth glowing in a circle around a faux sheepskin rug laden with cushy zafus, a platter of fresh fruit, a bottle of sparkling rosé in a bucket of ice with a couple of flutes and a crackling fireplace on a flat-screen TV. "What is all of this?" she whispered.

Griff wrapped his hand around hers, leading her toward their space. "I told you, I have us covered for tonight." He pulled out his phone and connected it to a Bluetooth speaker sitting on their unstocked wet bar, and soft music began to play. Luna peeked out of her cat condo as Griffin twirled Halley around and pulled her close, their hips touching, as she wrapped her arms around his shoulders. Griff placed his hands on her lower back, and they two-stepped slowly until the song changed.

Instantly, Halley's eyes widened at the sound of their song—the one that had made them both flinch only a month ago on their ride to the station. She leaned back enough to see Griffin smiling at her as H.E.R. sang about loving in every kind of way. Griffin pulled Halley toward him, dipping his head to kiss her gently. "What a difference a month makes," Halley murmured against his lips.

"I know you didn't fully believe me then, but I meant every word, Hal. There's nowhere I'd rather be—even if the sky was falling—I'd want to be right here with you. It took me a long time to realize that, but now I can't imagine ever losing you again." He stepped back from her and knelt on one knee, brandishing a box that made her gasp. "Halley Andromeda Oakes, named after comets and galaxies. You are my world, my safe space, my beautiful stargazer. Can we spend the rest of our lives chasing shooting stars together?" He opened the box to a twinkling diamond ring.

Halley's mouth dropped open as the warmth of the starry lights made the ring sparkle. "Wait, did you talk to my dad? You know he's old-fashioned."

Griffin smiled wide. "I have blessings from your dad, Nova and the chief. Nova helped me pick out the ring and is expecting a call after the all-clear. Chief has known about us all along, and he just asks that we remain professional on projects."

Halley's brow lifted. "Meaning no pedestal sinks or building forts?" Her smile turned sinister as Griff's gaze dropped to her mouth.

The corners of Griffin's eyes crinkled as he laughed. "What the chief doesn't know won't hurt him, babe." He leaned forward slightly, his brow wrinkling as he whispered, "I love you so much. Marry me, Hal."

Halley exhaled a breath she didn't know she'd been holding and perched on Griffin's other knee, wrapping her right arm around his shoulder. There were no questions left in her mind. "Then my answer is yes, Griffin Harper. I love you, and I cannot wait to marry you." Her hand cradling the back of his neck, she pressed her lips against his for an array of soft butterfly kisses. Halley opened her eyes to Griffin sliding the ring onto her finger. "You know," she whispered, "you're stuck with me now."

Griff stood, pulling Halley with him toward their starry circle of cozy cushions. He lay her down on the rug gently, her curls fanning out against a pillow as he propped himself up next to her, kissing her fingertips and her wrist before attempting to unbutton her blouse with one hand. "And I intend to take every moment possible to show you how happy that makes me."

★ ★ ★ ★ ★

ACKNOWLEDGMENTS

Taj McCoy

Disaster movies of the '90s and all the love stories that could have been were a huge inspiration behind this anthology, as was Veronica Park, who messaged me with a wild idea for a disaster-inspired "something" that I should pick up and make my own. As we spitballed our favorite movies and themes, *EITSIF* was born, and I am so grateful to V for believing I could bring the concept to fruition, for teaching me so much about the proposal process and for having the foresight to connect me with Errin.

To my incredible friends: Lane Clarke, Farah Heron, Charish Reid, Sarah Smith and Denise Williams, your talents are so far beyond anything I could have hoped for, and this project is better because each of you are a part of it. Over the last few years, I have learned so much from each of you and your respective writing styles, and I am so honored to have the opportunity to collaborate with you all. I'll never forget this experience. Thank you so, SO MUCH.

To my agent, Jem Chambers-Black, thank you for stepping into an awkward situation and immediately taking charge as firmly and as gracefully as you did. Your efforts to make this transition seamless did not go unnoticed, and I'm so blessed to have your guidance, support and friendship.

To Errin Toma, editor extraordinaire, thank you for understanding the vision and for even picking up the song references and vibes on that very first call. It's been a true joy working with you, and I hope this is just the first of many projects we work on together.

To Mia Sosa, thank you so much for graciously agreeing to introduce this collection! I am so grateful for your generosity and friendship, and I couldn't be more thrilled that you connected with the premise in such a tender way.

To the team at Canary Street Press: it takes a village! Thank you to Susan Swinwood, Kathleen Oudit, Erin Craig, Denise Thomson, Bradley Myles, Amy Jones, Ana Luxton, Lindsey Reeder, Heather Conner, Laura Gianino, Sophie James, Tracy Wilson, and the many other hands and voices who touched our collection along the way. To Adriana Bellet, for our gorgeous, swoony cover art—you are SO TALENTED!

To my family/friends/tramily/crew: thank you for your continued support. I know sometimes what I'm saying doesn't make sense until years later, but I appreciate your faith that *some*thing is coming and that you continue to support me no matter what. Your joy is absolutely everything to me!

To readers: thank you for believing that love can be born under the most precarious of circumstances and for chasing those happily-ever-afters even when the sky is falling.

Lane Clarke

To Taj—thank you for inviting me to join this project and being the big sister I always needed.

To G—we built our love story while the sky was actually falling. Thank you for being my disaster soulmate.

To *The Day After Tomorrow*—thanks for teaching a teenager who didn't think she could make it that survival is possible even in the worst of circumstances.

Farah Heron

I was a huge fan of epic disaster movies in the '90s, so I am delighted to be a contributor to this fun anthology! "Keep Calm and Curry On" was an absolute joy to write, and I am beyond grateful to Taj McCoy for giving me the opportunity to stretch my creativity and write something unlike anything I'd written before. Also, big thanks to Errin Toma and the rest of the Canary Street Press team for your enthusiasm and support! We all loved knowing this project was in such great hands. And thank you to my husband and to my family for being patient with me while I asked a million questions while I was brainstorming Maya and Tarek's story. I'm especially grateful that they nodded enthusiastically when I asked, "What if they had rival tikka sandwiches?"

I love connecting with readers! Find me on Instagram at farahheronauthor, or on my website, farahheron.com. And by the way, there is a paneer/chicken tikka recipe on my website that might not be as good as Maya and Tarek's, but it's close!

Charish Reid

Thank you, Taj McCoy, for coming up with such a brilliant concept for an anthology. Yes, there should have been much more kissing in movies like *Dante's Peak*, *Twister* and *San Andreas*. Thank you for rounding up a talented bunch of authors to make this happen. I'm so proud to work alongside Denise, Farah, Lane and Sarah.

Thank you, Errin Toma, for always asking me to dig deeper to find new ways of thinking about these characters. Under your guidance, I know I grow as a writer. Of course, I'm so thankful for my agent, Saritza Hernandez, for always supporting and advocating for me. Knowing that you have my back makes me want to take more chances and seek new creative avenues.

Lastly, I'm thankful that my husband shares my love for disaster movies and the Cold War. Thank you, Noah, for helping me with the strenuous research of watching how Gerard Butler saves his wife, his estranged child, the president and most of London while trying to bury his Scottish accent. There's no one else I'd want to grab my go bag and escape a "geostorm" with. God help us all.

Sarah Smith

Thank you to my amazing husband, my friends and my family for their love and support. I couldn't do this author thing without you. Huge thanks to all the authors in this anthology—working with you was a dream come true. To my fur baby, Salem, you were the best little guy. Thank you for cuddling by my side as I wrote all my stories. I'll love you forever. And to the readers, thank you for giving our disaster romance a chance. We love you!

Denise Williams

Thank you to everyone who made the last few years feel like I wasn't alone when it seemed the sky was falling. For my husband, there's no one I'd rather doomscroll next to. For Tiny Human, thank you for being you and being weird. I love us. Thank you to Mom, Dad, Jay, Amanda, Mike, Melissa, Barb, Tim, Bruce, Jean and everyone in my family, who are so incredibly supportive. Frankly, my cousins have always been the best at fighting imaginary spies AND adulting like bosses, and they always will be.

I'm lucky to have agent extraordinaire Sharon Pelletier in my corner, and the Dystel, Goderich, & Bourret team and Kristina Moore at UTA. Thank you to Errin Toma and Taj McCoy—it was a joy to work on this project with you and I'm so appreciative of the other authors, queens Charish Reid, Farah Heron, Sarah Smith and Lane Clarke.

Thank you to the friends I would happily destroy a vending machine for: Emily, Allison, Tera, Cass, Allie, Beth, Tova, J, Katie, Jen, Libby, Rachel and everyone whose DMs were a safe space the last few years. Finally, thank you to everyone who invited my words into their minds and hearts—I appreciate it more than you can know!

AUTHOR BIOS

Oakland-born law grad **Taj McCoy** is committed to championing stories that include Black and multiracial women of color, plus-size protagonists, Black love, Black joy, and strong senses of sisterhood and familial bonds. Taj started writing as a small child, enjoying her first publications in elementary school. When she's not writing, Taj may be on Twitter boosting other marginalized writers, practicing yoga, sharing recipes or cooking private supper club meals for close friends.

Lane Clarke has been in love with books since the age of two. Her stories feature Black culture and bighearted characters with self-doubts and big dreams, who—with a little laughter and good friends—can accomplish anything. She currently lives in Northern Virginia and works as an attorney in Washington, DC.

Farah Heron writes romantic comedies for adults and teens full of huge South Asian families, delectable food and, most importantly, brown people falling stupidly in love. Her books have been named as best books of the year by CBC Books, *USA TODAY* and NPR. She lives in Toronto with her family.

Charish Reid is a fan of sexy books and disaster films. When she's not grading papers or prepping lessons for college freshmen, she enjoys writing romances that celebrate quirky Black women who deserve HEAs. Charish currently lives in Sweden.

Sarah Smith is a copywriter-turned-author who wants to make the world a lovelier place, one kissing story at a time. Her love of romance began when she was eight and she discovered her auntie's stash of romance novels. She lives in Bend, Oregon.

Denise Williams wrote her first book in the second grade. That book featured a tough, funny heroine, a quirky hero, witty banter and a dragon. Minus the dragons, these are still the books she likes to write. After penning those early works, she finished second grade and eventually earned a PhD in education, going on to work in higher education. Denise lives in Des Moines, Iowa.